# TOP BANANA

# Bill James

# TOP BANANA

A Foul Play Press Book

W. W. Norton & Company
New York    London

Copyright © 1996 by Bill James

First American edition published 1999 by Foul Play Press,
a division of W. W. Norton & Company, Inc., New York

First published 1996 by Macmillan London Limited

For information about permission to reproduce selections from this book,
write to Permissions, W. W. Norton & Company, Inc.,
500 Fifth Avenue, New York, NY 10110.

Composition and manufacturing by the Maple-Vail Book Manufacturing Group.

Library of Congress Cataloging-in-Publication Data
James, Bill, 1929–
    Top banana / Bill James. — 1st American ed.
        p.   cm.
    ISBN 0-393-04718-0
    I. Title.
PR6060.A44T66     1999
823'.914—dc21                                                   98-49699
                                                                    CIP

W. W. Norton & Company, Inc., 500 Fifth Avenue, New York, NY 10110
http://www.wwnorton.com

W. W. Norton & Company Ltd., 10 Coptic Street, London WC1A 1PU

1 2 3 4 5 6 7 8 9 0

# 1

She could not read or write, but she could count. Her schooling ended a year ago, when she was twelve. She ended it. Even while she was still on the register she hardly ever went. Perhaps there were a few written words she would understand: very simple combinations that she had picked up in primary school, when her attendance was better; plus words she recognized through familiarity: graffiti words, placard words, pop music programme titles on television. But especially graffiti words, such as kid gang names like Zit and Saka; and produce names, like ganja, nut nuts, poppers, wash and Billy; and then the usual, of course: love, fuck, HIVSPIT, lootable, fRenZeeEee. She could write her name in block capitals. It was NOON. She had taken this from a group she loved, but which had come apart now. She liked to keep the memory of them in her name.

Before NOON she was Mandy, which she had hated. That was a baby name given her when she *was* a baby. The school had called her Mandy, of course, and the newspaper reports of her death did, too, because that was the way it came from the police. If she had been able to see these reports, and able to read them, this would have truly pissed her off. One of the papers did say she liked to be called NOON, but it was right down the bottom of the story, as though unimportant.

And if she had been able to see the report she would definitely not have been able to work her way that far through the words. It was the sound of the name NOON that she liked, and she had a pretty good idea of what it meant, too. Getting the crossbar of the N the right way, and making the Os join up gave her trouble, but she had stuck at it.

Even thirteen-year-olds up on their reading would have had trouble with some of the words in the news reports. *Fusillade. Courier. Intimidation. Convictions. Culmination. Tragic symbol.* The pictures, though, gave no difficulty. They showed the stretch of pavement outside a fruit and veg shop where she was found. Her body was not shown. Possibly the photographers arrived too late. Conceivably there had even been some self-editing by the Press in the cause of tenderness. A dozen Vs of glass hung from the top frame of the shattered fruit and veg shop window. Fusillade. There would be thin spikes in the broccoli: not good at all. One of the bigger papers did a series of street maps on page two, with white arrows: *Child killed here; Man One (white) shot here and pulled into exiting blue Carlton by Man Two (black) armed with automatic rifle, possibly a Kalashnikov; Man Three (black) drove; Man Four (black) possibly wounded in arm here and escapes on foot down Cave Street; Man Five (white and wearing beret) unhit and escapes into Simon Street here.* The maps had the artist's name in the bottom right-hand corner, like battle paintings. The houses and apartment blocks in these sketches looked good. They had style, even grace. That's how they must have been forty-odd years ago when

they were built: a post-war impulse to house the people decently. The slow slide into seediness did not show. The map placed the park at a junction of Cave Street and three others. It was represented by a few bushy-topped tree drawings and the wooden bridge over a stream. You could imagine it as restful, and in the 1950s it probably was.

Even ten years ago that park, Fulmar Gardens, was not too bad: usable. On some fine summer afternoons then, Mandy was taken there to play by her mother, and other mothers and children went, too, and even fathers. Later, when Mandy was NOON and busy, she had in her head woolly but nice recollections of those afternoons, and her feelings about the park might grow confused for a second. Of course, she knew it was not on to go into the park now, morning, afternoon or night, and especially when carrying what she might be carrying. This would be either one of the products or money she had just collected for the products. But the tidy, grown-up good sense of such fears could be shaken for a second occasionally by some of those far-off recollections and she would gaze at the trees and big clumps of bushes and think how nice they looked, never mind the dumped stuff all round, the old fridges and bits of car. She could just about recall great games of chase, and running yelling with no clothes on through the stream near the little bridge. She remembered how a breeze might shift the high leaves and let the sun flicker through on to her face for a second, a lovely hot glare, and then it would be shady again. She remembered a thick wallflower smell.

3

The park would have been a useful short-cut for her now when she was on one of her courier runs, but she would never let those pleasant old memories make her think Fulmar Gardens might still be all right. In the summer especially, when everything looked so beautiful, people hung about in there among the bushes, getting highs on, or planning something for the night or dividing up looted stuff. Someone told NOON it was not safe to run through the park in case you fell over mugged handbags and it was not safe to walk through there in case you were caught by lurkers. Once, NOON asked her mother did the park change all at once one day. But her mother only said, 'What?' She never seemed to want to talk very much about anything, and there was nobody else to ask. Most people did not like to speak about the park. They were ashamed of it and afraid of it. NOON heard a woman in the mini-mart say Fulmar Gardens was a mockery. This was one of those words NOON must have missed. The mini-mart kept its steel shutters closed in the day as well as at night, and the door was shut, too, except when customers came in or went out. They had a couple of dim light bulbs on in there all the time and there were shadows, so that NOON could not see the woman's face very well. But NOON could tell from her voice that mockery meant don't go in the park. The thing about Fulmar Gardens was it could be bad in there at any time, but the place near the fruit and veg where NOON was hit was not usually bad at all. It was very bad that day, that was all.

Although the reports had some awkward words, the headlines were almost as uncomplicated as the pictures, and NOON might have been able to manage them, given a bit of help.

*GIRL, 13, SHOT DEAD IN DRUGS GANG WAR*

*DEAD MANDY, 13, WAS DRUGS PUSHER*

*CROSSFIRE DEATH CHILD SOLD DRUGS*

*VICTIM: CHILD OF OUR TIME*

'Child of our time' meant, obviously, that she was no child at all, a little girl made adult too soon by deprivation and evil. It also meant there were others like her. But, yes, she *was* a child. Although she ran an efficient, pretty business, she liked sweets and dolls – slept with three dolls, and could not sleep without them – and had no interest in the produce she ferried. Possibly she even realized, or half-realized, that there was something wrong with her life. That is, not just wrong in a way which might have brought the police after her; but not right to have moved young into trade and skipped so much of growing up. She wondered whether what had happened to the park had happened to her: a dark, rushed change that would never change back. She would have asked her mother about this, but knew she would not get much of an answer. There was one doll she talked to most, a doll she took to calling Mandy when she gave up the name herself. In bed some nights NOON told Mandy of this idea of the sudden alteration to the park and herself. She would also talk to the other dolls sometimes, but for this special matter only Mandy would seem to do, because Mandy had the name NOON had when she was young.

*Little Mandy Walsh, aged only 13, was gunned down yesterday in broad daylight yards from her home, blasted to death in the crossfire of warring drug gangs.*

*Her small body was hit by possibly three bullets in a fusillade from a Russian-made Kalashnikov automatic rifle. She died on the pavement near a shop she often visited to buy sweets. Drugs barons on the estate where Mandy lived employed her to carry supplies to street corner pushers and collect cash. Police say she had £2500 worth of crack cocaine 'rocks' in a carrier bag when she was hit.*

*FULL STORY PAGES 2, 3, 4 and 5.*

The Press covered the details of the shooting very thoroughly, and most of them also looked at the tragic symbolism of NOON'S death. One paper said that in a good week she could make £250. Originally, she had been paid a wage for running supplies. Then she had asked for a percentage. This part of the article was where the sentence, *She could not read but she could count*, probably first appeared. *The child knew how valuable she was to the major drug dealers. Police would not suspect a pretty, smiling girl of 13 of pushing.*

One of the writers had been to Mandy's schools and discovered her attendance record. *From May 7 1992, her 10th birthday, Mandy had only four full days of schooling registered.* It was not clear how this figure had been arrived at. The article said that neither the schools nor the education authority would allow sight of the registers. Perhaps some clerk or some teacher had whispered the facts, wanting to highlight the difficulties of schooling in areas like the Ernest Bevin estate. The authority claimed it had done all possible to enforce attendance, but the feeling from the article was that she had been written off by teachers and officials who had too much else on their plates, and who were, in any case, afraid to get heavy on the Ernest Bevin.

*Mandy's father left her mother, Rachel, 34, when the child was a year old and disappeared. Police have so far failed to trace him to inform him of the death of his daughter. Honey-blonde, attractive Rachel Walsh says the only money coming into the house was from income support and child allowance. She denies that Mandy had earnings from drugs running and says that if she did none of it was passed from Mandy to her.*

*Mandy lived in a neat, 6th floor, two-bedroom flat in the Osprey tower. On her carefully made bed lay her three favourite dolls, including one which she had recently given her own name, Mandy, which she had abandoned.*

*Psychologist Emily-Marie Harbison of the Child Welfare Institute, which has a clinic on the Ernest Bevin estate, says that this rejection of a given 'official' name is typical in disaffected youngsters. 'And the shifting of that name on to a doll or pet or other cherished possession is also typical,' she said. 'The child wishes to quit childhood, or has been compelled to quit it by circumstances. At the same time, the child seems to recognize subconsciously that the premature loss of childhood is, indeed, a loss, and so will seek to embody that "younger" self elsewhere. A doll or other inanimate possession, rather than a pet, is the more common choice, because inanimate objects do not age.'*

*Comforted by neighbours, Rachel Walsh was too distressed to talk at length about her daughter's death, but said it had happened because the law no longer operated in that area, and the innocent were just as likely to be injured or killed as members of the battling gangs. 'We are intimidated and terrorized,' she said. 'The death of Mandy is the culmination of many acts of violence. There is constant crime, often involving guns, and no convictions.' She has had a police warning for possession and use of cannabis, but has never been prosecuted. She said that her boyfriend, Carl Sillers, loved Mandy as if she was his own child and would never even raise his voice to her. 'It was not home life that made her become so uncontrollable,' Rachel Walsh said.*

# 2

The Chief wanted to look again at the spot where Mandy was killed. Harpur drove him and Desmond Iles, Iles lying out on the back seat, slim legs crossed. He had on fine grey slacks and a navy blazer bright with silver buttons. For some crimes, the Chief would routinely do this: visit and revisit. To Harpur it looked like a kind of penance: the monk climbing and reclimbing a hill in the sun, the nun cleaning and recleaning a spotless floor. Crimes which drew the Chief to make these personal trips were always those that proclaimed to him a terrible and general message about what one of the papers had called 'our times'. Now, Lane wanted to stand exactly at the place where Mandy had lain, and Harpur guided him to it, a hand on the Chief's arm. Lane gazed about at the shops and tower blocks, empathizing. The Chief was a good, confused man, now and then able to fight his way to a clear and terrible vision. Today he wore one of his brownish suits which Iles said were made instead of mail bags by lifers in Zaïre. 'More than ever I feel this domain is coming apart, and that we do nothing,' the Chief said, his tired-looking skin more tired than ever. There was traffic noise, but Harpur heard him. 'And what happens to this domain happens throughout the country. And further yet.'

'It's called chaos theory, sir,' Iles replied, leaning against a pillar box. 'You'll know that Stoppard play, *Arcadia*.'

Lane glanced at him. It lasted a second. Lane did not speak. Then he looked away, as if afraid of encouraging the Assistant Chief to say more. Iles always accompanied the Chief on these trips to the scene of emblematic offences. Lane's life was mortally chafed by the ACC's brilliant rough mind and unstoppable tongue.

'A development of chaos theory, yes,' Iles said. 'That suggests there's a system in seemingly random reversals – a sort of order in disorder. That would be fine, of course, if the hidden pattern were benign. But what if it is an ordered decline, like troops marching in formation over a cliff? Some feel we are methodically regressing and will eventually enter the new Middle Ages.' A big grey 525 BMW slipped past them. Harpur thought he recognized a famed middle-rank supplier driving, gold finger furniture bright on the wheel. Iles, too, seemed to notice.

Lane continued to stare about at the drab buildings. 'This was a fine progressive architectural concept. Modern in all the best senses when it was built.' He smiled at a couple of old women on their way to the mini-mart. He was here to try to console people. They might not recognize him, but most would recognize Harpur and probably the ACC. They would deduce Lane was police, too, although he appeared so benign and crushed. Harpur knew the Chief yearned for these folk to believe that law and order would yet win through, even if on most days he could not believe it himself.

'Obviously, sir, the main comparison with the Middle Ages is the resurgence of plague,' Iles called out across more pedestrians out shopping. 'Aids as equivalent of the Black Death. Untreatable viruses. Then we have the education of the populace dropping to what it was five hundred years ago: a girl of thirteen who does not go to school and cannot read. And as for us, sir – you would rightly ask what is our role in all this – well, we are the equivalent of the king in those days. Ostensibly, we are authority, charged with the preservation of order. But we are miserably incapable of controlling the barons.' He pointed to the place where NOON died to illustrate. 'Robber barons in those times. Drugs barons now. They run the place.'

'Never!' Lane cried. A tall black woman pushing twins in a buggy stared towards him, then looked elsewhere and walked quicker.

Iles went and stood close to the Chief and in a moment bent down swiftly until his lips touched the spot near Lane's feet where Mandy was found. The ACC could go theatrical. Iles stroked the paving stone for a while, as he might have stroked her hair to comfort a child in agony. 'It's five times worse in France,' he told Lane, looking up along the brown trouser leg. 'Whole suburbs lost to villainy. The police don't go near. These are seemingly isolated areas of disaster. But perhaps not. Perhaps there is linkage. Perhaps these setbacks will spread, affecting one another and growing at each stage. They will become the norm.' He straightened. 'Harpur will tell you, sir, that there's little chance of finding those who killed the girl, and even less of bringing successful charges. That so, Harpur?'

The ACC expected answers to his questions and Harpur said: 'One of my daughters had that late-night Channel 4 shit on about chaos theory, sir, including the Froggy bit.'

'Will you get anyone for this child slaughter?' Iles asked. 'Will there be witnesses? Will they talk? Will they live?'

Harpur said: 'I loved that crazy moment where the imported don from Oxford, or was it Yeovil, said police would soon be forced to accept treaties with the drugs lords, the way the king had to with the barons. Neat!'

'Never,' Lane hissed. 'I do not treat with scum.'

Iles said: 'A controlled evil. Our job is order. We fail to get it because of accelerating chaos. So, we change the nature of what order is. It's no longer an arbitrary and abstract idea. We turn order into an agreement between powerful parties where predictable behaviour becomes not just possible but convenient. King, barons. It's really only a return to policing by consent – the consent of those with clout. The lawmakers used to have the clout – which meant the voters who elected them. Democracy. Not any longer. If we can get established satisfied villain firms it means peace. No illiterate little delivery girls caught in a bullet storm. Accident? Or were they gunning for her?'

'I'll never make deals with them,' the Chief said. 'That would indeed be chaos. Infiltrate. Get someone into one of the firms.'

Iles smiled. 'Infiltrate.' He shrugged. 'We've been here before, sir.'

Harpur would have to agree with that, but said nothing.

'Infiltration doesn't work and carries appalling risk,' the ACC said. 'Remember our young detective Raymond Street? Dead.'

'If it's the only way to get evidence, the only way to win and to remain winners, infiltrate,' Lane whispered. He walked back towards the car, dignified in his way, regardless of the suit and shoes. He was someone a child like Mandy could have trusted to do her no harm. But she should have been able to trust him to do better than that.

Back at headquarters car park, Lane walked to the building ahead of Iles and Harpur. The ACC said: 'Listen, Col, how did you suddenly get so fucking witty – "Oxford, or was it Yeovil?" The destruction of league tables by jumbling them. That's my kind of chaos joke and you pinched it, you pitiful jerk.'

'You've got a million, sir. You won't miss it.'

# 3

The Sunday Press stuck with the story. Because all details of the actual shooting had been given in the dailies, these Sunday papers moved on to deep profiles and analyses. Articles came in the full range of journalistic styles. A tabloid had bought up Mandy's mother. The papers knew they were writing about Britain, not just the death of a little girl or the dark troubles of one council estate.

*

*Things were never going to be easy for Mandy Walsh. Pressures on the child to look after herself – financially and in all other ways – began immediately she was out of infancy: the kind of accelerated move to self-preservation seen in young animals. 'She had street savvy at the age of eight,' one teacher said, 'She'd be sitting in the middle of a class, her eyes on you and apparently paying attention, but what her eyes told you was she was alone and that that was how she wanted it.' Like some other children on the estate, she seems to have regarded school as a luxury to be forgone. She would not let herself burden her deserted mother.*

*Psychologists say some children fear that a single parent resents them, as a liability and restriction. Mandy, who became NOON, probably adopted her criminal career to escape this resentment; and adopted her new name to signal the end of a dependent relationship with her mother.*

*

*Mandy lived in a sex empire, as well as a drugs empire. Many big-time pushers are also pimps. Girls go on to the streets to finance their habit.*

*Some of the streets where Mandy delivered drugs were notorious beats for prostitutes of all ages, some nearly as young as herself.*

*There is no evidence that Mandy sold sex. But, had she lived, the pressure might have fallen on her before very long to turn tart. If police had come to suspect she was a courier, her usefulness to the barons would be over. Then she might have been compelled to earn her money with her body.*

*

*Mandy Walsh was not the only child courier used by local drugs merchants. The system appeals to the barons. In addition to the youngsters' appearance of innocence, they tend not to be users, so are unlikely to run away with drug consignments or – in the case of cocaine – conceal a theft by cutting (mixing) the product with filler, such as baby powder. The children are also easy to frighten and control. Most live at home and are traceable if they behave out of order and have to be punished.*

*Major middle-rank dealers do not allow children to make their larger deliveries. These they handle personally. But for supplying the smaller, street-corner pushers, youngsters are ideal. Above these middle-rank dealers are the wholesalers who are by nature idle and arrogant. They exult in the title 'baron'. And they get kudos from employing young retainers to dispose of chickenfeed transactions. Yet to a child – and to some of their out-of-work parents – the possible earnings are dazzlingly high. Mandy's mother claims she never saw any of her daughter's earnings – in fact disputes there were any. But there is no doubt that the kind of money Mandy could bring home would be riches to a woman trying to run a home on State payments only.*

*On a typical day Mandy might have been carrying up to five or even ten grammes of cocaine at £50 a gramme. Or a quarter of a pound of cannabis costing £110 an ounce. Ecstasy pills could be anything between £7 and £15 each. But crack is easily the biggest earner, and she would have done at least two consignments of that per week. Crack comes in quarter gramme rocks at £25 a rock, and on some trips – including her last – she might push 100 of these. Mandy was believed to have secured a 3% commission. If she made eight or ten deliveries a week – about the norm – a return of up to £300 would be easily reached. In cash, of course. A good week might break down like this:*

| Delivery | Load | Value | Commission at 3% |
|---------|------|-------|------------------|
| 1 | 5 gms cocaine | £250 | £7.50 |
| 2 | 100 crack rocks | £2500 | £75 |
| 3 | " | " | " |

## Top Banana

| 4 | 4 oz cannabis | £440 | £13.20 |
|---|---|---|---|
| 5 | " " | " | " |
| 6 | " " | " | " |
| 7 | 10 gms cocaine | £500 | £15 |
| 8 | 100 crack rocks | £2500 | £75 |
| 9 | 50 Ecstasy pills | £500 | £15 |

*Couriers pick up their day's consignments from the car of one of the dealers, never from his house or office.*

*Delivery personnel are kept at arm's length. The rendezvous points change daily: couriers are told where to report tomorrow. All the pushers Mandy served probably operated within a mile's radius of Fulmar Gardens and she would generally travel on foot, though sometimes by bicycle. Girl couriers dress unobtrusively. To preserve the appearance of innocence they must not look older than they are. On the other hand, there is danger that a child seen in the streets during school hours might cause suspicion. But this is not a likelihood in Mandy's area because of general truancy. She carried the crack in a carrier bag, as if out shopping for her mother.*

*

*Even though so young, Mandy and her friends came to question the value of education, and to despise it. The people who employed them and paid them so well did not succeed through schooling. Children like Mandy decided this was the future, not books. These youngsters had landed in the category sociologists dub Status Zero: chronically truanting and with no prospects but the dole and/or criminality.*

17

*

### *Rachel Walsh talks exclusively to Malcolm Pitts*

*Until she was nine or ten my little Mandy was just a normal, happy girl and so full of fun and love. When I had time I took her to the park to play and I would read her many stories at home, such as fairy tales and about Uncle the grumpy elephant, which she loved.*

*Often she would kiss me and cry out in her tiny little voice that I was the 'bestest' mummy in all the wide wide world. This was so I would not feel so sad because Phil had left me. She would make me lovely little handicraft presents at school – once a cardboard serviette ring and another time a lovely little stationery rack.*

*I can't be certain when she started to change. Of course, I did not know she had stopped going to school, not until the attendance officer came. How shocked I was! Of course, by the time the attendance officer called, Mandy had been off school for months. They cannot keep up with it. I felt sorry for him. I pleaded with Mandy to return to school, explaining that she would regret it later, but she refused to listen.*

*I had various jobs as Mandy was growing up and was too busy to spend a lot of time making sure she did go to school and stayed away from undesirables, though I was able to take her to school myself now and then. I could feel this area where we live sliding, sliding, and I feared Mandy might be sliding with it. But none of us could do anything to stop that.*

*This kind of area – you do not get residents' associations,* which happens in some places. People do not like coming together in such ways. They are too ashamed of being here. They would be too afraid to form a group, anyway. Leaders of a group would be targets.

And the councillors – they're also afraid. You never see them, except at election time and even then they do not hang about for long. If you complain about the violence and threats and lack of police they just say it's the same everywhere, a blight of our time – like part of Nature. Do they get this kind of terror in those rich streets in Chelsea or Bath?

Romance would come into my life now and then and, although I never neglected Mandy and fretted about her all the time, I had my own life to live, obviously. Two boyfriends, including my present one, Carl, tried so hard to help me show her that what she was doing was wrong and stupid. They always treated her right in every way, nothing off colour. I would never allow that. I hated it when she took that name, NOON. It was like she had stopped being my daughter.

# 4

Infiltrate. Lane might have a case. The idea frightened Harpur, though, and he struggled to crush it. Iles who would generally ignore risk thought undercovering *too* risky, and Harpur agreed. Iles had never properly got over the death not long ago of DC Ray Street when undercover. And the ACC had never forgiven it, either. To penetrate a gang meant asking someone to put himself into the darkest kind of lonely peril and stay there. Or herself. Yet, even while he looked for ways to dodge the Chief's orders, Harpur short-listed in his head five or six people who might do, mostly women. No detective would refuse. Wasn't it a distinction to be asked?

But, God, could he ask, ask again? Anyone Harpur picked would know the tale of Street, murdered when exposed. It would not prevent acceptance. Wasn't the choice too heavy for a detective chief superintendent, and too heavy for anybody? All the same, he sensed it would eventually come to infiltration. Lane kept insisting. Previously, the Chief always discouraged such operations. Now even he saw no other means to claw back his dirty realm from the gangs, or to *try* to claw it back. It was not the blasting of Mandy Walsh that changed Lane but learning of the child courier network. The routine evil of it would sicken him: that system daily soiled his ground. Everyone had suspected something like it existed, everyone except the Chief. He was too wholesome to believe it possible, until he heard of NOON's rock-rich carrier bag.

*My name is Charles Ericson, proprietor of Alert, a company specializing in automatic alarm systems, based in London. At about 11.10 a.m. on May 25 I was standing outside the Post Office in Sphere Street on the Ernest Bevin estate. I was spending three days in this city to update the alarms of a large number of its Post Offices. I had just descended from a ladder outside the Sphere Street Post Office, having examined the alarm control box fixed to the wall. I saw a blue Vauxhall Carlton car approaching very slowly up Bateson Road towards the junction with Sphere Street opposite the Post Office. Its slowness drew my attention. I thought it about to break down. There appeared to be three men in the Carlton, two in the front, one in the rear. I would judge them all to be in their late twenties or early thirties. The driver was black and so was the man in the back, who wore sunglasses. The man in the passenger seat was white and also wore sunglasses. The Carlton turned left into Sphere Street and stopped opposite a jeweller's and pawnbroker's shop. I thought the engine might have failed.*

This from one of two witness statements. In his office, Harpur went over them again now. Both were given by visitors. Locals did not do statements. They never saw anything or heard anything, not even when threatened with a withholding evidence charge. Worse threats existed: the kind that did not need to be spoken because they hung permanently in the air, the way patriotism and belief in God did once. These hellish pressures would probably fit into Iles's chaos theory, except that for residents of the Ernest Bevin estate they were not theory but very actual.

Harpur longed to drag some identifications from these statements. Both witnesses had been shown dossier pix of all the domain's possibles, but unsuccessfully. The descriptions they gave did nothing for Harpur or for Francis Garland or for anyone in the Drugs Squad, or so the Drugs Squad said. That meant the men in this shooting could be invaders from London or Manchester or Leeds or Edinburgh or Paris or Antwerp, in search of fresh openings and earnings and more or less untraceable. But Harpur worked through the words in case even so late in the day he might suddenly feel something familiar in these pavement warriors' looks, clothes, business style, social style, weapons. Of course, the slow-moving Carlton had been stolen and offered no message. Harpur needed these people to be home grown. He could handle that. If he found an identification he would be able to work from this, and postpone the Chief's scheme or kill it off. And also kill off or postpone Iles's scheme for a 'working arrangement' with big villainy. Harpur was not sure which scheme he dreaded most. He would even settle for half an identification.

*I had expected one of the men to leave the car and look under the bonnet. This did not happen. I saw the driver and the man in the front passenger seat lower the car's sun vizors although there was no sun and it would have been behind them anyway. I assumed they wished to hide part of their faces from someone approaching from ahead. At this point I grew uneasy. I was aware of the reputation of this area. I watched carefully and memorized the Carlton's registration number. I suspected now that the car had moved slowly not because of mechanical trouble but to use up minutes before a timed rendezvous or interception; probably the latter, or they would not have needed to conceal themselves.*

A couple of days ago, the Chief had asked to see these statements and Harpur took them up to his room. Iles had been present. Lane read silently for a while and then stopped at that sentence, 'I was aware of the reputation of this area.' Raising his head wearily he had spoken the words aloud twice, turning once to the ACC and once to Harpur, as if impressing a text on Sunday School pupils. 'So, we preside over an area whose infamy is widespread,' he declared. 'This man has heard of our failures even in London, for God's sake.'

'Oh, Sphere Street Post Office gets done now and then, sir, like all Post Offices everywhere,' Iles replied. 'The Alert company supply and service the alarms, and Ericson will have heard the horror stories. He's bound to be jaundiced.'

'I can't bear to have people speak of a section of my – our – domain like that,' the Chief had replied. 'It sounds chaotic, like no-go for us.'

'There is, of course, an argument for keeping it localized, sir,' Iles said. 'Think of it not so much as no-go, but as an area where trouble is confined, sealed-off.'

'What argument for keeping it localized, Desmond?' Lane replied. 'The death of this little girl?'

For a moment then Harpur had thought the Assistant Chief would strike or more probably head-butt Lane. They were standing quite close to each other, and Iles took a quick step forward, bringing his face to within a few inches of the Chief's. Iles knew nutting and Harpur had seen him use it deftly once or twice. No, three times. Harpur had been sitting down but stood hurriedly and contrived a good stumble in which he barged Iles to one side. 'Oh, sorry, ' he said. You could not let even a venomous dandy like Desmond Iles drown his career in a Chief Constable's nose blood. Harpur believed a prime duty of all good officers was to protect his inferiors, and at self-control the ACC was inferior to most. Lane had walked back to his desk. Chaos theory took a rest.

*The man in the rear of the Carlton left the car and stood near it. He was carrying a brown holdall. He seemed to be staring south along Sphere Street, as if expecting someone. I confirmed he was between 25 and 30 years old, black, about 5 feet 10 inches tall, lean, with small features and possibly a small moustache. He wore a dark, two-piece suit and open-necked floral shirt, the background colour pink or red. Now and then he would bend down and speak through the passenger window of the car to the two men inside. He smiled a lot. He seemed at ease, full of jokes. His teeth were very good, even and bright. He was swinging the holdall playfully.*

The two in the front pull down the vizors to hide themselves. The one on the pavement, Kalashnikov in his swinging holdall, is relaxed and seemingly does nothing to conceal his face. He might be a stranger, then, another out-of-town visitor who would not be recognized; perhaps a big city import, untroubled by what he would regard as minor league, back-street stresses, and keen to calm the nerviness of the men in the car. That pair could be local, afraid they might get spotted by their target, targets. Harpur liked this reading. It brought them within his range.

*I feared that the man with the holdall would realize I was watching him. Therefore, I remounted the ladder and pretended to examine the alarm again. From this point I had an extensive view both ways along the length of Sphere Street and I looked to see whether I could make out whom or what they might be waiting for. I saw a girl of about 12 or 13 approaching at a quick walk. She had a carrier bag in her right hand. I now, of course, know her to be Mandy Walsh, the girl who was shot. At that time she seemed simply a child kept off school to shop.*

And did our waiting friend from the Carlton appear interested in her? It would have been hard to judge from up a ladder while play-acting concern for something else. Ericson would have tried to plumb eyes behind shades and directed mostly away from him. In any case, did it matter whether she had been hit by intent or accident? Either way she was dead and Harpur had nobody for it.

Oh, tell me, tell me, Mr Ericson of Alert Alarms, tell me,

do, about the two men in the front of the car who are shading themselves from no sun pre-noon and pre-NOON. Might I know them?

*I saw two other men now appear on foot from a side road a little way behind the child and turn into Sphere Street, walking towards the Carlton. One was white, the other black. The white, about forty, wore a half length plaid jacket, a black beret and training shoes. He was about 5 feet six inches tall, powerful looking and agile. The other was around twenty-five, over six feet and in a long grey overcoat, odd for May. He had no hat and he had begun to lose his hair. When I looked back to the man standing at the Carlton I found he appeared suddenly tense. The joking was over. It was like the moment of truth. He opened the zip of the holdall, though he produced nothing from it yet. I had the impression he might be talking to the men in the car through the open window, but he did not bend down to do so now. He was preoccupied. He stared ahead.*

At the two men? At the girl? At all three? Were they linked in some way? Had the two men and NOON been programmed to coincide like this in Sphere Street, and had the Carlton party somehow found out? Hence the dawdled approach, to get the timing more or less right: 'the moment of truth', to use Ericson's bit of gaudy phrasing. Were the two following NOON to some quieter spot for a deal? For a business conference?

Did any of this matter, either, though? Her chest and thin neck were torn open by two bullets, that was what mattered.

Both rounds had passed through her and had not been identified yet among all the spent shells recovered after the incident. And yet perhaps it *was* important to know the run-up to her death. This was not much to do with identification. But it could affect what the Chief and Iles had argued about: strategy, even philosophy. At their pay level they were expected to do some philosophizing. If NOON was accidentally shot in a battle between the Carlton people and this walking duo, Iles's comforting suggestion that the gangs fought only one another, hurt only one another, might stand up. The same was said of the Krays and their enemies. She would be a crossfire victim. The sort of accommodation with the gangs suggested on that Channel 4 programme might then be conceivable.

But if a thirteen-year-old child had been deliberately targeted along with the two men, Iles's analysis obviously nosedived – nosedived even though this thirteen-year-old had been portering two and a half grand's worth of crack on the day, and something similar on most days. Such a death could never be accepted as the price of stability. And there were other child couriers to get hit some time if this death was left unpunished. These were kids not gangsters: kids who had vigorously clambered their way into the neighbourhood's bad commerce, yes, but still just kids. If NOON's death was planned, the call by Lane for infiltration as the one hope looked desperately convincing. Yes, desperately. You could not blind-eye a ghetto where children were murdered, not even for the sake of peace everywhere else. And not even because chaos theory said you needed an under-standing with the gangs that they could run things how they liked, as long as they stayed in their territory. That is, stayed in one of those enclaves with what Ericson called a 'reputation'.

*One of the walking men – the white in the beret – seemed suddenly to spot the Carlton and the man waiting alongside it. He spoke to his companion and they stopped. The man in the beret put his right hand into the pocket of his plaid jacket. The black put his right hand up towards his shoulder under the long overcoat. They looked frightened.*

Probably. And the child? Had the child noticed anything? Did it look as if the men behind her called a warning?

*The passenger door of the Carlton opened and the white man came out quickly and stood with the holdall man. The white man had a large automatic pistol in his right hand.*

But tell me about him, tell me about him, his looks, his build, his gear. The shades hide a bit but not everything. He's out of the car now and visible because he'd seen that the two on foot knew what was happening: no point in concealment.

*The Carlton passenger door remained open. I saw the black who had been waiting by the car pull an automatic rifle from the holdall, and throw the holdall into the car. I have seen automatic rifles in television newsreels from Northern Ireland and Afghanistan and I thought I recognized this one as a Russian-made Kalashnikov. I began to yell then. I felt entirely helpless. I could see everything that was taking place, yet I was up the ladder and could do nothing about it except make a din. I wanted to alert people, tell them to get out of the street, into the shops, anywhere. Some of them seemed still unaware that anything was wrong. There were women talking in a group outside the mini-mart.*

Mr Alarm. Mr Alert. But he had done well. He could even have been in danger. If the men near the Carlton heard him they might have fired to knock him off his perch and shut him up.

*Both the walking men now had pistols in their hand. I don't know who fired first, except that it was a single-shot weapon, not the Kalashnikov. I had been looking at the little girl, not the various gunmen. There was terrible confusion now. The white man standing near the Carlton seemed to have been hit. I saw no wound and for a couple of moments he did not fall, but leaned against the car, one hand draped across the roof, supporting him. I think he had dropped the pistol. Then he did slide down to the pavement. He was still trying to keep himself upright by clinging to the car roof but I could see his fingers lose their hold and slip. His sunglasses seemed to get pushed off his face as he slumped. I saw him go down, dragging against the car as he went, and for a second I made out his face pressed against the rear nearside window. This was not a completely clear view. I was seeing him through two layers of glass and at an angle, since I was looking down on the car from the ladder. My gaze was through the offside rear window, the one nearer me, and then across the cabin of the car to the nearside window. Because of the angle I could see only the lower quarter of the nearside window and I glimpsed his face briefly as he crumpled down. He was clean-shaven, long-faced with sallow skin and pointed nose and chin. I saw that the sunglasses were still fixed to one ear and hung down against his neck on the right-hand side. I thought I could make out blood behind the sunglasses, perhaps running down from his head or from high on his neck. Seen imperfectly and fleetingly like that, the face could have been of someone of any age between 20 and 50, but probably not more than 30.*

Harpur had shown him all the mugshots of bony-faced people in the drugs files, but no use. He was a careful, conscientious fucker and had to be certain.

*When I looked up the road again, I saw that the girl had turned and begun to run back, away from the Carlton. I thought she was trying to get to one of the shops for cover, possibly the fruit and vegetable shop or the mini-mart. Instead of holding the carrier bag down at her side, she seemed to have gathered it up and was clutching it with both hands against her chest, like a baby. She had her back to me now, but this was my impression. Twice as she ran she glanced back towards the Carlton. I saw terror in her face. On one of the occasions when she looked back, she seemed to see me up the ladder. I waved her on, telling her to run faster, and I shouted at her to do that. But she was too far off to hear. It was simply that I had to offer her something. Perhaps, though, she feared I was part of it, one of the enemy. She might have thought it a Post Office raid, my job to knock out the alarm.*

*Then I head the automatic rifle fire. The black had the*

*weapon to his shoulder and was shooting in long bursts up the street towards the two men on foot. He seemed to me unfamiliar with the gun, unable to hold it steady. He should have supported it on the car roof. One of the two men on foot, the white wearing the beret, had turned like the girl and also seemed to be running for the shelter of a shop. The second man, the black in the long overcoat, came on towards the Carlton, but still on the other side of the street, the side where I was. He also was running now. He had the handgun out in front of him at shoulder level and fired at least twice towards the car. It was as if he had decided the best thing to do was take on the Carlton party.*

*The man with the automatic rifle ignored him at first, continuing to fire in bursts towards the older man. It's possible he could not immediately adjust to a new target. I think it was somewhere around this time, during a pause in the firing from the Kalashnikov, that I heard two more shots from what I took to be a handgun, rapid shots, but I could not tell where they came from. Then the man with the Kalashnikov did turn it towards the younger man in the overcoat and fired a short burst at him. It saw the bullets tear pieces of masonry from the jeweller's and pawnbroker's frontage next-door-but-two from the Post Office and I feared that if the man in the overcoat continued to run towards the ladder and me I could come into the line of fire. I now saw that this man had possibly been hit in the right arm. His face was knotted in pain and I made out a stain high up near the shoulder of his coat. He held the gun in his right hand, but did not seem able to raise it any more.*

*It hung to his side. Perhaps he changed his plans because of this wound. He did not go across the street to confront the Carlton men, but stayed on my side of Sphere Street. He kept running, though, and went past me and the ladder towards the park and Cave Street. Looking down on him, I could see he was almost bald. I heard him gasping with exertion or pain as he passed. He was slim built but very wide in the shoulders. The overcoat was tight across them, as if the garment was not his.*

*The man with the Kalashnikov had not fired again, and I wondered if his ammunition clip was exhausted. I thought I recalled from television that the Kalashnikov held up to forty rounds. He pulled open the rear door of the Carlton and threw the gun in. The car had begun to move forward. The man outside yelled. The street was silent now. People had hidden from the shooting and at both ends car drivers who had seen what was happening had stopped and blocked the road. The black near the Carlton was shouting: 'Wait, you fucker, you fucker.' My view was obscured by the car, but I saw him bend and knew he must be trying to get the other man, the injured white, into the vehicle, lifting him from the pavement. The man behind the wheel did not help. He was gazing about, apparently eager to leave. The black outside backed his way into the rear of the car and I could then see through the window that he was dragging the white in after him, holding him by the shoulders. The white man might have been unconscious. He looked a dead weight. I think I started to come down the ladder then. The Carlton began to move again, though the rear door was still open and the injured man's legs must have been trailing outside. This time the Carlton was in reverse. The driver might have seen the end of Sphere Street ahead was blocked. He backed towards the junction with Bateson Road. When he reached there, he drove forward into Bateson Road at high speed and soon went from my sight. Just before it disappeared, the rear door was pulled shut.*

I know what happened to the child, but tell me now about her, just the same.

*When I looked back up Sphere Street the white man in the beret had disappeared. I did not know whether he had reached shelter, or whether he had been hit. The little girl lay on the pavement just outside the door of the fruit and vegetable shop. She seemed to be hunched over the carrier bag. There was nobody near her. I thought she made a small movement, perhaps twice. I wondered at first if she had simply gone to ground to avoid the fusillade and was protecting the bag. Children know such tricks from TV war and crime films. But these small moves were the only ones I saw her make. She did not stand up or try to, although the shooting had finished and people had begun to emerge into the street. I saw a woman stand up from behind refuse bins near the mini-mart where she must have taken cover. I came the rest of the way down the ladder and ran towards the child. She struggled to say something as I reached her, and then became unconscious. What she said was: 'Oh, shit.' Her eyes were open, and I think she could see. The police armed response vehicles and ambulances arrived soon afterwards and traffic began to flow again.*

Nobody tried to get the crack rocks from NOON, so the shooting was not about robbery. There were people who would kill for a couple of grand plus, though probably not using a Kalashnikov. Harpur still could not make out whether she had been shot deliberately. NOON might have been connected with the two walking men somehow, and therefore on the target list; but Harpur saw no certain proof of this. According to Ericson, the black from the Carlton looked useless with the Kalashnikov. NOON could have been caught by bullets meant for the two men.

Harpur turned to the other statement. It had been given by a saleswoman for a mail-order firm based in Liverpool, on the estate that day trying to sign up customers. She had just stepped out of the mini-mart after buying some cigarettes when she became aware of single-shot firing. As soon as the Kalashnikov opened up she cowered behind refuse bins and heard some of the bullets bang into them.

*I saw two men walking on the pavement a little to my left. Both held handguns. One man, who was white, wore a black beret, a half length lumberjacket-style coat and training shoes. He was about 5 feet 8 inches tall and strongly built. I'd say he was forty. His back was towards me. He and the other man seemed to be shooting towards a large blue car parked about 100 metres away on the opposite side of the street. I could see—*

Iles knocked and came into Harpur's office. The ACC looked ungenial in one of his superb single-breasted grey suits and a murkishly striped tie that would be some mighty London club's: the kind of what-the-fuck-are-you-staring-at tie meant to cow the masses by tastelessness. He was still doing his hair *en brosse* following a late-night season of Jean Gabin films at one of the cinemas. He gave Harpur a kind of smile, an Iles kind, fat with insult. 'I popped in to thank you, Col,' he said.

'Sir?'

'For stopping me defacing Mark Lane.'

'That's all right, sir.'

'Well, no, it's not all right, you smug shit,' Iles replied. He came and sat on the corner of Harpur's desk, kicking repeatedly and hard at the front panel with one of his magnificent black slip-ons. 'Suddenly, a little alliance between you and pale Marky, is there? All at once you are his minder, then, you quaint hulk?'

'I was minding *you*, sir. I've done a course on caring for Assistant Chiefs gone apeshit.'

Iles picked up Ericson's statement and read something from the last page, perhaps the death of NOON. He dropped the papers to the floor. 'You and Lane are going to plant someone, are you? Regardless.'

'I haven't—'

'His wife told him to do it that way. She'll be mouthing all round. Thought of this?'

'Sir, my own feelings are that—'

'Lane would never be capable of such a decision, especially after his totally deserved breakdown. His wife cares even less about what happened to Ray Street than he does.'

'I'm going through the statements in case—'

The desk was metal and the ACC would never be able to kick a hole in it, but the noise seemed to give him solace. 'Have you considered that one of our people – maybe more than one – might have been bought, Harpur?'

'Well, sir, I—'

'How could sweetly running firms and a courier network like that exist unless there was a purchased friend or two in Drugs?'

Harpur said: 'I thought you approved of a tolerated villain economy, to contain things.'

'Yes, but *I* decide what's to be tolerated – not some no-rank nobodies on the take. This is a thing for judgement, balance.'

'Sir, I—'

Iles began to shout. His brilliant suit no longer seemed quite right: the frenzy in his face could have done with a secure-ward smock to set it off properly. 'So you're going to ask in your slimy, minion-minded way whether I, personally, could be deemed to have balance.'

'Sir, I—'

Iles pulled a photograph from his wallet and threw it on the desk. It showed the ACC looking demure among rose bushes in an ornamental garden somewhere, perhaps a stately home. It would not be the garden of his own house, Idylls in Rougement Place, which was a tip. 'Examine the

good nature in that face, Harpur. The warmth. Some puckishness, yes, but civilized puckishness, I think you'll agree. This
is a snap taken by Sarah, who brings out the best in me,
sweet girl. And I'll tell you this, you nit-picking prick: at
conferences of the Association of Police Chief Officers I am
always known by one of two nicknames: either "Empathy
Iles" or "Mr Balance". I've earned those titles from perceptive
people, and I'm proud of them. I'm proud of "Empathy Iles"
more, possibly, empathy being so modish, but "Mr Balance"
is a worthwhile accolade, too.'

'Certainly, sir. Would you like me to call you either of
those in future? Or are they only for people of Chief Officer
rank?'

Iles stood and paced in front of Harpur's desk. Quite apart
from the great tailoring, he did not look like a policeman at
all. He was slightly made and only just up to regulation
height. When calm, his face and features at some moments
could appear almost refined, and he might have been mis-
taken for a costume period actor or owner of amusement
arcades. 'And do you realize, Harpur, that if there's someone
in Drugs on the take the hint could leak out about our
putting someone undercover, even who it is?'

'Yes, of course I've thought of it.'

'Fucking liar. Do we want another disaster? Who breaks
it to the next of kin?'

'But I'll—'

'You'll go ahead with it, just the same, because Marky or
his cow wife tell you?'

Harpur said: 'If I put someone in it will be the last possible—'

Iles held up two hands, then came closer to Harpur's desk, bent half over and thrust his face forward. There was a bracing odour of mouthwash. 'You think you can speak to me how you like, don't you, you biodegradable lout, because you once had my wife? Once or twice. Garland's the same. Well, I can definitely tell you she—'

'How *is* Sarah, sir?' Harpur replied.

Iles straightened up. 'Ah, wonderful, Col. Whatever little distinction and joy I have in life I owe to her.'

'Grand. And your daughter?'

'Fanny? Wonderful, too, Col. Such beauty.'

'Wonderful,' Harpur replied.

'She's undoubtedly mine, you know.'

'Sir, I—'

'Absolutely, no question,' Iles replied. He crouched again until his eyes were level with Harpur's. 'I know Sarah did some sleeping around under bad stress – you, Garland, that crooked bastard, Aston. Especially him. But the child's all mine.' He whispered this and might have been close to weeping. 'Now and then I imagine you with her, and Garland, the libidinous jerk. On an accelerated promotion programme, is he? We'll see about that.'

'No hospital reports anyone with gunshot wounds,' Harpur replied. 'Yet Ericson makes this white outside the Carlton sound badly hurt. So does the woman's statement. Injured but not dead. She saw him sit up for a second in the back of the car as they reversed.'

Iles said: 'Somebody in Drugs possibly sweetened by two firms, even more, and knowing their programmes. That would explain how the Carlton team could coincide with these two foot soldiers and the girl in Sphere Street.'

'Yes. I wondered about that: someone helping the Carlton people to a monopoly, possibly to consolidate his/her payments into one big salary from one big unchallenged firm.'

Iles said: 'They're not going to disturb the company profile by taking the white guy to a doctor, and so to us. They'd let him die. Think of *Reservoir Dogs.*' The ACC smoothed down the lovely suit, then passed a hand affectionately over his cropped grey hair. He picked up the photograph of himself and gazed at it for a while with real wonderment before replacing it in his wallet. 'You side with Lane and his bulbous mate against me, Col, and you're just bones in a box,' he said. 'But you know that.'

'Plus we have the other one, the black in the long overcoat, possibly wounded badly in the arm,' Harpur replied. 'This lad's going to be in pain. Yet he seeks no treatment?'

Iles nodded and seemed to consider this. He said: 'Now tell me, Harpur, how is *your* daughter? I've been unthinking.'

'Which daughter?'

'Well, the older one, I should hope.'

'Hazel? Still virtually a child, sir.'

'But when do they leave childhood these days, Col? This girl, NOON, running a business at thirteen. Did you know

Hazel once described me to a friend of hers as "the feral loony"? But you probably told me.'

'Hazel thought that up alone, sir. I didn't prompt her.'

'You wouldn't have the perceptiveness or vocab. This is a girl with gifts, Harpur.'

'Thanks, sir.'

# 5

'This was our own kid, am I right?'

'Well, yes, she was a girl used by Bulmer on a regular basis, Mansel. If I may say, not *our* kid. You're a major wholesaler. In fact, *the* major wholesaler here. You're patently not a, as it were, street person, Manse.' Alf Ivis chuckled. 'You employ people at various levels below, and one of these, Stefan Bulmer, seems to use a child or children as runners.'

'Fucking chaos. Didn't I always hate the use of kids?' Shale said.

'Well, you did, Mansel. It's on record. But Stefan Bulmer—'

'Stefan, my arse. Where'd he get a fucking name like that? What's his real name? Where's he from, from Hungary or Peru, somewhere like that, with a name like that? His real name's Justin or Percival I could bet.' Shale would often rubbish people for their names. It really went right to the innards of things. 'A kid blasted like that on a thoroughfare with folk around shopping for their legal wares. This can't do us no good, Alfie. This will bring activity. Think of Harpur. Think of Desmond Iles. Whatever they're up to these days, shagging and warring among themselves, those two are bound to notice the killing of a kid on a piece of normal commercial pavement. A death like that got to fall within police business. Plus a thick bag of produce. This is volatility.'

'That was not usual, Mansel. I mean the value. Mainly this kid did grass and very minor coke consignments. This was bad luck – the particular day,' Alf Ivis said.

'Bad luck? Bad luck? Don't I know it's bad fucking luck? This is one of our own kids with two bullets in her from one of our own chartered people. Friendly fucking fire. A Kalashnikov – I mean, Christ, Alfie. We commission this black to come in and do a limited task for us, a properly laid out definite task, and then suddenly there's a Kalashnikov banging off among an established community and one of Bulmer's freelance staff on the end of it. Me, I'll never call the sod Stefan. He *looks* like a Percival. Or Anthony. That line of things. This kid, from all I hear now – now, when it's no good at all hearing it – I hear she was a star runner. Acumen. Always delivered, and no tampering with the produce or filching cash. Enthusiasm, yet also careful – never short-cutting through that jungle park, Fulmar Gardens. One thing about that lazy slob, Bulmer, he spotted talent. This was definitely a percentage child from all I been told.'

'Well, NOON was a gifted kid, yes, Mansel, by all accounts.'

'The word I've heard about her – it's that word saying she's ahead of her age, you know.'

'Precocious.'

'This was a flair,' Shale replied.

'But believe me there are others eager to look after your interests. The girl was outstanding, yes, but she comes from a general level of competence and dedication that has developed very nicely on the Ernest Bevin. Traditional employment is not so easy for modern youth, and these children have adapted early. There's a pool of these slick runners, the way some villages had a mining tradition or trawlermen. Well, it's as if it's already in the blood, Mansel.'

'Didn't I just tell you I'm against kids?' Shale replied. 'As a rule.'

Ivis said: 'Obviously, they've got to come off the routes for a while now. You're right – that bag with the rocks in is a factor. This is what I meant, unlucky. Well, it's going to make it tough temporarily for a courier child up there to look like just a harmless youngster. You could say the more innocent they seem the more it'll be assumed they're freighters.' He chuckled again: 'And we want a forever ban on carrier bags, I think. You're right, Mansel – Stefan's going to have to roll out of whoever's bed he's in these days and nights and make more calls himself, even with the minor loads.'

'Wowing birds by telling them he's called Stefan, the fucker.'

'But, with respect, Mansel, what we can't do is shut down all youngsters for all time. This would be unforgivable waste. Yes, I do think, unforgivable. Well, it would be to spurn a real bonny reservoir of skill. Plus, we might get maverick trouble from the children and their families. They know a lot about our operations, sensitive matters. Look, Mansel, these young people are used to good money, and some of them might well be breadwinners. Runners are central to the local economy. This is a society dependent one way or the other on produce. They could devise things against us, against trade, if we cut them out. Also, the shops would notice a drop in customer income should people find themselves suddenly flung back on allowances. If we flatten their business some of them could put words where, frankly, Manse, we don't want words put. Oh, yes, we've worked out a very decent system for keeping people helpfully quiet, but, as you know, it's always vulnerable, and if enough of them were offended over a widespread loss of purchasing power we'd face difficulties. Certainly we require a pause now on the use of children until the racket over NOON fades out. But it will be important to let the youngsters and connections know it's temporary only. This is a communications priority.'

They were in Alf Ivis's big greasy sitting room drinking gin and pep from mugs with fairy tale pictures on them. 'This kid's funeral,' Mansel replied. He waited a moment and tightened his jaw to get the sob out of his voice. 'I hate the idea of that funeral. There's nothing worse than a small coffin. I hate to see a vicar crouching over a small coffin in all that black, like some crow crowing over the kid because the kid's dead early and this vicar's still there quoting.'

'I don't know if you're thinking of going to this funeral, in the circumstances,' Ivis said.

'I'd like to get some respect somehow to this kid. Do you realize, Alfie, a kid like that could of thought the whole world was like Bulmer or that fucker with the Kalashnikov. He's dead when I find him. This fucker is with two of our own long-time people, including Neville, but they don't control him. Do you understand how that could be, Alfie? It's too late to tell this kid the whole world is not like that, like Bulmer or this black, but I'd like to do some gesture of respect.'

'Well, Mansel, you could obviously send big flowers from a make-up name.'

'The make-up name won't be fucking Stefan, I'll tell you that.

'And maybe slip some decent sum to the mother, who's an off-and-on user and must have expenses. A grand or two, cash. Or cash and some produce.'

'Yes, of course. But it's cold, so cold, heartless, Alfie – flowers, money, produce. I'd like to do some really warm fucking gesture. Something . . . something in line with the kind of person I am, Alf. I think I can claim that. Like my presence at this sad occasion. But if I'm in the church and I break down seeing this small coffin, and maybe yelling hate jibes at the vicar, this would all draw attention and ruin the atmosphere, I see that. This kid's entitled to atmosphere. Harpur, Iles are probably there. They pick up signs. I never met the kid, of course, but I'm supplying Bulmer who's using her to supply street level. People like Harpur, Iles, they'd work out the link, if I'm into spotlight at the funeral.'

'Or additionally offer to pick up the tab for the funeral and casket,' Ivis replied. 'Explain to the mother that you can't attend owing to pre-arranged commitments but tell her that you have been moved by the terrible incident and would like to show support, out of citizenship. Well, this is only what's true, Mansel. There would be no need at all to intimate a connection with NOON, since, in fact, there was not one, nothing direct.'

Shale considered this a useful idea, the kind he paid Alfie Ivis to provide. This was a great relationship that went back and back to more difficult days when they both had needed to be a lot rougher than now. Alfie had a real way with handguns then. He was always brilliant and serene when speaking in his home, this mad, abandoned fucking lighthouse he had bought and converted more or less by himself. Parts of it were nearly quite comfortable now. Scruffy but comfortable. Alfie had moved into this high-class accent and so on, but his furniture was shit and the carpets as thin as smoked salmon and with the same sort of smell. To suppress that odour Shale usually lit up a cigar as soon as he entered Ivis's place. They were sitting in the big ground-level area where the dynamos and amplifier gear for the fog horn used to be. The sea was grey and rocky out of the window. The thing about sea and rocks was they went on and on, and to Shale it looked like a lighthouse was still needed. Yet now all they had was Alfie and his family. There were things to be said for a lighthouse. When Alfie had stress and wanted some beautiful uninterrupted views he could climb up to the top of the tower on the iron staircase and voyeur couples having it off in the beach dunes. Alfie had had some great education in his youth and he was the one to ask about law, the body's structure, accounts and the history of the Royal Navy right back.

'We're certainly looking for Kalashnikov man for you, Manse, believe me,' Ivis said. 'Well, what else? I mean, he's got Timmy with him injured, hasn't he? We hope only injured. Earl, he's called.'

'Earl, bollocks. When I say he's to be killed, this Earl . . . oh, look, Alfie, I'm not some wild tyrant who thinks in blood only, am I? But this black has cost us a bucketful. He's got to be spoken to. There's Timmy and the dear pavement kid, plus what's worse, this general disturbance of the scene, livening the police. This was a situation of peace that took years to create, and a lot of the credit goes to you, Alfie. Now, what I hear from W. P. Jantice is it's not just Harpur and Iles, but Marky Lane himself into rage.'

'Well, Jantice is not that kind of rank. This will only be rumour around the building. I—'

'Someone like Lane, a through-and-fucking-through Catholic, he's certain to get damned fed up about a girl knocked over by a Red gun. Micks got this lovely reverence for the female, dating right back.'

'Jantice says there's no identifications.'

Shale stared at the sea for a while. Jesus, there was a hell of a lot of it. 'You live in this lighthouse, Alfie, and I like to think of the great beam that used to go burning out from here. I like to think of it burning into the soul of someone like this W. P. Jantice.'

'He's all right, Manse.'

'All the time I have to worry. I have to worry that I've bought him, and I'm still buying him, but have I bought him because they wanted him to be bought and he's telling them more than he's telling us?'

'I'd swear he's no plant,' Ivis replied.

Alfie had the sort of face you would never trust all the way, yet it was the kind of face that made you want to trust it all the way. It was meaty and solid-looking with trimmed dark eyebrows and youngish skin. Alfie did a lot of gin, yet his skin kept this honest polish.

Shale said: 'You're the boy who talks to Jantice most one to one. I've got to listen to you, Alfie.'

'Nothing but sound stuff from him.'

Shale could hear Ivis's children somewhere outside, playing and laughing. One of the voices was Alfie's daughter. It seemed wrong to Shale to be talking about the killing of a girl around the same age as that child, like two different kinds of life. 'All right, if the Kalashnikov fucker had shot the two he was supposed to shoot and then the girl as well by accident I could see some point,' Shale said. 'But, what I hear, they both got clear, the one they call Sailor Billy with his fucking beret not even hurt, and the other nothing serious, an arm or lung. These are people who come into our realm from outside trawling for gain, no question, so we're absolutely entitled to tear their heads off, and we engage what's supposed to be a supreme expert to do it, also from outside. But instead of that this sod finds space in a tiny self-employed kid for two missiles from a Kalashnikov. I'd probably call that ironic. We ought to locate that black before Harpur does, Alfie. This is for many reasons. There's Timmy to think about.'

Ivis said: 'Well, Manse, Neville's with the two of them, don't forget. He seemed all right, not hurt, was driving well on the exit. Nev's not going to let that black dispose of Timmy just because he's hurt and a liability. There'd be a loyalty matter involved, probably. Nev and Timmy have worked together a long time.'

'This black's got a Kalashnikov. He can't use it right, but he's got it and close to even he could spray where it counts. I've got responsibility to Timmy, a responsibility although it sounds to me like he helped fuck things up, too. I mean, the black couldn't hit Sailor Billy nor this other one, Joseph Quant, if that's the bugger's name, but why couldn't Timmy instead? He carrying a .45 and the distance is not impossible. How could it be impossible, when he got hit himself by them, and he's behind a car? This whole operation makes me a prick, Alfie. And then if I go and collapse into weeping at the funeral, even more so. This is no way to run an enterprise. Yes, I see chaos.'

# 6

Alfie's wife brought the children in then and Shale stood up from the rough old armchair where he had been sitting and gave them all a good greeting and some chatter about guillemots and so on. He thought these children looked right for a lighthouse. There was something jumpy and too clever about them, and they had a way of talking too fast and moving their heads about a lot. Shale did not hate them – Christ, you could not hate a major colleague's kids! – not hate them, but he did think Alfie would be more comfortable when he could get the three away to boarding school well up north. There was the girl about thirteen and two younger boys with all sorts of names. The mother was taking them to archery, or something like that. This was the kind of special sport Alfie would prefer. He was always looking for style, except with the furniture and carpets, which probably he would think too middle class to bother about much.

When they had gone in the Land Rover, Shale remained standing. 'We ought to visit Timmy's mother, Alfred,' he said. 'I see a great family like yours and it's bound to make me think along those lines. The bonds.'

Ivis had been out to the yard to see the family off but now sat down again, like for a long session. He said: 'She's not going to know he was in that incident and hurt. She won't be worried, believe me. It's a typically kindly thought of yours, Mansel, but I feel we could wait.'

Ivis reached up behind him to a bit of a drinks shelf and was going to pour more gin and peps into the Brer Fox mugs, but Shale stopped him. 'He's a boy who kept in touch with her, I know that,' he said. 'Fucking eyeshades nonstop, but he was very close to his mother.'

'Well, yes. Timmy's dutiful.'

'The word. Christ, it must be sweet to have vocabulary. Timmy's got to stay out of sight, Alf. That's the best we can hope for. This good lady's going to be uneasy about no contact. This is a widow.'

'He could probably ring her.'

'They might be living rough. They'd ditch the Carlton. No mobile phone. He's hit. Can he walk to a booth? You got to ask that. Can he even dial? Can he speak? Plus he could think to himself that if he rings and he's sounding weak or full of blood or fragments how's that going to affect her? If someone's been shot somewhere central a mother will pick up the flavour of that on the phone and get distressed. I would not like to be talking to any child of mine on the phone if I thought he had bullets in him, and I'm a man. Or, in any case, is this Kalashnikov black going to agree if Timmy says he just has to slip into the village from the woods to phone his widowed mother, and maybe draw attention, if he's bleeding in a general way?'

'My fear, Manse, is that they might be watching his

mother's place, knowing from the dossier that Timmy thinks so much of her.'

'But W. P. Jantice would of tipped us to that, wouldn't he?'

'Well, W. P. only knows so much. He's just a sergeant. He's valuable but limited.'

'He said no identities.'

'He did, but things move on, Manse. And even without IDs they'd have a shortlist of likelies. This is how they work. Timmy could be on that list. My feeling is that at this stage you should avoid all overt associations that might bring embarrassment to you personally and to the company. As things stand – happily stand, Manse – there is nothing to link you in any way to the disgraceful death of this child, for which you have heartfelt and very obvious regret. I would advise against this visit and attendance at the funeral. Perhaps it would serve if you telephone Timmy's mother yourself. I wouldn't think there'd be a tap. Not even Iles could get permission on such slight grounds.'

\*

In Shale's Jaguar on the way to see Mrs Montain they kept the driver's partition glass shut. 'Phoning her was a fair idea, Alf, and definitely worth consideration, but what I got to think, isn't it, is that we're really going to see her in case it turns out bad, I mean the worst. Known as the bottom line. We got to get some support in, in advance. This probably requires face to face. Loss of blood or this mad black –

Timmy might be dead somewhere, or dying. We could be into one of those rolling tragedies.'

He opened the partition and told the chauffeur to take his cap off and drive right through the street on the first approach, so they could have a look around in case of surveillance. He closed the partition. 'Neville's with them, yes, and he's great, of course he's great, but if they're running, changing cars, Timmy could be such a drag. You say loyalty and I agree, I prize it – in fact we live by it, Alf – but Timmy blitzed could be such a drag. I got a duty to a woman in this position, surely. How I regard it – we are surrounded by chaos, can see it everywhere. And with break-up like that all round it's so important to look after the good links left in life, such as a widowed mother's regard for her son.'

'Does she know you, Manse?'

'Oh, yes. Timmy took me out here once before. I like to meet those close to my colleagues. Likewise your children and Zoë. These are like ... well, like windows. You can't really know someone unless you know those near to him and loved by him. If there's one business rule I live by and cherish, Alfred, that's the fucking one.'

Of course, the big Jag would be noticeable and the number was in every copper's mind, but Shale was not going to sneak up to the house on foot or in some rented banger, was he? Taking the cap off would make things a bit less obvious, and driving through and not stopping was just a bit of sense. That would have to be enough. He had a right to call on a widowed lady, for Christ's sake. He did not agree with Alfie that just because you called at some widowed lady's house this meant the world thought you had laid on the death of the kid in Sphere Street. He'd like to hear Harpur try and get away with that on a jury, though he'd tried worse. Alfie had a lot of insights and was worth the money, but someone with a face like that and kids like that, you could not just follow everything he said. A ruler overruled.

Shale opened the partition again: 'We're looking for the usual eye parties, Denzil,' he told the driver. 'People in parked cars, front or back on to the house. Or bedroom windows if they've got in a property opposite somewhere. If it's Harpur himself he'll be in some absolute wreck, supposed to be the perfect disguise. Look for a fucking hulk in rust.'

But they saw nothing to trouble them and came around the block and stopped a little way from the house, then walked. 'Mrs Montain, this is a very fine friend of mine as well as a business colleague, Mr Alfred Ivis, who looks after quite a few sections of my business. As a matter of fact, some sections in which Timmy himself is concerned.'

Shale had thought about flowers, but what did flowers say to a widow and a widow under strain, for God's sake? He was keen on flowers himself, but they could send out a difficult message of brightness and misery mixed. He took quick sharp looks into Mrs Montain's face to see if she knew from this visit that things might not be absolutely great for Timmy. Or she might have known it even before. This was a woman with a round face and slant eyes and good arms, like the best sort of Russian peasant from TV programmes about wheat out there. This was a strong face, someone who could put up with a big-headed twat like Timmy. She was around forty-five and with women this was not an age when things started brightening up. 'I said to Alfred that it was important for the running of the business that he should meet not just all staff – that's obvious – but those close to staff, also. It gives a dimension. And naturally one of the first people I suggested for him to meet was Mrs Montain in her lovely home.'

It looked like Ivis was going to say something, swallowing and so on getting his smile right, but Shale gave him a swift frown. Ivis with all his majesty and words was terrific when it came to breaking it to kin about a death, but Shale did not want that here yet. Timmy might still turn up in some condition. At this stage, this was only a meeting to say things could be worse so she was teed up in case. Shale said: 'Plus as well as introducing you to Mr Ivis, we're a bit concerned about Tim at present, Mrs Montain. It would be fair to say we've lost touch.'

'My feeling is I don't want you or any of your associates in my house,' she replied.

'Mrs Montain, Timothy *is* an associate, and I'm proud of that fact,' Shale said. Yes, this was a strong woman. You could see that the way the neck bones stuck out now. They were talking in the hall of this little villa. Her voice was just ordinary, although speaking this abuse, not quivering or screaming. She had not asked them into a room. The front door was still open, like they were not stopping.

Alfie said to her: 'Is there some stress, Mrs Montain? Remarks like that, they do suggest stress. Perhaps there's something we can do.'

'This was Timothy in Sphere Street, wasn't it?' she replied. 'Engaged on some filth for you. The career. And hurt for it. Perhaps badly hurt.'

Here was the trouble with a boy like Timmy, close to his mother and open by nature. Often Shale had worried about it. A fine mother like this could probably read her boy. She might even have known ahead of the disaster that he had some special task that day. This would be the same kind of sensing something as when she might pick up any wounds by phone. Mothers *felt* how things were. They were a sodding pain. She would realize anyway that this boy had some hazards in his life, and knew he was not, say, a librarian. Then she reads the papers, sees the TV News reports about Sphere Street, hears of a white boy, shades, in his twenties, knocked over and dragged into a Carlton by a black – and all credit to the ambulancing bastard, even if he was a dingdong plague handling a gun. Then she would wonder and turn savage in a mean little hallway like this, despite a pleasant earlier meeting.

'I wondered if he had made contact, Mrs Montain,' Shale said.

'How could he make contact? He's dying somewhere, isn't he? Or dead.'

Shale wished she would cry, but she looked like she could not cry, this strong hefty face, and the slant eyes so full of suffering they had given up crying a long time ago. If she cried they could try to help her out of her sorrow, and get rid of her viciousness with some genuine caring. This was where Alfie worked wonders. He had that wordage. He had been pretty terrible with a gun not many years ago, but now he had turned to grand conversation. She did not even sit down. There was nowhere to sit down in this thin little hall with its pale picture of a second-class stream somewhere, and she did not take them to a room. There was nothing wrong with her clothes. He had seen much worse than these on all kinds of women, but he would have liked her to be really dressed up and crying, to make the grief seem important and easier for comforting, more of a worthwhile target.

'And you've got him firing at some child,' Mrs Montain said. Her voice was thick with hate. 'How could you make him do that?'

Shale struck at the emulsioned wall under the picture. 'No, no, dear lady. That child should not of come into it in any way. This child was not on our agenda in any way, was she, Alfred?'

'Mr Shale is as distressed about that appalling incident as anyone, believe me,' Ivis said. He gave that maximum.

'Is he dead? Are you here to tell me he's dead?' she replied.

'It's entirely possible he's perfectly well,' Alfie said. 'This could be tactical.'

'He's shot,' she said. 'Every paper said so. I bought them all. Diagrams. Diagrams of a child's death and perhaps my son's death.'

'It's true he was shot, apparently,' Alfie replied. 'But there is no reason at this stage to assume that this was a grave . . . that is, serious injury. There are what is known as flesh wounds, Mrs Montain. These are very common.'

'He couldn't get into the car alone,' she said.

Shale said: 'There's a bitterness in you. I can understand that. I hope I prize family as much as you. These are not peaceful times. What we got to have, Mrs Montain, is any tip as to whereabouts, if he's in touch. This would be of benefit to us all. I mean including you and Timmy himself. It's important for us, that's me and Mr Ivis, to reach Timmy before any others. Or any contact at all – the news of that could be important for us. This is a boy we want to do well by.'

'Obviously, we would prefer it that, if he makes contact, you notify us, rather than, say, the police or even seek medical help,' Alfie pointed out. 'This is not a situation where outside involvement would serve.'

Shale said: 'There has been a mistake or two, no denying that, but this is a boy we could get back on his feet and even in great smiling form again, as we all love to see him, and as we all like to think of him. Yes, we'll get him back there if we get some nice luck and early news from you of hearing from him, in any form, by phone or letter or even arriving at the front door. This is a boy we got obligations to, Mrs Montain. If he phones, listen for what's in the background if you could. This can sometimes tell us the place. And, of course, you can dial back on the find number, but he will probably be in a box and the find number don't always work with them. Or he might have done the cancel thing, anyway. Or his colleagues might of made him do that. It's important to listen in case of trees or a train, even shipping. These would help a search. I've got good people to run a search, but narrowing down the area would be useful. He might say where he is, but I'm not sure he will. It might be only what we name a "holding call", to give you peace of mind.'

'They'll stop him telling me where he is?' she asked.

'These are his good friends,' Shale replied. 'Neville and this other colleague. Currently they could have a bit of strain, though.'

# 7

Lane grew obsessive about the NOON case. Harpur recognized the symptoms, and they turned abruptly worse when Timothy Astor Montain's body was found. Although that had always been a possibility, Lane seemed badly ravaged by this second shock. The Chief's reaction to it appeared even more frenzied than to the child's death. Thin lines of fright or rage or both quivered momentarily in his sallow face and forehead. His voice went out of control and for much of the time he spoke in a blare, as if determined to dominate, but not sure he could. He never had on this manor, except when Iles was distracted by problems at home or went on leave. Harpur hated seeing Lane so troubled. He would have hated seeing anyone in that state, but it seemed especially sad in the Chief. Lane had once been a clear-headed, fine detective on the neighbouring patch, and Harpur had enjoyed working with him occasionally. But this top post, plus Iles, had begun to shred him. He had already suffered one breakdown and suddenly looked liable to another. Iles would provide no therapy. Why didn't the Chief treat himself to a holiday? No, of course he wouldn't, not now. Mission. He had to save the rotten realm. His face might be sallow but he could bring true resolution to it now and then.

## Top Banana

News that Montain was dead came near the end of a meeting called by Lane with Harpur and Iles, plus all Drugs Squad officers who knew the Ernest Bevin well. The Chief wanted what he called a 'comprehensive update', though it turned out to be an update that amounted to not much. When Francis Garland entered the conference room to give his message, Lane had been summing up with reasonable poise regardless of his clothes and in his usual moderate tone. He emphasized his determination to have no unspoken alliances between the police and big-time traffickers or wholesalers. He had even laughed briefly and said: 'Or small-time, for that matter. But above all I will not tolerate "corporate understandings" with crack and grass magnates in the supposed interests of street peace. A price not to be paid.' It was meant mainly for Iles, though only he, Harpur and the Chief would know this. He was proclaiming that whatever results Iles forecast from his 'chaos theory' Lane meant to fight them. And fight Iles. In a way it was a bonny, brave show by the Chief: almost as if he had at last thrown off his terror of the ACC. Perhaps there would be no breakdown after all. While the Chief risked this challenge, Iles devoted himself to scratching and realigning his balls inside the narrow cut of the grey flannel trousers. The ACC kept a pleasured smirk on his face.

Then Garland had come in and stood at the back of the room, as if keen to hear Lane's words of policy. When the Chief had finished, though, Garland approached and whispered briefly to Harpur.

'Well,' Iles asked, lounging further down in his chair, 'what the fuck is it?'

Garland said: 'A departmental matter of some urgency, sir. I thought I'd—'

'Has one of the Sphere Street people been found?' Iles replied. 'Dead?'

Harpur said: 'Francis tells me it's Timmy Montain.'

'Ah,' Iles said. Harpur watched him do a rapid dossier scan in his head. 'Twenty-sevenish? Shades? Would he fit our picture of the lad shot alongside the Carlton?'

Lane now began to shout, and a line of red snaked fast across his cheek and down his nose like night-sky tracer bullets in war movies. 'But how did you know this, Desmond?'

'Know what, sir?' Iles murmured.

'Know this was the information brought by Francis.'

'I didn't know, sir. I intuited. At Staff College I was fondly dubbed "Intuitive Iles". People said it was a happy result of my feminine streak. Of course, we all have traces of the other gender. I'm sure Mrs Lane would endorse that.' The Drugs Squad people lounged back and watched and listened enraptured, but none spoke.

'And how do you know this man?' Lane replied, still with his voice at between a snarl and a yell.

'Timmy would be known to most people in this room, sir. He's a trivial part of the local trade scene and has been for aeons. Lovely widowed mother, forty-fiveish but spruce.'

'*Part of the local trade scene?*' Lane said. '*For aeons?* How has this been tolerated?'

The Chief knew, of course. Or knew once. Now, in the big job, though, he had to pretend that villainy in all its forms should be instantly annihilated.

'Why tolerated, sir?' Iles replied. 'Oh, that customary gap.'

'What gap?' the Chief said. 'Oh, are you going to tell me again about—'

'The gap between knowing it and proving it to the satisfaction of a feeble-minded, bought, anti-cop, intimidated British jury,' Iles replied. 'I speak truth, don't I, Harpur?'

'Tim Montain was found in one of the abandoned houses off Valencia Esplanade at the docks. Francis says he had two gunshot wounds in the upper body but appears to have been killed by a bullet in the head fired from very close. This is a very long way from where the Carlton was located.'

'My God,' Lane yelled. 'Jungle.'

'Executed,' Iles said. 'This was always on the cards.'

'What is happening here?' Lane bellowed. 'Eliminated by his own crew? But didn't that black save him during the street incident?'

'During the street incident he might have, sir,' Iles replied. 'Things change. People's patience with the wounded can fade. Or Montain might have been in such pain he asked for it: they wouldn't risk a hospital, so this was their next most merciful resource. In any case, perhaps it's not quite proper to assume he was shot by the Kalashnikov black. There's a driver.'

'I'd better go and look at the body, sir,' Harpur said.

'Of course,' Lane replied. 'Do you know, Colin, I feel I must come, too. This death – oh, the implications of it. The cumulative implications of this and the child. It's my duty to be present.'

The Chief was eternally on watch for what he saw as cumulative evil. He lived with the dread that lawlessness in his nominal territory would gallop ahead and take over. Perhaps even while denying it he believed in the ACC's chaos theory, if chaos theory meant that whatever happened it would probably lead to self-aggrandizing disaster. In fact, Harpur had the feeling that Lane's fears went further than anything Iles envisaged. The Chief thought evil might win on a world scale and would most likely start its victorious progress from here, his patch, if he failed to reverse it. Lane had all those heavy Catholic notions about responsibility and guilt. Harpur's older daughter, Hazel, said one day that the Chief reminded of her a Graham Greene character, whatever that meant. Well, she told him what it meant: she thought Lane searched out failure as a way of making God pity and love him more.

'Yes, it might be best that the three of us should go to see Montain,' Iles said.

Oh, Jesus.

The ACC stood, ready, aye, ready in one of his double-breasted navy blazers as advertised in *Tailor and Cutter*.

'It's a pity we have to break up the meeting, sir,' Harpur told Lane. 'I was finding it very profitable.' Well, sort of:

some rumour had surfaced, some speculation, some names. No question a few of the Drugs Squad people here knew pretty much everything that could be known about trade in the Ernest Bevin and beyond: there was Sophie Pole, Peter Lace, Wayne Patterson Jantice – or W. P. as he liked to be called – Naomi Anstruther and Daphne Ann Calt. While he listened, Harpur had found himself thinking that if it came to infiltration the Anstruther girl would probably suit best. She had been on his list of probables from the beginning and watching her and hearing her today he almost definitely decided she was the one. She had the kind of jumpy, nostalgic looks that seemed to spell a one-time habit. Someone had been slack letting her into the force – or wise. A lot of people trading produce had come out of addiction, or were still in it, and her disorganized appearance would be an asset. Her brain was quick, and when she spoke about the structure of the businesses it was with what sounded to Harpur like brilliantly thorough understanding, even affection. People with a habit or the memory of a habit did feel affection for the system that catered for it, and bugger the expense. Her clothes were ramshackle, yet not so ramshackle you'd think she was an undercover cop.

'We can always reassemble,' the Chief stated. 'But I think Colin is right and that this second death has to be a priority now.' He stood too and gave the room a bit of profile for a moment. It was quite like leadership.

Iles said: 'We're so lucky here to get hands-on Chiefing, aren't we, Col?'

'I think Montain often worked with a lad called Neville Greenage,' Harpur replied. 'Mansel Shale sometimes used them as a pair.'

'Less these days, sir,' W. P. Jantice said. 'They hire themselves out elsewhere. My information is that Mansel didn't trust those two any longer.'

Lane said: 'You know it all at ground level.'

In the car with Harpur and Iles, the Chief said: 'I liked the look and sound of W. P. Jantice. I mean for possible planting in a firm. He has the subtlety and the knowledge – current knowledge, with its shifting complexities. He would very soon pick up the feel of any outfit. And that's so crucial to his safety, my prime anxiety. In fact, the prime anxiety of us all, I know.'

'It's what's always said about you, sir,' Iles replied. 'Loudly.'

Montain lay in rubble on the ground floor of one of the big derelict old villas in Hawser Street off Valencia Esplanade. Arc lights had been rigged over the body and at other points in the large room. A couple of men were searching through debris near the door, though not in any organized way yet. There was a lot of debris near the door: bits of plaster and masonry, old take-away cartons, timber, cans, bottles, withered condoms, aged and filthy pieces of clothing. Anyone who moved sent up a wall of dust that took minutes to settle again. You could get used to the smells after a time. Montain's head had bad damage. That might mean hefty calibre or just the closeness. Harpur crouched over him. He could see the bulk of a shoulder holster under the left lapel of Montain's jacket and the butt of something heavy. A lot of Harpur's detective career had been spent looking at corpses, armed and unarmed, in these once noble properties. The city would clear them all and rebuild when the money was about. It had not been about for the last five years at least. And each year these houses slipped a bit further into decay. Most were boarded up. But boarding up did not keep out the winos and dossers and tarts with their clients, and people on the run, and people looking for a quiet spot for a killing. These houses had been built in the last century for rich merchants. In those days, Valencia Esplanade must have seemed the right sort of happy name for a seafront road bright with success and promise. Now, 'Esplanade' had come to sound grandiose. People usually called the area simply 'the Valencia', and there was no magic in their voice when they said it.

Garland was with them and started to instruct: 'He's carrying a .45 Smith and Wesson Model 645 automatic. Formidable weapon. Double action trigger, eight round magazine.'

Iles said: 'Has it been fired?'

'I thought I'd better not check it until Scene of Crime arrive,' Garland replied.

'Absolutely not,' the Chief said.

'Ask him if it's been fired, will you, Harpur?' Iles said.

'Has it been fired, Francis?' Harpur said.

'There's only one round in the magazine,' Garland

replied. 'Yes, the gun smells recently active. There are fragments of quite fresh bought food about in this room. The three might have camped out here the whole time since Sphere Street. They would know we'd have road blocks out immediately after the shooting and possibly thought it safer to go to ground. Of course, they'll have stolen another car and we're checking on anything missing from around where the Carlton was found. We're also looking at vehicles parked around the Valencia. It would probably be close. Montain might not have been able to walk far.'

'Shops?' Lane said.

'Naturally we're visiting everywhere they might have bought supplies,' Garland replied. 'But it's a moving population in these houses, and the food remains are not necessarily theirs. Oh, not necessarily theirs at all.' Garland, this whiz kid on the fast route to the top, loved intoning. His voice banged out and echoed from the peeling walls. Iles used to say that if Garland ever had to leave the police he could always get a job as a steel band. But he was right about Hawser Street: all sorts might spend a night or two here, then move on. There was nobody else in the house now. There wouldn't be. The sound of a shot would frighten most lodgers away. And the knowledge that a body lay here would get rid of the rest. They would be out before the law swarmed.

'We should search these houses as a routine, after any incident when suspects disappear,' Lane said.

'We did, sir,' Iles told him. 'How we found him.'

'But sooner,' Lane said.

'Next time a kid's shot in the street we'll come here first,' Iles replied.

Harpur said: 'We had to concentrate the opening trawl near where the Carlton was found.'

Lane bent down alongside Harpur, staring at the wound and the dust stains on what remained of Montain's face. 'And was he from this city?' the Chief asked.

Harpur sensed that something profound and maybe religious lurked here. Lane wanted know how a local youngster had been allowed to tumble to where he had tumbled, a mean end in a ruin. Was it a second young local who had slipped towards rough death? This was normality on his domain? Guilt, responsibility – yes, they never ceased to badger the Chief. They gave his tone a tremor now.

Iles said: 'Perhaps Harpur can be in attendance, but I'll notify the mother personally.'

'Oh, Desmond,' Lane replied, straightening, 'is that—'

'This requires finesse,' Iles said. 'Montain was a fucking nothing crook, and thank God for one fewer. At the same time, he is undoubtedly a son, quite as much as we are sons, sir: you, myself, Harpur, even Garland.'

# 8

In the Granada on the way to see Mrs Montain, Harpur restudied the short-form postmortem report on NOON while Iles drove. From the wounds and recovered bullets they had now worked out what killed her.

*The child was struck by two 6.35mm rounds, both entering the body from the left. One penetrated the lower neck on an upward trajectory and lodged in the right jaw. This bullet carried away half of the trachea and all the larynx and would probably have caused death within two or three hours. The other bullet entered her chest just below her heart, breaking a rib. The bullet lodged 3mm to the left of the heart. A large fragment of rib ruptured the heart and caused death within ten minutes.*

So they had been wrong to assume she was hit by the Kalashnikov, either intentionally or by accident. The calibre was too big for the 5.45mm AK74 Kalashnikov model used: they had found plenty of its spent rounds. The firing from this rifle seemed to have been almost farcically incompetent, except that the balding black in the long overcoat might have been winged by a burst late on. Yet all the reports on the AK74 said it was easy to keep on a target when firing full automatic and had little recoil.

The gun in Timothy Montain's hand as described by Ericson also sounded too big for that 6.35mm calibre – only about .25 inches: Montain's sounded more like a .45. Of course, Ericson was some distance away and up a ladder, and, as he had said, knew only about guns he had seen featured on television. A .45 Smith and Wesson ACP, though, had been in Montain's holster at the Hawser Street house. It appeared at least probable that this was the gun he had in Sphere Street.

Did it look now, then as if NOON had been shot by one of the two men on foot, the white in the beret or the long overcoated black, both still untraced? The witness reports could not specify what calibre weapons these two carried. Although Harpur probably knew a bit more about armament than Ericson, it was not all that much, and he took advice: Percy Wate at the range said the most likely 6.35mm pistol was a P230 SIG-Sauer automatic made in Germany. If the shooting had happened nearer the centre of the city there might have been overhead cameras to settle all these unknowns, but this was a shopping street at the edge of a far-out council estate. Everything depended on witnesses, and witnesses at this far-out council estate were always rare.

The possible new reading of the incident produced more difficulties. As the witness reports told it, when the firing from the Carlton started NOON had turned and run back towards the two walking men, who were behind her. That is, she would be head-on to them and if one or the other had shot at NOON the bullets would have entered her body from directly in front, not from the left, as the postmortem found. There was nothing in the witness statements to say either man had moved to the left. For a second, Harpur felt as if he were conducting in miniature the kind of unresolvable guesswork that continued about Jack Kennedy's assassination. Had there been another gunman, unaccounted for by either witness? This one would be positioned to the girl's left, perhaps hidden between parked cars, and probably in a crouched sniper stance so that the neck bullet was rising when it hit her, despite the fact that she was a small child. There would have been appalling confusion in the street, and, although both Ericson and the woman were careful and sharp witnesses, they might have missed this sixth marksman, or woman. Did that mean NOON had definitely been shot by intent?

The idea that one of the two walking men might have killed NOON also clashed with Harpur's general interpretation of the scene. He had thought the girl and this pair might be somehow acting in agreement. They would hardly want to hurt her. The Carlton team were the enemy. That's how it had looked to both Harpur and Garland and to several of the Drugs Squad. Were they all wrong?

Iles had seen the short-form postmortem report, too, of course. Harpur was not clear what the ACC made of it but as they approached Stipend Road where Mrs Montain lived Iles said: 'Mr Kalashnikov brought in at no doubt mighty cost and looking full of aplomb yet can't use the weapon properly, or won't. Thought about that, Col?'

'He might have panicked, even an expensive imported black with aplomb.'

'Although we hear of a big war between major powers, the only immediate death is this sad little flying bird, hit twice with fine efficiency inside a diameter of about four inches, lower neck and chest.'

This did not seem to require a reply.

Iles said: 'A child like that, padding about across the district – she'd see and hear all sorts, a lot of it very confidential. Suddenly, she gets regarded as a risk by someone with fine shooting skills, because of what she knows. And the someone might be aware a nice camouflaging street battle is scheduled.' Iles took his left hand from the wheel and flicked the report on Harpur's lap. 'The autopsy completely changes the direction of inquiries. But, of course, you realize that, Harpur.'

'I'm going to talk to the mother again.'

'We spend our time talking to mothers.'

'I want to discover names of people who might have been frightened of what she could tell.'

'There'll be a million,' Iles replied. 'The mother claims to have known nothing.'

'Mothers are always tricky,' Harpur said.

Iles left the car a good distance from Mrs Montain's house. The Granada was unmarked, but everybody knew the police had these big Fords and it might cause some interest if parked near her place. Now and then Iles would have such surprising moments of consideration. Empathy Iles. Intuitive

Iles. They walked together up the little front garden and Iles knocked the door. He was in civilian clothes, including a Royal Enclosure-style brown trilby. He took this off in a modest moment when Mrs Montain opened to them and said: 'Madam, may we speak to you for a moment?'

'Law?' she replied.

Harpur did introductions. 'Can we come in?' he asked.

'To do with Timothy?' she said. 'Something wrong with Timothy? An Assistant Chief doorstepping? Des Iles himself? Tim's dead?' Her face stayed strong and her grey eyes direct: no sign of weeping or break-up, but the questions raced from her. It was a demand to be told the worst and told it fast, so it would be over. She had a good face, round and balanced, with a firm, short nose: Eskimo-like, Harpur thought. This was the sort of complete woman always liable by some freak of genes to generate a piece of nonsense like Timmy.

Iles said: 'I think I can say I understand grief, Mrs Montain. This is why I asked my colleague if I might accompany him on this call.'

'He's dead. Where?' she replied.

'Would it be better if we all sat down?' Iles said.

She led them into her bright, unluxurious living room. Framed photographs of young Tim Montain in a school blazer hung on one wall above a scarred upright piano. A couple more pictures of him, older and wearing a tracksuit, stood on the piano. Iles took her arm briefly and directed her towards a brown hide armchair. He put his trilby on top of the television set and then walked over and rigorously studied the photos of Tim. 'Ah, one can spot the degeneracy even so early,' the ACC said. He leaned out and touched some part of the schoolboy face for a moment, perhaps an ear, or his forehead or nose. 'See it there,' he went on. 'Above all I hate the use of tracksuits by people like this to suggest physical wholesomeness.' He sat down in another chair of the suite opposite Mrs Montain. Harpur took a place on the sofa. There were small fat green cushions. The carpet also was green and not new. Undoubtedly it was the kind of home Tim Montain would have been desperate to buy himself out of.

Iles leaned forward sympathetically and spoke to Mrs Montain: 'At a time like this the nature of the life in question hardly seems to count. We are certainly not here to try to force information from you about Timothy's career. Yes, career. But, tell me, were you expecting bad news about him? You seemed . . . well, almost prepared for what we have to say.'

'He hasn't been in touch lately. And then, like I said, an Assistant Chief and Detective Chief Superintendent. It's not for riding a bike without lights. Where?'

'This was in a property in the dockland area of the city,' Harpur replied.

'The Valencia?' she asked. 'One of those big shit-tips? He finished there?' The tone was still clipped. Perhaps she had told him that could be his end.

Iles said: 'We think that his death would have been very quick.'

'Eventually,' she replied, her voice quiet and even. 'Do I see him?'

'Mrs Montain, of course,' Iles replied.

'Now?' She stood and brushed down her heavy grey skirt, as if wanting to look svelte for the dead on a shit-tip.

'Well, not immediately, Mrs Montain,' Harpur said.

'This will be at the morgue, when he's been cleaned up and repaired, will it?' she replied.

'It's the normal thing,' Harpur said.

'Please,' she replied. 'I need to know it all.'

Iles said: 'It's a rather unkempt spot, Mrs Montain, and I wouldn't—'

'Mrs Montain will be all right, I'm sure,' Harpur said.

'Will she?'

'It's natural, sir, that someone mourning should wish to see all the circumstances of a death,' Harpur said.

'Thank you. Oh, thank you,' Mrs Montain replied.

'Who the fuck suddenly turned you into a bereavement counsellor, then, Harpur?'

'Everyone knows this about mourning,' Harpur replied.

'It's I, I, who knows about bereavement,' Iles yelled. 'Why I'm here, for God's sake. In my previous post I was known as "Desmond the Comforter" . . . Off and on.'

'Let's go, then, shall we, Mrs Montain?' Harpur replied.

She brought a coat. The three of them were in the hall when someone tapped the front door. Harpur opened it.

Mansel Shale and Alfie Ivis were waiting outside, Shale's Jaguar with the chauffeur at the wheel parked behind.

'You call at a bad time, Mansel,' Harpur said. 'How's trade?'

'Why are you here?' Mrs Montain asked in a rough whisper. 'Go away. You're interfering.'

'We're taking Mrs Montain to see the body of her son,' Harpur said.

Shale looked catastrophically startled. 'Oh, my God, this is terrible,' he cried in a high, aghast voice. 'What happened? Timothy dead? Is this a motoring accident?'

'Kalashnikov man has been in touch and told you, has he, Mansel?' Harpur replied. 'Or Neville Greenage. Tim worked with him, didn't he? You're here to warn Mrs Montain not to talk. Been visiting her quite a bit lately, urging silence?'

Ivis said: 'This is such a shock. Please accept the deep condolences of Mr Shale and myself, Mrs Montain.'

Iles said: 'Was Timmy on your current staff, Mansel?'

'Current? Oh, dear, no,' Ivis replied. 'A long time ago, quite years, Timothy did have some contact with Mr Shale as a freelance employee, I believe. Is this important?'

'But how did it happen?' Shale demanded in another shriek. They were all clustered around the front door, Shale, Ivis and Harpur outside, Mrs Montain and Iles still in the house.

'Timothy, such a well-loved and respected young man. Oh, yes, and athletic.'

'So what version of his death were you given, Manse?' Harpur asked. 'This would be eye-witness stuff. We're always short of that, as you know.'

'Mr Shale and I will withdraw now,' Alfie Ivis replied. 'As you said, Detective Chief Superintendent, this might be an unfortunate time to call. Mr Shale would not think of imposing on you, Mrs Montain. But if in need, any need at all, please do not hesitate to be in touch.'

'Naturally, we're looking for Greenage and the other,' Harpur said. 'What intimations or even sightings, Manse?'

Ivis said: 'Neville, yes. One had certainly heard of him. Black? And my recollection like yours is that he might well have colleagued with Timmy in those far-off days.' He and Shale walked back towards the Jaguar, and Harpur, Iles and Mrs Montain went down the path after them. The chauffeur did not leave the car to open the door for Shale and Ivis but leaned out of the window and managed it like that. To Harpur it seemed disrespectful. Alf Ivis slammed the door shut when they were inside. Iles raised the trilby as they drove away.

In the Hawser Street house, the lights were off over the body and it was now covered with a canvas sheet. Iles helped Mrs Montain across the rubble until she was standing alongside Montain. Harpur switched on and then removed the canvas. Iles had kept hold of Mrs Montain's arm for support. She gazed down for a long while at the shattered head and face – perhaps for a full minute – but did not crouch to be nearer. Apart from the occasional grunts of traffic outside and some rushed movements by rats or mice in the room above there was a decent silence. Iles stood with his head bent forward, his eyes possibly shut. He seemed to be muttering some prayer or curse. Mrs Montain's breathing remained quiet and steady. 'Thanks again, Mr Harpur,' she said. 'There'll be pictures of him like this, will there?' she asked.

'Now the photographs have been done he'll be removed,' Harpur replied.

'I'd like one.'

'No,' Harpur said. 'I don't think so.'

'You'd realized from news reports that he was at the Sphere Street incident, had you, Mrs Montain?' Iles asked.

She drew herself free of him. 'Can I go home now?' she replied. Harpur covered the body again and switched off the lights.

# 9

Shale and Alfie Ivis were in Shale's own place tonight, not the lighthouse, a good big room he called 'the den'. W. P. Jantice would be joining them soon to give a deep run-through of things from the police angle. It was vital to keep informed when you had a situation that changed so fast. No question at all, this skinny sod Jantice was an asset, with genuine, good inside stuff, but what you had to decide – same as with all assets – what you had to decide was whether the asset was worth what you paid for it. The crux of business. Shale did not like the way Jantice used initials instead of a name: It seemed fucking stand-offish and expensive.

Shale knew Alfie considered it quite an error to have been discovered like that calling on Mrs Montain, but Shale himself was not too troubled. You had to take a bigger view. Life was a more complicated business than Alfie seemed to realize sometimes. 'I consider I'm entitled to visit the dear widowed mother of a lad who's just had half his fucking head blown off in poor surroundings, Alfred,' he said.

'With respect, Manse, there are dangers through association. The Press have been describing Timothy pretty accurately as someone police want to trace after Sphere Street. Jantice tells me Harpur's got two good witnesses. This is always a danger – people coming in from outside the area or even the town and regrettably ignorant of our silence rule. If you recall, we took pains not to be seen by any surveillance on our first visit to Mrs Montain, because of linkage risks. Now, here we were driving straight up to the front door and unfortunately running into those two officers.'

'This was a sympathy visit, for fuck's sake, Alf.' They were in fat Victorian red leather armchairs, part of a suite that Shale had paid a lot to get re-covered. He loved stuff that seemed to recall better times. In those days nearly every trade was expanding beautifully. Now, you had to be in drugs or privatized water if you wanted to be sure of the future.

Ivis said: 'Well, a sympathy call, yes, of course, Mansel, and attempting to seal off a situation. But, with respect, how did we know so soon that sympathy was called for? This is what Harpur and Iles will ask.'

'Smart-arse sods, leaving their vehicle out of sight.' A *Tristan and Isolde* CD was on, the sound low. Shale listened to that without speaking for a while, getting the extent of the tragedy again. 'Tim Montain's death goes right to my fucking holy soul, Alf, so even if I already know about it I still feel like I've been thumped by the news again when someone mentions it. It's like listening to *Tristan* over and over down the years, but it still touches me like fresh.'

Shale let the stricken singing voice shake him thoroughly for another spell. His son, Laurent, came at a gallop into the room and stood beaming in front of Ivis. There were good pieces of furniture about from several countries, including eighteenth century, and Shale disliked the children running in the house. But he did not shout at him now. 'Uncle Alfie,' Laurent said, 'Matilda told me you were here, but I didn't know if it was just a joke, because sometimes she just says things for a joke, but you are. Yes. So are you going to tell me some more about the Royal Navy and wars?'

Ivis was good with the boy and often did tales for him about the Battle of the Nile or Jutland, that kind of quite reputable old knockabout. Alfie knew it all from top to bottom. You mention mine sweeping for D-day to him and he could give you the full yarn, magnetic and all sorts.

'Not today, Laurent,' Shale replied.

'Oh, Dad. Why?'

'We've got someone else coming shortly. This is something a bit important. Uncle Alf can talk to you another day.'

'The *Graf Spee* – when she was you know what-do-you-call-it at the River Plate?' Laurent said.

'Scuttled,' Ivis replied.

'Off you go now, Laurent,' Shale said. He liked to be as easy as he could be with the boy and Matilda, his sister. It was a while now since their mother left and although she sent Christmas presents and that sort of thing it was not the same. Sometimes Shale thought it might be time to look around for someone else long term, not just casual, for the sake of the kids. Something like that with their mother taught you to be careful, though. Shale had a lot of respect for family. When Laurent had gone, Shale struck the arm of his chair lightly. 'Did you ever hear of Law taking a lovely, widowed bereaved parent to some murk hole in Hawser Street to see the smashed-about body of her son? This will be that fucking Iles. He thinks, Get her in there among all the bat shit and old bandages, force her to view her reduced son and then when the morale's a bit down turn on the interrogation. This is a fine, steady-based woman but a creature like that could leak all sorts if she's made to feel a trifle low by circumstances. Impossible to keep spirits jaunty, choked by brick dust. So fucking Iles says to her: *We know Timothy worked for Mansel Shale Incorporated, Mother Montain. What did Timmy tell you about the way things had been planned for Sphere Street?'*

Ivis twitched that plate-of-beef face. 'Timothy was not one to confide such matters to his mother, Manse. This was a boy who was certainly very close to her, but he was also a boy with deft mercantile instincts and a flair for confidentiality, believe me.'

'Here's Jantice.' Shale had heard a car on the gravel of the drive. His house was in its own grounds on the edge of the town. Jantice could drive into one of the stable buildings and close the doors so his car was hidden. It would take a few minutes. Shale and Ivis were drinking gin and peps again. Shale would have preferred some decent glassware, but he did not want to show up Alfie, so they used Cinderella and Tom Tom the Piper's Son mugs here. Jantice would always come into the former rectory by a side door. Shale left it open for him. Laurent and Shale's daughter, Matilda, were supposed to stay in the front drawing room or upstairs. Jantice would not want to be seen by either of them.

Shale said: 'Probably it was wise of Nev and the other to finish Timmy like that, being an undoubted liability in a go-to-ground situation. And there could be a definite humane element in it, owing to wounds and pain. Didn't they say so on the phone? Yes. But there's bound to be a hasty feel too, Alf. Timothy was a boy who had his points. Forget the fucking shades. I mean everybody needs a little gimmick to help out with their personality, especially if you haven't got one, like mummy's boy Tim. Think of Roosevelt in American history with that wheelchair. I'm upset Timmy had to go that way.'

'Of course, Manse. We have to trust the judgement of the people on the ground, Neville and Earl. They seem to have exited very efficiently without him.'

'They were ringing from Hull or Lytham St Anne's, Neville and the other, the fucking cataracted marksman. Somewhere like that. So, is that cow going to gab?'

'Mrs Montain? I don't think she could if she wanted to.'

Shale sipped and groaned briefly: 'First we had NOON's funeral to think about. Now Timmy's. I don't know how I'll play it, Alf.'

Ivis did not reply at once. Then he said: 'Well, with respect, my feeling is, absent yourself from both. Remember, Manse, W. P. was going to stress at headquarters that Timmy had no present connection with your companies. Frankly, I feel this to be wise. Your presence at the funeral might seem to contradict what W. P. tells them. It would be as imprudent to attend his funeral as the girl's.'

Now, Shale heard footsteps and went to the side door to welcome Jantice. This kind of courtesy he considered crucial, especially living in a rectory.

'W. P.,' he said, 'here's a pleasure.'

'I love this house,' Jantice replied. 'The feeling of space and solidity. The grey stone.'

'Well, thanks indeed, W. P.'

'And you keep everything so beautifully – grounds, interior.'

'Thanks again, W. P. Just stay one fucking step ahead of Harpur and you should be able to buy a place like it yourself soon, the amount you're milking me for. Do come in and relax. Alfred's here, too, being cogent and so on.'

At the door to the den Jantice gazed about in delight, as if he had never seen the room before. He let his eyes climb the pastel green walls to the high ceiling and then brought them down just as slowly to admire the desk and some neat Regency straight-backed chairs. Christ, though, he could do a role. Afterwards, he gave some good looks to the paintings which according to where Shale bought them were all definitely old and in tip-top taste. He liked a good portrait. He liked the idea of a personality inside a heavy frame, it gave control. Jantice sat down on the suite settee and Shale did him a gin and pep and more for himself and Alfie. Some said you should not say settee but sofa, but sod them. 'So tell us how much of a disaster we got, W. P.,' he said. 'This kid up

Sphere Street and now Timmy. Give us the genuine police voice.'

'They suspect a lot, can prove nothing,' Jantice replied. 'The usual. I've had a long look at the statements. Piss poor on descriptions. We're all right. Keep a distance from Tim Montain, obviously, and Neville.'

'What Alfie's been saying.'

'It's basic, Manse,' Ivis replied.

'I been thinking about the funerals, W. P. – the girl's and Timmy's. I really don't know. It seems only right – I mean, at least Timothy's. So, if he's supposed to have been with us a long time ago and not now, he's still somebody in my knowledge, isn't he? I mean, Alfie, we've been calling on Mrs Montain, and Harpur and Iles have seen this. What you term the connection is known. Putting it very simple, boys, I feel ordinary fucking decency says I got to go.'

'You're too sensitive to these things, Manse,' Ivis said.

'I'm with Alfie on this, Manse.'

Often Shale thought, yes, he *was* too sensitive. But he regarded this as a nice fault, human. He stood and paced. He had a big partner's desk in mahogany at the centre of the den, and he circled it slowly, speaking at Ivis from all angles. He had bought the desk with the house, plus some other old handsome items. Probably the final vicar in here used to do his sermons at this desk. It was something to think about. 'Let these worthwhile rituals such as funerals go and where are we?' Shale asked. 'Into chaos, that's where. I find myself speaking this word so often lately. Heartfelt funerals and things like that, they're what keeps a sort of order and shape to matters. Do animals do funerals for one another? This is one area where Man's superiority really fucking shows.' Alfie had a bright mind for many important aspects, such as money, gunplay, tactics, discretion, but he could not see the wide issues. He was not in the biggest way a thinker, he was a sort of accountant and a sort of lawyer, a nitty-gritty person only. 'Mrs Montain already thinks I'm pus, and likewise you, Alfred. She'd think W. P. was too if she knew about him, which she never will. What's she going to feel, Alf, if you and I fail to show for her boy's last journey?' The Wagner boomed and jangled. There was scale. He sat down again.

Ivis said: 'My feeling is we should prepare for possible future problems, not undertake additional risks, no matter how nobly motivated such risks might be. We have to think that they may pick up Neville and the other one, Earl.'

'Nev's not going to talk. Nev is loyalty right through. They're well clear. They've got money. Nev said so. I don't know anyone I'd trust more than Nev, except for you, Alfie. I love Nev, really love him. He knows absolutely if he opened his fucking mouth even the smallest he's going to finish worse than Timmy, and that girlfriend of his. Get someone to go around and see her – make sure she's all right for funds now her man's away. Oh, I do value loyalty, Alfie, W. P.'

'They'll focus on child couriers for a while,' Jantice said.

'What Alfie said.'

'Basic, Manse,' Ivis replied.

'Just get the kids lying low for a while,' Jantice said. 'The heat will pass. Let them know it will all resume. There's a lot of budgets depend on child runners.'

'What Alfie said.'

'Basic.'

'So what do I pay this bastard for?' Shale asked. 'He tells me what I been told. I hear the Chief himself's so upset he's suddenly hands-on.'

'My feeling is he wants me to go undercover,' Jantice replied.

'He fucking what?' Shale yelled.

Jantice nodded. He started to laugh. Then Shale laughed, too. In a while even Alfie joined in. Jantice said: 'I noticed at our conference he thought I had a good instinct for the inside of the trade.'

Shale laughed again. 'Instinct and more. If you don't know the trade from inside what bugger does?' He left his chair and went to an early nineteenth-century American Salem desk and bookcase. It stood against the wall under a portrait of a nice plumpish woman who somebody said was Dutch, or up that way. He opened the bookcase's glass doors and removed some genuine books. Behind, the back of the bookcase had been taken out and there was a wall safe. Shale unlocked it with two keys and picked up a roll of twenties. He secured the safe and replaced the books. He handed the money to Ivis who counted it and kept the roll on his lap. Shale mixed more drinks and then sat down again.

'If it happens, I'm going to have to con my way into one of the firms, Mansel,' Jantice said.

'Oh, my God, my God, am I finally going to be penetrated?' Shale cried in a womanish voice, clutching at his groin.

They all laughed for a while more. Shale hated to see Ivis laugh. It did not look right for his face. 'No, no,' Jantice said. 'I'd have to come up with some real insider material for Lane and the rest. You wouldn't want me revealing your all, would you? I might try Panicking Ralph's outfit. Or there's Keith Vine and Stanfield or even Misto's. But Misto's pretty down for now.'

'Keep him there,' Shale said.

'This is hazard, W. P.,' Ivis said.

'When my Chief calls I must answer,' Jantice replied. He did a cub salute, then took a long gulp of the gin and pep. Jantice always seemed cocky, but there were nerves there, also. He was about thirty-two, tall and very thin, with long, thick fair hair nearly on his shoulders. He had a face that Shale thought many would call sensitive, being long and good for showing wonder. His eyes were big, brown and friendly and you knew you could trust them totally to keep that friendliness when he was sinking you and taking a nice fee for it. His clothes were like a student's – sweaters or T-shirts, boots, the oldest jeans. They said he was brave and much stronger than his body showed. Shale knew that already, or Jantice would not have been able to carry the money he took on these calls. Jantice always made Shale feel the approach of defeat. He was one of those officers who probably started out honest and full of pride but let themselves get pulled on to the take, driven desperate by the hopelessness of what they were trying to do. They saw law and order could hardly ever win, so why not win for themselves, personally, instead? It was useful, yes, and so sad.

'If you're planted it could be handy,' Shale said. 'About time we had some good news.'

'When I'm in and collecting info about competitors obviously some of it could come your way, Mansel,' Jantice replied.

'More fucking expense,' Shale said.

'These could be invaluable commercial glimpses, Manse,' Ivis said. 'Panicking's accounts and personnel or Vine's.'

'Harpur, Iles – they agree with Lane you should be planted?' Shale asked Jantice.

'Probably not. Well, maybe Harpur. He's hard to sort out. Iles and he are hand-in-gloving most of the time. But Harpur likes Lane, wants to protect him from the very worst.'

'That's Iles, isn't it?' Shale asked.

'Most likely,' Jantice said.

'If Iles is against, Lane can't do it. And *you* can't do it. The Chief can't defy Iles. Not even the Chief's wife.'

'Lane's turned very powerful. Suddenly, he's out in front. It's despair that's driving him,' Jantice said. 'He fears a total end to law and order. I don't blame him.'

Like Jantice himself. But Lane would still try to fight.

'It should be made known that Mansel is always ready

to hold constructive discussions with the Chief on such matters.'

'Right,' Shale said.

'This would be a commonsense alliance,' Ivis said. 'Indeed, a common*place* alliance. It's happening everywhere.'

'Do I want bullets on the street, for God's sake?' Shale asked. 'I've always sought compromise and accommodation.'

'You have, you have, Manse,' Ivis said. 'These might well become more attractive to the Chief now his salary is performance-related. Events like the street murder of a child or execution of an also-ran gangster are bound to cut bonuses.'

Shale waved an arm to indicate the comfortable room and respectable art. 'I would be prepared to conduct one-to-one discussions with Mr Mark Lane here on a totally private basis, with a view to agreeing responsibility for the creation and maintenance of peace on this complete manor, W. P. I don't really believe these tales he's run by his wife. Lane and I, we have so much in fucking common, W. P. It's only that we come at it from different angles. All that's necessary is a commitment to see the other's point of view and be ready with concessions.'

Jantice nodded and flashed the brown eyes sincerely. 'I'll bear this in mind. Obviously, I could not approach him with such a proposal now. I'm not supposed to be in contact with you, Manse, am I? Perhaps a more convenient time will come. Meanwhile, I must hold myself in readiness to infiltrate.'

Ivis said: 'But you're known around the Ernest Bevin and so on. Can you be acceptable?'

'The eternal problem, Alfie,' Jantice replied. 'To infiltrate you need someone who knows the scene. But if the someone knows the scene the scene is likely to know the someone. So the someone has to seem to drift into a habit, or put it around he's sick with money troubles, and is ready to act for a firm on the quiet, in return for payment in cash or the commodity.'

'The way you do with us,' Shale replied.

'Only cash,' Jantice said. 'And I don't carry insights from here back to headquarters.'

'I do hope not, W. P.,' Shale replied.

'Of course not,' Ivis said. He tossed the roll of twenties to Jantice who carefully counted the notes.

# 10

At home in the early evening Harpur's daughter Jill took one of those telephone calls. 'Dad,' she yelled out of the living room window, 'it's your favourite fink,' probably without covering the mouthpiece: she thought it funny to be heard at the other end. Harpur had just left the house. He wanted to look for a spot in Sphere Street where a concealed sniper might crouch low and fire two 6.35mm bullets on a rising path into the neck and chest of a four-feet-tall child. He almost hoped he would find nowhere that fitted. Such evil should be unthinkable.

Jill had opened the window and called to him as he was about to drive off. When he came back into the room she said: 'You know the sort of thing, Dad – no name given, of course, and *I wonder, little lady, if I might speak to Detective Chief Superintendent Colin Harpur, should he be at home? A routine matter. I could always call back should he not be there now.*' This bit she spoke in a soaring servile whine. 'Lots of creepy shoulds.'

Harpur waited for her to leave the room. When he picked up the receiver, Jack Lamb said: 'Delightful girl, Col. Jill? What age now?'

'Thirteen.'

'Polished.'

'Thanks, Jack.' Harpur always let him lead these conversations. Jill had it right and Lamb *was* Harpur's favourite fink, though Harpur might prefer some other word. Informant would be fine. Tipster wasn't bad. Even snout or nark or grass were sweeter than fink. In fact, Jack Lamb would have been any detective's favourite informant. Nobody was better at it. Yes, there were conditions for this exclusive service, and Harpur accepted them as part of the soiled, sanctified bond between a sleuth and his grass. Basically, they meant that Harpur put himself in Jack's hands. Lamb spoke, Harpur listened, with an occasional question, which Jack might or might not answer. Mostly not.

'We need a meeting, Col.'

'Yes?'

'Don't you feel it? A sort of thinness of achievement. On your part.'

'I'm used to that. No longer notice.' A security procedure had been established that Lamb could use Harpur's name in telephone conversations but Harpur could not use Jack's. There did not seem much logic to this, but Harpur agreed because Jack wanted it. His skin and life were exposed, not Harpur's. On security, Lamb had all sorts of fierce, contradictory notions.

'Say Number Three at 8.30 p.m.?'

'Right.'

'I'll be able to move things along for you, I think.'

'Oh, good,' Harpur replied.

'Regards to Jill from your favourite fink.'

Harpur would have time to take in Sphere Street on the way, and he drove there now. When you were looking into the annihilation of a child of thirteen by shooting you hesitated to get nasty with your daughter of thirteen merely for insulting a prime tipster. People older than Jill failed to see that without informants detection was dead. But he thought he would ask Jill at least to put her hand over the mouthpiece when she shouted.

Across the street from where NOON was hit, Harpur found a narrow service lane leading to a yard at the back of several shops. The lane was not wide enough for vehicles, but would take a hand trolley. It would take a crouched man, too. There was an alternative exit, through the yard and leading away from Sphere Street. For some seconds Harpur did crouch at the mouth of the lane. Both sides of the street were No Parking and, except for moving traffic, he had an unbroken view of the piece of pavement where NOON fell. On the day, there would have been no moving traffic, because of the battle. For anyone who knew how to shoot it would have been simple, even with a handgun.

He stood, then turned quickly and leaning against the wall threw up very fully, spattering his shoes and the bottoms of his trousers. As he crouched, he had seen NOON in his head with vile clarity, and had seen the neck bullet do its damage – its lesser but more obvious damage. He had watched her fall, and for a second had felt as if he were holding a SIG-Sauer automatic in an efficient double-handed aiming grip. That's what had made him sick: the illusion of responsibility for it. Perhaps something similar but larger in scale had helped make Lane ill: his grandiose illusion that he had responsibility for the slide of the domain, the country and the cosmos into hell.

Primly, Harpur moved away from the vomit, back down the lane again towards the yard. Christ, but that was a trite bit of sentimental feebleness: he could actually dream himself into nausea! He cleaned his lips with a handkerchief, then used it to get what he could off his shoes and trousers. He returned to Sphere Street. Everyone in all the shops – customers and staff – had been questioned about what they saw, and they had all seen nothing. But they had been questioned only about the five men, the Carlton and NOON, not about an extra gun. Harpur decided he must mention this possible sixth man in the lane. Quickly he revisited all shops still open from which the sniper might have been visible. As he expected, he heard that nobody had seen anything. People were sorry about this. In the newsagent's a girl assistant said she would not have noticed anyone at the mouth of the lane because she was distracted by shooting among the five men in the street. But when Harpur nodded understandingly and invited her to tell him about these instead, it turned out she had not seen anything she could remember of that, either. He bought some mints from her all the same to spruce up his breath. He knocked several doors of flats above the shops where residents might have had a view of the yard. They had been questioned before, too, but not about this retreat route. However, none of them had spotted anybody withdrawing that way after the sound of shooting. This was the kind of inveterate, untreatable local blindness which made Jack Lamb and lesser Jack Lambs so crucial. Somehow, they did see and did hear and did speak. It was also why Mark Lane had lately come to believe in undercover work.

Harpur drove to Number Three. Jack was already there. 'I might have a location for you, Col,' he said.

'Good.'

'This is a location of someone you've been trawling for.'

'Great, Jack.' Lamb liked to control the pace of disclosures. It was power.

'But you'd need to go solo in the first instance, I'm afraid.'

'Right.'

'This has to be something you as it were find for yourself.'

'Right.'

'Otherwise things point to me.'

'Which things, Jack?'

'Like Deep Throat in *All The President's Men*,' Lamb replied.

'Right.'

Lamb leaned forward and gazed at Harpur. 'Death of a child, Col. Can I stay quiet? Could anyone?'

'Some.'

'Your daughter in her playful way calls me fink, Col, but I'm not really one for that. Well, I don't need to tell you, I hope.'

'No, Jack.' Occasionally, Lamb would spend some time or

more than that explaining his gospel of grassing. Harpur knew it right through, could have written a book about it, but remained patient. Jack was entitled to his conscience.

'I don't just inform for informing's sake, Col. Or for favours' sake, either. That's your real fink. I know of a thousand things you'd like to hear about, but you won't because I've got no cause to tell you. These are people running their own little desperate illegal lives, and I'm not going to put the law on them.'

'Thanks, Jack.'

'But some crimes, Col – some crimes reek. Death of a child.'

'Yes.'

'Sickening,' Lamb said.

'Oh, yes.'

'My silence is not available for that.'

'Thanks, Jack.'

Number Three was a code name devised by Lamb for a Second World War concrete blockhouse on the foreshore which they used as rendezvous now and then. Harpur had an idea that criminals sometimes came here for secret get-togethers and share-outs, too. Police work, crooked work – there were bound to be overlaps. It was the same world. Another factor understood by few outsiders.

He and Lamb did not go inside the blockhouse at once. Jack paced and noisily breathed in the foreshore air. He liked the military touch and would often come dressed in army surplus gear to match the settings. There was rain about and he had on a voluminous khaki cape tonight, and a khaki peaked cap displaying some kind of regimental badge. Jack's love of costume seemed to make all the security drills pointless. He was over six feet and eighteen and a half stone plus. Harpur was big, but standing near Lamb felt like standing under a cliff. Jack would be conspicuous in a suit, let alone dressed for D-Day. He carried a leather-coated swagger stick with which he occasionally pointed out to sea, as if he had sighted the invaders, somehow delayed since 1940. Harpur never said much about the garb or the performances. If that was how Lamb wanted things that was how they should be. Harpur knew his place. In any case, now and then he would turn out in special gear himself, though not military. He had a morning suit bought secondhand which dated from early in the century, and he liked to parade in that occasionally. It drove his daughters berserk.

'I heard about your two witness reports, Col.'

'Oh? How?'

'They're marginally helpful,' Lamb replied. He drew his cape closer around him so that in the twilight he looked like a gigantic monument temporarily swathed against riotous vandalism.

'These two walking boys, Col.'

'I've heard of them,' Harpur said.

'This is what I mean – a location for one. I can point you.'

'Brilliant.'

'I can't come with you in support, Col.'

'That's all right, Jack.' He would not want aid from anybody in a cape.

The rain increased and they went inside the blockhouse. Harpur had worked out a technique for filling up
with fresh air before he entered and afterwards breathing
only very small quantities the atmosphere until he
grew used to the stacked stenches of fifty-plus years. At
least his stomach was empty. He had nothing else to bring
up.

Immediately Lamb went to one of the loopholes, as he
always did. He examined the mud flats and distant sea, in
case more of the enemy had come up since he last looked.
He pushed the cap back, so he could get closer to the gun
slit and improve his vision. There seemed something about
the way the cape hung proudly from his shoulders that
proclaimed his love of Britain and his readiness to die on a
beach today to save it – or in the past, if only he had been
born sooner.

After some minutes, Lamb turned away from the loop-
hole, his sentry duty over. He said: 'This is Sailor Billy I'm
talking about. White, 42, wears a beret.'

'Sailor Billy?'

'You wouldn't know the name. He's from outside, obviously. But you recognize the description. It's in both witness
statements.'

'Is it?'

'These intruders from other realms bring such trouble,
Col. I'm surprised you boys haven't come to an agreement

with local barons to keep the streets serene. This would be an element in what's known as "chaos theory".'

'New to me,' Harpur said.

'A sort of *realpolitik*.'

'Where's Sailor Billy?' Harpur replied.

'He's in a safe house. William Charles Rich. The Yard will give you all you need on him.'

'Londoner?'

'They look for new lands. They're colonists.' Lamb fumbled under the cape and produced a short-barrelled revolver. 'Look, Col, you won't be able to draw an official weapon, will you, because . . . well, because you won't officially be going into the house at all?'

'Sailor Billy is armed?'

'Of course he's fucking armed,' Lamb said. 'You know it. Take this. Only a .32.' He held the gun out towards Harpur.

Harpur said: 'I'd better not, Jack.'

'I don't say fire it. Just have it with you. Let him see the pocket bulge. It's a deterrent in case he tries anything, and he might try something.'

'I'd better not, Jack. Not British. You know the rules about firearms.'

'Fuck the rules.'

'You can say so, Jack. Not me.'

'Pious fucking liar. You run your whole life like that.' He let the gun hang down by his side and his mind seemed to switch suddenly. 'It's not the first time I've heard her call me fink, Col.'

'I'm going to speak to Jill.'

'Their mother didn't think much of me, either, did she?'

'Megan had her views.'

'Megan sadly died, yet the tradition goes on, mother to daughter, daughters.' Lamb waved his stick compassionately. 'Oh, Jill's just a kid. Let her alone.' He turned and faced the sea again. 'There's general ill-feeling, you know, against those who offer information to the police.'

'Is that so, Jack?'

'I've read of a survey. Money from the Economic and Social Research Council.'

'Survey into what?'

'Use of informants. The findings are hostile. Question the whole system.'

'Oh, dear.'

'Researchers found some police use tipsters without putting their superiors in the picture.'

'My God, that's appalling. Totally against guidelines, Jack.' The rules laid down over and over that an informant belonged to the police force, not to any one officer. A Handler, maybe a Co-handler, a Controller and a Registrar were all required to run him. Fuck the rules. Jack was his, only his. The bargains between them were unshakeably personal and intimately dangerous. 'So where do I find Sailor Billy, Jack?'

'You don't, if you refuse the gun. Who's going to look after me and my business should you get killed?'

'True.'

Lamb stepped forward, like a moving pylon, and thrust the .32 at Harpur again. He took it.

# 11

Lamb gave him the address and Harpur wanted to look at it straight away. He drove there now from the blockhouse. As usual, he was in an ancient car from the police pool, for disguise. He had the snub Charter .32 in his jacket pocket, ready to provide that happy deterrent bulge Jack mentioned. Lamb often fussed over Harpur's safety – considered him naive and liable to underestimate the world's untiring malevolence.

The house was in a clean, sedate avenue of big semis. They blared optimism. These villas would have gone up in the 1950s, a happy statement that the Second World War was safely won and things might really be all right from now on. Yes, really might: this uncertainty meant the confidence had to be spoken louder, and you could see it in the proud width of the double-bay windows and the baby doric columns posing in the porches. Harpur regarded himself as acute on architecture. Night had come now and as he passed in the Lada he saw lights on behind drawn curtains in the two front downstairs rooms and in one bedroom above. He kept going. It had to be a late-night job. He would go home and one-parent for a while, then possibly sleep.

When Jack Lamb told you something you'd better believe it, but what he told you might be no more than part of it.

Jack did not know everything, only nearly everything. Sailor Billy would probably be in the house, as Lamb said, but he might not be alone. The long overcoat had been with him in Sphere Street. Although they had seemed to separate, this house called 'Kimberley' could have been the chosen reassembly point. The overcoat might be there, possibly injured, but also possibly still able to shoot. And there could be others with these two. Conceivably, the house was headquarters for an invading team: gangs pressured by drugs police and competitors in London or Manchester or Edinburgh came here looking for easier trade, softer opposition. Some of them liked a nice masking touch of suburbia, especially with a flash of old Empire in the house name. Intruders often brought trouble, like Sphere Street. They did not realize or did not care that the city had been deftly divided up between local trading gangs to produce standoff, and even a kind of peace.

Harpur felt that if he could find and hold and talk to Sailor Billy and anyone else in Kimberley it would be possible to sort out what the battle of Sphere Street meant, and how the child tied into it, if she did. It might then also be possible to persuade the Chief he no longer needed to send someone undercover. Harpur still agreed with Iles on that. The risks were gross. Normally, the Chief would have been the first to see it but terrible anxieties and swelling guilt had begun to fracture his judgement, and even his humanity.

Harpur adored breaking into other people's property illegally on his own and nosing and nosing and learning and learning. It was the swiftest way he knew to truth, for want of a better word. He saw it as easily the most rewarding aspect of his job. A target's life and soul were on show in his home. Harpur thought of this penetration as like psychiatry: a shrink peered behind the furniture of the mind and Harpur peered behind furniture. But a bit of care was needed. When you were wrongfully on someone's property you might get rough retaliation if caught. And tonight's intrusion would not be just a spying jaunt. The object was to land Sailor Billy, and any of Sailor Billy's shipmates. Surprise was crucial. Obviously Harpur could not risk entering while all those lights shone. In fact, for a couple of moments as he passed the house he regretted his promise to act alone. This was white knighting at its craziest: one man with a pathetic block about guns tackling God knew how many, probably all of them armed. He did not understand why Lamb feared he personally might be spotlighted if a police platoon invaded the house, and not if Harpur went solo. But Harpur had agreed to do it that way, so he would. Always you put the informant's neck before you own, and vows in the cause of concealment were sacred. That is, *almost* always and *more or less* sacred.

When Harpur arrived home, his daughters were still up. They had half a dozen friends in for a music, cider and whatever session. He joined them briefly and stole some of their Strongbow to mix with his Plymouth gin. He had heard worse music, but not since the last time Hazel and Jill hosted friends. Jill danced alone, some neck-bobbing, arm-snaking caper, her face blank. Darren, her boyfriend, seemed to be asleep on the sofa, a spilled glass alongside him. Harpur could smell no weed, but then not everything usable had a smell. This room gave on to the street and although the curtains did not quite meet Harpur went and closed them as much as they could be. During a pause in the music, Hazel said: 'The general view, Dad, is that police have lost the battle.'

'What battle?' Harpur replied.

'Oh, you know,' she said.

'What general view?'

Hazel waved her hand to take in the lounging or dancing red-eyed youngsters and Darren. 'Plus some of their parents think so, even those pro-police.'

'I've heard of pro-police parents,' Harpur replied.

Hazel's boyfriend, Scott, muttered: 'My mother says they do what they like.'

'Police?' Harpur asked.

'No – the drugs biggies. Like Sphere Street.'

Scott's mother was not pro-police. She hated his connection with Harpur's family, for safety reasons mainly. Harpur could half sympathize. They were all in the big sitting room, still lined with packed shelves of Megan's books. Megan was bright, but had believed in all that kind of thing, even *Dombey and Son* by Charles Dickens. He was going to get rid of virtually the lot any day now. It had not seemed too bad when Megan was alive to take the blame for her books, but now they had no role and embarrassed him. It would be a bit of a wrench to clear them, all the same: one of the last traces of Megan.

Jill had stopped dancing and crossed the room to stand supportively near him: 'Take no notice of what they say, Dad.' She nestled against Harpur. She touched his jacket with her hand. 'This a piece?'

'Stop that cheap telly talk,' he replied.

Jill said: 'You'll win, won't you, Dad?' She still had her hand on his pocket. 'Are you going out later?'

'Me for bed now,' he replied, finishing his drink. He set his alarm and slept for four hours until 2.30 a.m. When he awoke the house was dark and quiet. He dressed and wondered about the .32. He was gun trained but had always loathed carrying one; loathed even more firing one. This squeamishness Iles regarded as glib affectation, and he knew about affectation. Tonight, anyway, Harpur did take the revolver. Jack was right to fret. Quietly, Harpur moved on to the landing. He had reached the top of the stairs when Jill's door opened and she came out in her pyjamas and took his hand. They walked down to the ground floor silently like that together, he one stair ahead with his arm stretched behind him to her. Near the front door, she touched his pocket once more and then put her hand back into his. They stood for a few moments in the dark hall.

'I can't come, can I?' she asked.

'You're not dressed.'

'No. But couldn't you take, say, Mr Desmond Iles with

you? Give him a ring. You know – somebody mad and sort of fierce and quite clever.'

'That's Mr Iles. I won't be long.'

'It's the battle, is it?'

'It's a call I have to make.'

Jill lowered her head and he thought she might cry. But almost immediately she lifted her eyes to his and grinned. 'I'll do a really good breakfast.'

He bent and kissed her forehead, then let himself out.

Kimberley was also in darkness. He parked in the next street and walked. As much as possible he had to be a silent part of the night, and he wore rubber-soled navy running shoes, dark dungaree trousers and his navy suit jacket. These streets looked the sort of middling-moneyed area where bloody Neighbourhood Watch would be *qui viving* given half a chance, even so late, frantic about possessions. Harpur's habit was to break in through the kitchen. It made sense, because the kitchen was usually at the back of the house and, if the garden had trees, he could be shielded. Sometimes, too, you might find a kitchen table laid for breakfast, telling you numbers. But if this was a men's base camp there probably would be no neat domestic touches. In any case, he did kitchens really because . . . because he always did kitchens. He had his way of working, the same as most burglars, and he needed the comfort of a routine, the same as most burglars. Efficiency did come into it but was not prime. One day he might qualify for a Criminal Records dossier, and in the section headed *Modus Operandi* it would say: *Enters generally via forced or broken kitchen window. Because of physical bulk and diminishing nimbleness a large window is necessary.*

He entered now via a jemmied kitchen window. Because of physical bulk and diminishing nimbleness he did a casement window in front of a metal draining board full of dirty cups and other crockery. He had to spend a few minutes shifting much of it aside to make himself a quiet pathway in. This garden had a couple of eucalyptus trees and that was all, so he might be visible to anyone in the houses at the rear who was insomniac or up for a pee. There was a moment as he rested from his work on the window when he thought he heard something from behind one of the trees, up near the fence. It had been a small rustling sound over almost instantly. He froze and stared into the darkness but could make out nothing: perhaps the breeze or a stalking cat. Turning back to the window, he climbed in, and managed to avoid the rearranged crockery. He pulled the window to behind him, though it was not relockable now. He dropped to the floor and stayed flat there for at least a minute, listening and simply keeping his head below the windowsill. He put the jemmy back into the deep pocket of his dungarees. The amount of unwashed crockery seemed to say what the lights all over the house had said – that there were several people here. He did what Jill had done and touched the gun through the jacket cloth. Yes, the pistol was a good idea. In fact, perhaps he should have asked Lamb for some extra rounds if he had to take on a barracksful.

## Top Banana

He heard nothing and the house stayed dark, but he considered that a man or men who had been in a fatal street fracas would be very alert. Although these houses and this district were a long way from Sphere Street, Sailor Billy, the long overcoat and any of their friends would know that police sweeps moved out from the site of an incident to the surrounding districts and then out again and again, day and night. Eventually select Kimberley and its neighbours would be reached. Did these boys have a sentry somewhere, waiting, but waiting in the dark, so the house would look as innocently restful as all the others?

Harpur raised himself on to hands and knees. The moon gave a little light occasionally when clouds passed, and he could make out the door that would lead to the rest of the house. It was closed. He crawled towards it. He would stand once he was away from the window, and possibly bring the .32 from his pocket. Although he was right-handed, he had put the gun into his left pocket, as a sort of hindrance to using it. The floor was mucky and his spread fingers stuck to the lino tiles now and then. The grubbiness spelled men.

Reaching the door he got up. He turned the knob and opened it slowly. There was a passage – or what they would probably call a hall in this kind of house – a passage with two more closed doors on each side, and stairs ascending to the right. Moonlight reached in through the coloured glass of the front door, diamonds and rectangles of blue, red, orange and green. He stood for a moment listening again. He heard his heart – steady enough. That was all.

It was all for a moment. But then, suddenly, there was the loud noise of several violent movements and a crash. Something struck his dungaree trousers just above the ankle. The sounds did not come from the rooms in front of him or from upstairs. They were behind. Shock paralysed him briefly. When he did recover and found some control again he swivelled his head fast to look, and just as fast brought his right hand and arm up to protect his head. He should have been going for the .32 across his body. In his alarm he behaved like a victim. Dismal. At once he saw where the noises had come from. The window he entered by had been tugged open again. A man standing outside in the garden was slumped forward, head, shoulders and an arm resting on the draining board. One pile of the crockery had been knocked to the floor. He guessed that what had hit him was a flying piece of broken china. The loudest sound had been the crockery smashing, but just before that had come a heavier impact, which he thought now must have been the man's head pitching forward helplessly on to the draining board. In a good burst of moon he saw blood coursing from the scalp or face down the draining board and into the sink. The man spoke. He did not raise his head and the words went towards the remaining dirty dishes. 'Col, I couldn't let you do it alone after all.' The voice was faint and choked by liquid, probably more blood, but it was clear enough and recognizable.

'Jack,' Harpur whispered. 'What's happened? Who's here?'

Then Lamb did try to straighten. Harpur saw him press down with his hand on the draining board, struggling to lever himself upright in the window space. And it began to work. He was able to lift his head and face a little and then his shoulders. His eyes were open and staring, perhaps seeing Harpur, more likely not. As his body started to straighten he lost the support of the draining board. Harpur realized that only the ninety-degree bend forward over the sill had stopped Jack from slipping to the ground outside. He lurched slowly to the left now. His head banged hard against the white wooden upright of the window, leaving a smear of blood. He could not get his balance back and slipped down out of Harpur's sight. He heard the big body land on the concrete, a terrible, yielding weighty sound.

Harpur's first instinct was to get to him fast. He remained where he was, though, and stretched over and brought the revolver from his pocket. The noise must have reached everyone here, even if they were all asleep. In the kitchen doorway to the rest of the house he crouched down again, as he had in the service lane off Sphere Street, but this time really holding a pistol out in front of him. He waited for sounds of movement, most probably from upstairs. Was he entitled to shout 'Armed police!', when he was here illegally and with a non-police weapon? Would these people take any notice if he *did* shout 'Armed police'? Only if they imagined he was part of a battalion, and how did he make them believe that?

But, although he waited for at least three minutes, he

detected no sounds elsewhere in the house. All he heard was Lamb's appallingly laboured breathing from where he lay outside the open window. It sounded like a tired fight for life. Harpur realized then that the place was empty and thought he realized why. Jack must have come earlier, intent on giving Harpur support. He had been discovered lurking in the garden, and perhaps shot, or more likely beaten unconscious. Shooting would have roused the neighbours. Perhaps whoever had beaten Jack thought he was dead. He must have been lying somewhere out there when Harpur arrived: had possibly spotted him enter. Had Harpur heard him shift or try to speak? The people in here must have left as soon as they dealt with Jack for fear he had backing.

Through the open window now, Harpur saw that lights had come on in two houses behind the garden. The din of the crockery falling would have carried. He stayed where he was, the pistol still in his hand. After a few minutes a beam from a flashlight shone on the back of the house. He thought it came from the garden immediately at the rear and was directed over the fence. It paused for a while on the open window and then went lower. Jack was big enough to be very visible. The beam was raised again and moved about the kitchen. Harpur concentrated on stillness. Soon the light withdrew. Harpur thought he heard slippered feet running up a path.

He dropped the revolver into his pocket and left the house quickly through the front door. He could not go to Lamb. And he attempted no search of the property, even though there might be good findings if people had baled out at a rush. He ran to his vehicle and after four attempts got the bugger started. He drove fast away from the district. At home, both his daughters were up and in dressing gowns: 'A phone call from the nick woke us,' Hazel said. 'The man sounded urgentish. Well, nearly 4 a.m. I suppose he would.'

Harpur rang the Operations Room. 'A man's been found badly injured in a back garden in Letchworth Avenue, sir. A neighbour heard noises and called in. Apparently the house has been used by several unidentified men lately. Why Inspector Beale thought you might be interested. I mean, the trawls after Sphere Street.'

'Yes, thanks. Who's the injured man?'

'No ID yet, sir. He doesn't seem to be carrying papers. He's badly injured about the head and face. It's touch and go, apparently. Possibly beaten. The ambulance is there now.'

'Give me the full address, would you, and directions?'

Harpur made some grunts, as if writing it all down. 'When we couldn't get you we rang Mr Iles, sir.'

Jesus. 'Right.'

He put the phone down and Jill said: 'The piece is in your other pocket now. There's trouble?'

'We told them you were probably out on some close surveillance,' Hazel said. 'Isn't this the phrase to cover your love life, Dad?'

'We didn't say you were carrying anything,' Jill said.

'You'd better get some sleep,' Harpur replied. 'School in four or five hours.'

'Are you going out again?' Jill asked.

'Briefly.'

'To the same place as you've been already?' Jill said. 'You're ahead of them?'

'Of course he is,' Hazel replied.

As soon as the children were back in bed Harpur replaced his jemmy in the tool box and then went upstairs and put the .32 into one of Megan's handbags. Three of them still stood on a wardrobe shelf above some of her clothes. There'd have to be a clear-out here soon, too. He changed from his break-in gear and put on the brightest white shirt he could find, a silver tie and a light grey suit. He had to be someone else now. He washed the tackiness from his hands, then drove back to Letchworth Avenue. There were lights everywhere: in Kimberley and a lot of the other Kimberleys. He could see pairs of officers doorstepping neighbours for information. Marked and unmarked police vehicles clustered near the house. The ambulance must have left. Dawn made its first moves.

Iles was in the hall. He had on a soft brown leather bomber jacket, tan cord slacks, brown Doc Martens and a brilliant red scarf. Except for the boots, he looked like someone modelling casual winter wear for the older man. There should have been an Irish setter. Enthusiastically the ACC shook Harpur's hand. Vivid congratulations were in the grip. 'I knew, absolutely knew, you'd turn up, Col,' he said. 'I mean, eventually. The others all said no, you'd be engaged somewhere warm and accommodating for the night and deliberately out of touch, as usual. Out of touch with us and your children, obviously, not with whomever. But myself, I have eternal faith in C. Harpur.' He shouted into one of the front rooms: 'Viv, Alec, Gordon, Sid, Jane – here's Harpur now, trouser fly perfectly zipped. How unkind you were to declare he neglects his duties and his children in the mere cause of pussy. Col's principles always get him home for breakfast. Well, Harpur, I think he might live. Heavily hammered out the back. It looks as if he had been hoping to break in. A kitchen window. Perhaps he was heard trying it then chased up the garden. Garland is looking at some indications near the fence. All these other folk are searching the rooms.'

Harpur said: 'A lot of them go in through kitchens.'

'I've heard that,' Iles replied.

'It will narrow down the possibles, though.'

'Oh, good.'

'I—'

'Big for a burglar,' Iles said.

'This is why some of them do kitchens. There's usually a large casement to let out cooking odours.'

'Yes, it *was* a casement,' Iles said.

'I'm not surprised,' Harpur replied.

'I wondered if you would be. We don't think he got in, though.' He began to snarl in that way of his. 'What the hell *is* this, Harpur? *You're* supposed to brief *me*. He might have pushed a pile of dishes off the draining board. Not deft, Col.'

'Who lives here?' Harpur replied.

'We think three, possibly four men. This is from neighbours. Probably renting. We're looking for the owner. Whoever they were they've cleaned up traces damn well. Nothing
left. Apparently, there was activity around 2.15 a.m. A
car departed in a hurry. And then over an hour later we
hear of some big laddy dressed overall in black leaving
from the front door and at a pretty frantic run. Rubber-
soled. Another neighbour – at the rear, the one who 999'd –
he thinks this big laddy in black might have been crouched
in the kitchen for a while. Then in the next street we've
just been told a car was started at the third or fourth
attempt and driven away fast at about 3.30 a.m. Look, is all
this news to you, Harpur? You weren't out girling after
all?'

'The house was a rest centre for an incoming team?'
Harpur replied.

'This is possible.'

'I should have a look at the garden,' Harpur said.

'Of course you should. If you'd been earlier you could
have seen the injured man *in situ*. But you've got a life to
live, Col, a dick to follow. Maybe. We couldn't really keep
him death-wheezing on the ground out there until you
managed to show up, could we? Mark Lane's in the garden
now wearing one of his garments.'

'Oh, I didn't—'

'The Chief's left standing instructions he's to be told
immediately about anything with a bearing on Sphere Street
and NOON. This qualifies, apparently.'

Yes, Jack had thought so, too.

Iles said: 'Naturally, Lane's been asking about you, Col. Head of CID and all that. Should show interest. I said probably close surveillance somewhere, and necessarily out of radio touch.'

'Thanks. Yes. Hazel told Operations that.'

'Ah, how we look after you, Col, she and I. There's quite a little spiritual bond between her and me, you know.'

'Yes, and fucking well keep it that way, sir – spiritual,' Harpur replied. He walked down the hall and into the kitchen. The piece of cup that had struck his trouser leg lay where it had fallen then. He scuffed the floor with his shoes as much as possible, in case he had left hand prints in the muck layer. Then he went through the rear door into the garden. They had rigged some lights. Lane looked bad. He was in an orange-to-ginger three-quarter-length car coat. It was the kind of thing a peep-show doorman or schools inspector might wear. There had been a slump to the Chief's face, perhaps from loss of sleep, perhaps from more panic. His mouth hung open and very much to one side, like an injury. Under the glare of the lamps his eyes looked as black and dead as slate. He moved spasmodically back and forth between the place under the window where Jack had lain and one of the eucalyptus trees at the end of the garden. Francis Garland was busy there, examining the tree itself and the ground nearby. 'This is where he seems to have taken the beating,' Garland told Harpur. 'There's a concentration of blood in the grass and some on the trunk and on the fence. He might have realized he'd been heard and was trying to climb it when they caught him.'

Lane approached on his criss-cross journeying. 'This was a decent, quiet avenue, Harpur. I know people living nearby. Yet now we have . . . Where is it leading? Where?'

Garland said: 'Charlie Mates thinks he recognized him: Jack Lamb, an art dealer. He lives out Charlie's way.'

'Art dealer? My God,' the Chief cried. The first birds responded.

'I think I've heard of Lamb,' Harpur said.

'He owns a manor house apparently,' Garland replied.

'My God,' Lane said again. 'This sounds a man of some status, accustomed to fine things, yet sordidly beaten perhaps to death in a suburban back garden. Why was he here, Francis?'

Well, Lamb was here because of NOON. And he was here also because he and Harpur had their noble, long-time complicity which the Chief could not be told of. Nor could anyone else. Harpur looked at the tree. On the trunk he saw what was possibly a hand mark in blood, as if Jack might have clutched at it for support after being dragged back from the fence. He must have been still behind the tree when Harpur broke in. Why hadn't he called out? Possibly it was beyond him then. Or possibly he feared bringing the same violence on to Harpur. Jack was a gent, in his way.

Lane lowered his voice: 'Doesn't this make it so obvious that we must infiltrate, Colin, Francis? These people do what they want. We are powerless.'

'My daughter's boyfriend's mother says the same, sir,' Harpur replied.

'They can be beaten only from within. I shall possibly call you out to a little meeting at my home in due course, Colin,' Lane said. 'It would be better there.'

'Certainly, sir. What would be the nature of the meeting? In case I need to prepare myself.'

'It might be wiser not to mention this to Mr Iles. I mean at these early stages,' Lane replied.

'Early stages of what, sir?' Harpur asked.

'Naturally he would be brought up to date as soon as it is necessary,' Lane replied.

Iles approached. The Chief began his walk back to the stained area of concrete under the window. The ACC said: 'Did I hear a name?' he asked.

'Possibly Lamb,' Garland said.

'Fill me in on him, Col,' Iles replied.

'Francis says he's an art dealer with a manor house,' Harpur said.

'Mean anything to you?' Iles asked.

'Just that much,' Harpur replied.

'Yes?' Iles said.

This was a question and required an answer. Harpur said: 'The window forcing looks pretty skilled.'

'We've found no jemmy,' Iles replied.

Lane did not make his full tour this time and returned almost immediately. 'Francis, I'd like a note of the names of all neighbours who have helped us on this. I will write individual letters of thanks.' His body twitched very force-fully inside the ginger coat. 'It's so important to encourage fine behaviour in a disintegrating world.'

'Francis abhors praise for others, sir, but I'll see the pompous bastard does it,' Iles replied.

# 12

This terrible Kimberley incident on top of everything else really affected Mansel Shale. It was bound to. As soon as he heard of it he knew he must go to the girl's funeral and Tim Montain's. He asked Denzil to drive him up to Ivis's lighthouse right away to tell him. Not something for the phone. They strolled the cliff path in overcoats chatting, while Denzil waited in the Jaguar. God, how Shale loathed all this – the sound of the sea and the gulls and the sight of rocks getting their smug brown edges up through breakers. Nature told you it had been there so long that business didn't count – everything would sort itself out. Bollocks. You had to *do* something. No good admiring reefs or diving gannets, you needed enterprise, and you needed to take care of people, or smash some other people if they got in the way – which was the same thing, because you smashed some so you could look after yours. Nature and all that timeless stuff could go fuck itself.

But Ivis liked a walk, so Shale would go with him now and then. Alfred looked about at it all, the grey spray and ferns and dull mud, like the whole scene belonged to him, like an extension of the lighthouse. 'I mean, things slide and slide, Alfred,' Shale said. On this path Shale always called him Alfred in full because Ivis thought he had dignity in this setting and you ought to play up to humour people if possible. 'Someone got to take a stand for decent values.'

Although the total picture on Kimberley was unavailable, Shale felt there could be nothing helpful. 'We're not talking about some rough old spot like Sphere Street, Alfred. This is Letchworth Avenue. I'm not saying money or real class, but these places have their bits of dignity. You know this word decorum? What damn decorum if heavies come from God knows where to soil an honest little house in a clean street? Plus this bitter violence to a local among eucalyptus trees. I got to make a gesture against all that.'

'Well, with respect, Manse, the local you speak of is Jack Lamb, who's—'

'Oh, crooked as an S-bend, but that don't mean outsiders should attack him in a tidy neighbourhood. Civilization depends on the busy plodders who live around there, Alfred, maybe even more than flash-in-the-pan private businessmen like self.'

'Oh, Mansel,' Ivis cried, 'I'm sure nobody regards—'

'I know what you and W. P. Jantice say about caution, but a city's got to get itself together against such naughtiness. And if the Chief sees me at these sad ceremonies he will know what I'm saying to him. I'm saying I value traditions and long to stand square alongside him to defend such values against abuse from intruders. Alfred, this is how the grand police-Mansel-Shale-Incorporated alliance could come about. The Jag will give a bit of style to these mean rites, and I'll make Denzil wear his black chauffeur cap. I got a duty to take fine tailoring to their scruffy bereavements. It's expected.'

'But, Manse . . .'

They turned back. Shale had had enough of coast. 'Alfred, I'm thinking a lot about those two on the run – the Carlton driver – you know the boy – black, about Timmy's age and—'

'Neville. Neville Greenage.'

'Yes, Neville. And Kalashnikov man.'

'Earl.'

'Earl, arseholes. I'm sure they would want me to do a farewell to Timmy Montain, their fine colleague. And, yes, to this little child. They'd see the need for something meaningful from our firm, Alfred. You'll say one of them must of put the bullet in Timmy's head in that dump and one of them probably knocked over the girl, but we don't know the full circumstances, do we? I feel I owe my presence at these services to them personally and to our whole . . . well . . . our whole culture.'

Ivis said: 'I do appreciate your thinking, Manse, yet things could go so very awry.'

But nothing did go like that, or not until the second funeral was absolutely over. This was Timothy's. Shale never regretted attending either. The girl's was Gospel Hall and Timmy's Church of England, the day after. Shale did not object to one place or the other. Probably they both had their roles. He was glad the girl's was not in the church, because this meant there was no poncing vicar in robes flapping his wide black wings over the little box. It was just some ordinary lad doing the service here and at the grave-side, a dark suit and tie, but not even a dog collar. Shale found he did not need to yell out any protests, despite the smallness of the coffin. On the walls of the Gospel Hall he saw good, happy words about life after death, most probably from the Bible or that kind of old publication. It was a help to think of these words when you were staring at a tiny casket with a small battered kid courier inside, because this did look different from everlasting life on the face of it.

What Shale guessed was the girl's mother was there, up near the front. She was seated with two men and a woman. The man on her right in the black leather jacket might be the girl's stepfather. Shale thought he had heard the mother's present partner worked overseas. Alfie would have it in the records. If this partner had come back for the funeral a real distance with expense it showed a pleasant touch of caring. Some of these families could be quite wholesome, despite everything. The mother wore dark blue, not black, with a dark scarf with orange lines in it over her hair. Shale thought this was reasonable these days. The other man and woman in the party were young. The man had on a suit and the woman was in a cream blouse and red leather skirt, not much to do with mourning. Shale and Ivis stayed at the rear of the hall and during the service he could only see the mother's group from behind. He wondered if the young man and the woman were her brother and sister. Outside in the road he had a look at them head-on. They seemed full of shit and edginess and he guessed then they were London reporters from the paper that had signed up the mother. They were there to write about the funeral and look after their buy. The Press had an important role in many aspects of life. Obviously, Shale would have had to do something for her cash-wise if the journalists had not come in with funds.

Although Ivis still had doubts, he went with Shale to the funerals. Shale made sure they did nothing that might look like he was taking over the events. 'We sideline ourselves, Alfie,' he remarked. This was why they took seats far back. Shale sent flowers to both, and the cards had his true signature on them. He wished he had been living with a woman at the time, so there could be two names, giving a family feel, but Laurent and Matilda's mother was miles away with some broker or surveyor, that sort. She picked those fucking names. He got Ivis to send his own tributes. Shale did not want a card with 'From Manse and Alf' on it like a pairing, though he had nothing much against gays. Ivis put a made-up name on his cards. Rex someone. That's the kind he was, so cagey through knowing a bit of law, and liking that word Rex, meaning king, which he would never be – he was a baggage man. The Chief, Iles and Harpur were at the girl's service, but not Montain's. Shale knew Lane had seen him, even though he did not limelight himself. Partnership offers would bud.

Denzil was not keen on the cap but he wore it both times and looked brilliant – still ugly, but really solemn. Shale promised something extra in his pay as funeral driving was extra to chauffering. It was Denzil's face that first told Shale they had bad trouble. This was outside the crem around 11.15 a.m. after Tim Montain was concluded and a crowd exiting, including Mrs Montain, not a tear start to finish. Denzil brought the car to the kerbside to pick up Shale and Ivis. He drove nice and slowly and with full respect, but Shale noticed Denzil looked upset now and he seemed to be signalling something with his eyes. He stopped the car and jumped out, then walked around fast to the nearside, like to open the doors for them, so gracious. Until now the tired shit had always refused, and Shale thought he must be making another special show today. Good lad. But when Denzil pulled open the front door for Shale, he said, 'Neville and friend in the back on the floor.'

Shale got in but did not turn around and look down. Christ. He heard Denzil open the rear door for Ivis and mutter the same words. Then the door was closed and Denzil got behind the wheel again. They drove away, still with the correct sort of slowness. Shale looked about outside but carefully, trying to find the police observer, maybe a camera. He did not spot anyone. He gave a small, friendly wave to Mrs Montain, but she only stared past, that style she had.

'Lucky you left your coats, Manse, Alfie,' Denzil said. 'They're under them.'

'Stay there, boys,' Shale said over his shoulder. God, it was no time since he was talking to Ivis about them as a nice distant idea, and now here the buggers were, like employees.

'Didn't I know for sure you'd be at Timmy's finale, Mr Shale?' Neville Greenage replied. This was a lad who never used Shale's first name. It really showed something, what people called other people, like calling Alfie Alfred on the path, and Neville always calling him Mr Shale. Neville was a bit of a youth, really. He said: 'The kind of splendid chieftain you are, Mr Shale. You'll give your message to the world. Were there police inside at the funeral – Harpur and so on?'

'They wouldn't go to that kind of occasion,' Ivis replied.

'Which?' Neville asked.

Ivis said: 'Where it's a business death. The girl's, yes.'

'But she *was* business,' Neville replied.

'It's different,' Ivis said. 'So young.'

'And sort of symbolic of our time,' Shale said. 'The decline. They'll watch, film.'

'The way they work,' Neville replied. 'Why we were really careful, Mr Shale.'

Shale could hear him all right, despite it coming through quality overcoats and from so low. They were good thoughts.

'Earl said—'

'Who?' Shale replied. He was not going to take that name without giving some trouble.

'You know. Mr Shale – Earl. I'm with Earl here now on the floor.'

'The fucking Kalashnikov?' Shale said.

'Things didn't go too brightly there,' Neville replied. 'I

said to Earl you'd definitely be at Timmy's send-off, which we read about in the Press, but he thought you'd never risk it, because of what you said – connections. I told him he did not know Mr Mansel Shale.'

'That's what he said,' Earl remarked.

'So we came out and waited. Then I saw the car and Denzil under that crazy cap. We definitely were not spotted getting aboard the Jag. I wouldn't think of coming to your house or Mr Ivis's, things being as they are. That could bring attention. I haven't even been to see my girlfriend, Mr Shale. The police know Tim and I worked together. They could be watching Edna's place.'

'I don't see I could have kept them out of the vehicle,' Denzil said.

'Of course not,' Shale replied. 'They had needs. Edna? Do I know her?'

Ivis said: 'Neville and Edna have been together twenty-eight or twenty-nine weeks, haven't you, Nev? I'd have a note somewhere.'

Neville said: 'This is long-term, Mr Shale. She's great, and never a talker. But I thought, stay away. She'll be worried, but stay away.'

'Wise,' Shale replied. Often it was amazing how thoughtful the young could be, white or black, he hated racism.

There was a bit of movement at the back, but he still did not turn around. 'No, stay under the coats for now,' Ivis told them. 'We're close to the crematorium. Other cars are leaving.'

'It's money, Mr Shale,' Neville said. 'We wanted to get abroad out of your hair. Still want to. But where's the money? Not wishing to embarrass you in any way, please believe it. We'll disappear. Those two in the street, Sailor Billy and Quant, they're going to be looking for us after such an incident. They'll be looking for you, too, Mr Shale. You're exposed – I mean, the rectory. It's wide open. You should be careful. Anyway we know this is not the place to be. A bit of help and we're gone.'

'Gone,' Earl said.

This was crude pressure, and probably Alfie would like to throw the sods out of the car. But Shale wanted to be understanding.

'Earl knows folk in Portugal,' Neville said. 'Just getting there and some accommodation. Maybe Edna could come later.'

'So where do I take the bastards?' Denzil asked. He had put the cap on the shelf now. 'I thought Alfie's place. Nobody about. Just sea and sheep shit. We can drive right up to the door in his yard.'

Ivis said: 'Well, I'd be glad to host such dear friends, believe me, but—'

'Go to the fucking rectory,' Shale said. 'We'll be all right.'

'Can we come out from under now, Mr Ivis?' Neville said. 'There's Earl's breath.'

Ivis said: 'Well, we're still going through areas where—'

'Yes, you'll be fine,' Shale replied. Now he did turn and as Neville and Earl moved up on to the back seat he shook their hands with definite warmth. They should never have come back here, and they were trying to lever some cash now, yet Shale saw he was the only one who might help them. He believed in duty. Plus, Nev had the consideration to warn him about Sailor Billy and so on. These two in the back did not look too bad despite everything. It was obviously a tonic for them to see him. Then Ivis shook their hands, too. Neville had one of those faces you could get in blacks, very neat and sensitive, full of a kind of genuine thought.

Earl said: 'How could I shoot right? There's this little girl in the way, this little running kid. Even when Joe Quant is dashing at us I couldn't work properly any longer. Maybe I clipped him, but I was all over the place because of this kid.'

'You hit her,' Shale replied.

'Not me,' Earl said. 'Not me, you hear?' He was yelling suddenly, his lips curled back and his eyes half mad. It was wrong for an executive vehicle. Neville began to shout at him to go quiet. The voices were high and seemed to echo, like car alarms chatting in a multistorey.

'It could not be me,' Earl bellowed.

'Well, somehow she's dead,' Shale said.

'We saw on TV News,' Neville replied.

'They won't find my bullets struck her. Couldn't be, man,' Earl said. He had gone subdued now. 'I know that Kalashnikov. Am I going to rip a child?'

'Where is it?' Shale asked.

'In a river,' Neville said. 'We thought about selling it for funds or a clothes change, but Earl—'

'It could draw looks,' Earl said. 'It's not your usual barter.'

'Good, Earl,' Shale replied. You had to give credit, even to someone who went wild. 'And Timothy?' Shale was still turned towards them. Faces could tell you a bit now and then. He did not like that moustache on Earl. It looked like a white's moustache, too small and clerky. A black needed a moustache that said up yours.

'Timmy?' Neville replied. 'Mr Shale, we had to. We hung on, but eventually—'

'We did hang on,' Earl said.

'Couldn't you of done an anon 999 and left him for the ambulance?' Shale said.

'He didn't want it,' Neville replied.

'He didn't,' Earl said.

'You saying he asked to be finished?' Shale asked.

'If we couldn't take him, and we couldn't,' Neville said.

'That's what he said to us,' Earl said.

'Yes?' Shale replied. 'Who did it to him?'

'Tim said you'd believe us re his death, because you knew him so well, his kind of behaviour, Mr Shale,' Neville said.

'Yes?' Shale replied. 'Who did it to him?'

'This is what he said,' Earl stated.

'I did,' Neville said. 'He wanted that. A friend.'

'I'm nearly a stranger to him,' Earl said.

'I think of his mother,' Shale replied. 'The hard-looking ones suffer the most inside. Or that's the fucking tale.'

'He mentioned her,' Neville said. 'Just before. He said to tell her he loved her and there was no other way. Then he took hold of the barrel and put it against his own temple.'

'This is right,' Earl said.

'You saying suicide now?' Shale asked.

'No. I did the trigger, Mr Shale,' Neville replied. 'One shot. You can see stuff on my sleeve.' He was going to show the staining.

'Stop it,' Shale said.

Ivis said: 'Timmy had real strength.'

'He had *inner* strength, Mr Ivis,' Neville replied. 'By then he was only just strong enough to lift his hand and the gun to his head. What we did was necessary. It was a bad setting.'

'Fuck the setting,' Shale replied.

At the house, he cooked them all some early lunch, a spaghetti tuna with a few boil-in-the-bag Madras curried chickens mixed in. He liked food with a bit of scope. They ate it with heavy gin and peps. This meal would set Neville and Earl up for any travels. You had to consider your people, black or white, regardless, and bringing them to his home was the kind of risk he accepted. Ivis would not let them near his place, but Ivis was not the one with responsibility, he was only staff. That was the point – never Rex, king. Denzil did a lot of holidays in France and Italy and asked for wine instead of the gin and peps with his spaghetti, so fuck him. If he wanted Europe go live there. He was ugly enough.

Once they had got through the gates to Shale's grounds

the hedges hid everyone, as good as the lighthouse. For security, Nev and Earl had gone back under the coats on the floor for the last couple of miles. Shale would not have made them do it, it was juvenile, but this was Ivis's advice and Shale did not like to put Alfie down too often in front of followers – poor man management.

Shale wanted Nev and this Earl away before the children arrived from school at 4.15 p.m. Nev and Earl could have some money. There'd be a few grand around the place in pots and shoes and so on, and Alfie usually carried a good wad of fifties, in case the Second Coming did second come all at once and he had to buy past the Judgement Seat. These two grand lads, Nev and Earl, were entitled to cash aid as well as the meal and drinks after their problems, and it would be great to get the scrounging bastards out of sight abroad.

They ate in the proper dining room. Probably those two, Nev and Earl, had never seen anything like it, the long Regency mahogany Cumberland table and a breakfront side cabinet. This whole experience would get them feeling bonny again when they journeyed. Shale did not want any misunderstandings. They could not stay. There'd be a block soon on the gin and peps or they would get too comradely to move.

'That wasn't you two in the Kimberley house, was it?' Shale asked.

'Kimberley? What's that, Mr Shale?' Neville replied.

'No, I didn't think so,' Shale said, 'but I had to ask.'

'An incident?' Neville said.

'Give me and Alfred the detail on Sphere Street, will you?'
Shale replied. 'This was organized by people at a lower level
of the business for me and I never heard the total ins-and-
outs.'

Neville and Earl were both eating like starved rats. You
could see they'd had difficulties. Shale felt glad to be caring,
even for lads who did threats. Neville said: 'Three of us in a
Carlton – that's Timmy and me, and Earl brought in for
special skills, brought in and bought in, I believe.' He chewed
chicken for a while. He had good style with chicken, determined but not spittle all over the place while talking. 'Mr
Shale, we had it planned to meet these two invaders. This
was to knock them over before they could establish themselves more – them and their outfit. The idea was, hit two
and the rest would get a fright and quit. The usual. This
looked like a really nice piece of scheming. We knew what
time they were moving and the exact route. We knew who
they were – that's Sailor Billy and Joe Quant. There'd been
first-class research.'

'And then the girl turns up and none of it's so neat any
more,' Earl said. 'As soon as I saw her I knew disaster.' This
looked like real sadness all over his face. It might be
believable.

Shale said: 'But *how* did you know all this, Neville? The
information. Timing. Routes. Where's it coming from?'

'This was from a lad who had really observed their outfit,
the way it worked, even though it's new here. He's trained.
He'd done some talking to one of them. He's got himself

half inside. These people were looking for local contacts, the way they always do. This lad took advantage. Mr Shale, you know the lad, naturally.'

'This is W. P. Jantice?' Shale replied.

'Our officer,' Neville replied.

'He set this up?' Shale asked.

'It was beautiful. It could have been perfect. But then this accident,' Neville said.

'It's not down to Jantice – the fuck-up,' Earl said. 'Like Neville says, an accident. This kid in the way.'

'There's always the danger of an outside factor,' Ivis said.

'He's got a real gift, W. P. Jantice,' Neville said. 'He can organize, he can get trust. He's with us, but he can get inside them, too, and all the time he's keeping the police happy, as well.'

'Yes, it's flair,' Shale said.

Ivis said: 'Mansel picked him out as a good one a long, long way back. Mansel's got such an eye for ability.'

'Don't they know it?' Shale said, with a big laugh. 'How else would they be with us, Alf?'

They all did the washing up and then went into the den for coffee. Shale left them for a few minutes while he harvested some money from here and there in the house. When he came back he put about a quarter of it on the partner's desk and emptied his wallet on to the pile. Tipping out a wallet always looked lavish. Ivis added just over £750. The full total was £3800. If they had got in touch from out of town, Shale might have sent them five grand or even six. But they came here to try leverage so he had decided in the car it would be a bit less than four. This was compromise. Get rid of the buggers but don't let them squeeze you too hard.

'Were you paid your fee, Earl?' Shale asked.

Ivis pulled out his notebook and glanced at it. 'That's all been taken care of in advance. Attendance and use of his Kalashnikov.' He flipped a page. 'Yes, twenty-nine weeks, Neville and Edna.'

'You don't owe me a cent,' Earl said.

He could yell, he could talk like a fucking dove. Shale did not mind him too much. The moustache could always come off and his eyes were usually behind shades, though not today. Yes, he might be telling the truth about the girl's death. 'Equals then,' Shale said. He counted out the two £1900s and handed them over. 'I'll be able to get Timmy's message to Mrs Montain eventually, and we'll try to see her all right for a while.' It was 1.15 p.m. Shale said: 'Look, Nev, I don't like you being on the manor and not seeing your girlfriend. Don't seem fucking right, not at all. She going to be at home now? In work?'

'She works nights. A croupier,' Greenage said.

'Give her a ring. See if she's there. I could send Denzil up to bring her here for an hour. We could give you privacy.'

Ivis said: 'This might be dicey, Manse. It's like you – generous and full of feeling – but it's dangerous. Even the phone.'

Shale said: 'They wouldn't be able to get a tap authorized on his girlfriend. The link's too distant.'

'Iles doesn't always wait for authorization, Mansel,' Ivis said.

'Oh, I'd love to see her, Mr Shale,' Neville said, his face so tense and hopeful, those neat features aglow.

'He talks about her all the time,' Earl said.

'It's natural,' Shale replied. Probably Alfie could not see the way it worked. If you were warm-hearted and let Neville bang his bird upstairs somewhere in a short interlude it meant these two, Nev and Earl, would go on thinking of Shale as grand, even though the money was not much. 'Be brief on the phone, Nev,' he said. 'Just let her hear your voice and tell her to get to some spot a few streets away where Denzil can pick her up. You know the geography. Say to look behind now and then in case of a tail. Don't scare her, but just to be careful. She bright, know the score? You'd better describe Denzil so she's ready for that kind of fucking face and don't get terrified.' He took Neville to an extension in the hall and left him. After a couple of minutes, he returned, beaming and nodding.

'Take the Escort not the Jaguar, Denzil,' Shale said. 'We don't want a show.'

'He's to bring her here?' Ivis asked. 'Really?'

'It'll be all right,' Shale said. 'We got a debt to both, Alfred, a debt of humanity.'

In twenty minutes Denzil came back with her. Shale, Ivis, Earl and Neville were still in the den having more coffee and discussing the business. Neville stood up and she ran to him on heels and they stood there, arms around each other, kissing, a real kiss, yes, probably part of something long-term, as Neville said. Shale knew he had done right. She was white and about twenty-two, quite pretty, in good jeans and a black and silver blouse. He loved to see the races getting together like this, it was healthy and how the future was bound to be. Oh, he knew people said white girls only went to blacks for dick size, but he did not accept it. He thought it was an insult to women and to blacks. It made it sound like that was all there could be between then, and he did not know if it was definitely proved about bigger dicks. Anyway, he sincerely believed quite a few women thought about other things than dick. This girl looked like she had true emotions and a deep personality. She needn't have called herself Edna. Shale said those two could go anywhere else in the house for ninety minutes, while he and the others played cards and chatted in the den. He told Neville and Edna they deserved this. There would still be time to get them all out of here before the children came home. He could see the gratitude all through both.

At the end of the time, Shale sent Denzil into the hall and told him to beat the big dinner gong. Neville and Edna soon came downstairs then. They played it fair. Denzil would take her back to near her flat and then return to collect Neville and Earl. 'When they're fixed up in Portugal, we'll get you over there, don't worry, Edna,' Shale said. She and Neville kissed again and she cried a bit, that style most of them have, but then she went with Denzil.

Shale returned to the kitchen and filled two carrier bags with pork pies, bread, tins of beans, Mars bars and four bottles of gin. 'Picnic stuff,' he said returning, and gave one bag to each of them. 'You'll have to buy your own pep. Where do you want Denzil to take you when he comes back? Airport? Station?'

'Will they still try to pinch the trade, Mr Shale?' Neville asked.

'Who?'

'Sailor Billy, Quant and so on.'

'They can try,' Shale said. 'It's strange, but I see us stronger because of all this. I see a brilliant alliance on the way.'

'Mansel's a strategist,' Ivis said.

# 13

Harpur made a late Saturday-morning call on Neville Green-age's girlfriend. She worked nights and should be at home and out of bed by now. She might have heard from Neville; might have heard from him something about Sphere Street and the girl. A man would want to tell his woman that he did not shoot down a child but knew who did, or thought he knew who did. Harpur would settle for that. What else did he have? When Jack Lamb was unavailable, Harpur always felt weaker. One of his chief sources had gone. Lamb was alive but not properly conscious yet. In any case, he was in hospital, and unvisitable – unvisitable by Harpur: to visit would be a statement, the wrong sort of statement. Perhaps there would be a call on the hospital pay phone eventually. Harpur had to do something before then, though.

There was still no firm identification of Neville as the Carlton driver, but he was black and fitted the witness Ericson's age guess. Neville did job-drive for people, and he always worked with Tim Montain. Plus, crucially, he had disappeared, possibly straight after Sphere Street: a local boy gone suddenly absent. As soon as Montain's body was found, Harpur had sent people to check Greenage's flat. Only the girl was there. And only the girl was there on later calls. She had said nothing or as good as nothing: Neville was out of town, she did not know where and she had no contact, expected none. Were they breaking up, then, she'd been asked. What happened to love? And she had replied that he was out of town, she did not know where and she had no contact. She invited none of the officers into the flat and conducted all interviews on the tower block landing. Francis Garland said the ice was thick enough to land a Jumbo, and Garland never threw praise about. Neville was young and in some ways raw, but he knew how to train a woman. Maybe terrorize a woman. But she might cave in to someone of Harpur's rank. That's what he told himself, and half believed. For comfort he muttered the portly words of his title to himself as he climbed the tower block stairs: *Detective Chief Superintendent.* The lift was out, perhaps for ever.

Of course, Neville might be hiding inside, which would make terrorizing her easier and more immediate. Possibly this was why she admitted nobody. Harpur did not think so. She knew police could come back with a warrant if they decided Neville was there. Harpur had put a watch on the flat but Neville did not appear. He would be far away, knowing he could have two deaths against him. As Harpur visualized the Sphere Street aftermath, the three had hidden for a while in that Valencia wreck while Montain was dying. Then the surviving pair had somehow managed to clear the city, maybe in a different stolen car, maybe otherwise. Conceivably the girl was telling the truth and he had not been in contact. But this was a serious relationship lasting six months or even more according to the Collator. There should have been a phone call.

She stood in the doorway of the flat wearing denim and looking pretty good, despite the night work. There was shit music coming from behind her, probably right up-to-date. 'I wondered if Nev had been in touch at all,' Harpur said.

'What do you want?' she replied.

'I'm Detective Chief Superintendent Harpur.' He gave it full boom now.

'Fine.'

'I wondered if Nev—'

'I've answered on this already.'

Then Harpur went louder on the landing, so she would have to ask him in. She might not mind neighbours hearing up and down the stairwell that Greenage had been in a street battle, par for the course here. But what Harpur gave big volume to was the hint that Nev killed Timmy to ease escape. People would feel harsh about a villain who shot a comrade villain, and would feel harsh about his bird, too. In a block like this you wouldn't want to stir hate. 'Nev didn't invent convenience killing, of course. I've heard the Japs did it in the war,' he said. 'They'd finish off their wounded so as not to be slowed down.'

'The Bomb finished off more.'

'There were two lads – Nev and a visitor. My feeling, though, is Nev. He was always liable to go a bit desperate under pressure, wasn't he, Edna?'

'Cheers,' she replied and shut the door. Through the

frosted glass he could and did watch her jolly behind take its frigid leave of him down the little hallway.

Harpur drove back up to Sphere Street. He wanted another look at the service lane. And there would be more shops open than when he last made the trip, with plenty of weekend customers about. Now he had a brilliant chance to question many additional folk, and find they, also, had seen nothing, heard nothing, knew nothing, cared something but still knew nothing. He walked the lane slowly again. This time he did not go into a sniper's crouch. He would be conspicuous in the middle of the day. And very conspicuous if he sicked again. Nobody had tidied up after his last visit. Where was street cleaning – lost in that chaos Iles theorized about at third hand?

Harpur had begun to grow obsessive about this extra gun. He felt it and struggled to resist. Christ, the marksman had become an emblem, and Harpur was not paid enough to handle emblems. You had to be a Chief Officer. The Sphere Street inquiries looked appallingly different now. The horror had been high enough before, but lately it had moved on to infinity. Iles had seen that. This was not a kid knocked over in a routine bit of gang battling. She had been targeted, executed. The postmortem said so. Sniper's alley said so. Was it trade rivalry? But would someone old enough and experienced enough to shoot like that fear competition from a child? Or was the killing to keep her quiet, as Iles suggested? Would the child know enough to require her death? It was possible.

Yet, oh, Jesus, it should *not* be possible. He could mock Iles's borrowed diagnosis of our times, but now and then recently Harpur wondered whether chaos really had arrived and was already beyond treatment: beyond treatment, but not beyond treaties, with the lawless. He had had that feeling when Neville's Edna shut the door on him. He had it again now when the shops he could not try last time gave him the same effortlessly polite blankness. How else to guarantee some sort of safety on the streets except by a sly accommodation with the powerful? He wanted to yell in some of these shops: *Don't you ever look out of your fucking window?* Of course they looked out of their fucking window. What they did not do is talk about what they saw when they looked out of their fucking window, and especially not talk to someone with a face, build, suit and haircut like Harpur's: 'Cop written all over you', Hazel would tell him, 'spelled H-E-A-V-Y.'

*This would be to do with the recent death of the little girl? Well, obviously. Terrible. And we'd love to help. But it all took place so quickly, and at a busy time of day for us, you see. But perhaps one of the other shops. Have you tried the chemist?*

Yes, perhaps, and yes, he *had* tried the chemist. The chemist had nothing to kill the ache.

When he reached home, Jill must have been watching through the sitting room window and saw him drive into the street. She came to open the front door and they spoke for a minute quietly in the porch. 'A visitor,' she said. 'She's been waiting, but we've looked after her. The Earl Grey tea bags with one extra for the pot and Hazel popped out for good biscuits on the bill. Plus making her feel at home through friendly conversation, obviously, Dad.'

'Great,' Harpur said. It could be troublesome when his daughters made people feel at home through friendly conversation.

'This is the girl's mother,' Jill replied.

'NOON's mother?'

'Her name was Mandy. NOON's silly. Her mother is worried about the investigation. I think she thinks you've been bought, Dad.'

'Thanks.'

'Have you?'

'Stop talking like television again.'

Harpur began to move towards the sitting room, but Jill grabbed at his hand and held him back. 'She looked at me and cried. Really cried, Dad, asking how old I was.' Jill's voice shook a bit, but only a bit.

Harpur put an arm around her shoulders. 'Yes, I see.'

'It's not fair for her, is it?'

'It's very bad.'

She had tucked her face into the side of Harpur's jacket, perhaps to hide how upset she was. Now, she twisted her head up and stared at him, her eyes solemn. 'What's that mean, Dad?'

'A child dead. It's bad.'

'Meaning you can't do anything?'

'Of course we'll do something.'

'Honest?'

'I've been doing something this morning.'

'Honest?'

Honest? No, it would not be honest to say he had done anything. 'Honest,' he replied.

'We told her you would. Even Hazel said that.'

'Thanks.'

'Hazel said you and Mr Iles were the greatest team. Well, you know the way Mr Iles comes on to her. Sometimes she hates him, sometimes not at all, though.'

'It's silly,' Harpur replied.

'We know it is, but does Mr Iles?'

Harpur went into the sitting room. Rachel Walsh was with Hazel on the big sofa. 'It's not just Mrs Walsh who doesn't trust you, Dad,' Hazel said.

'Oh?'

'The Press.'

'That's really why she's here,' Jill said.

'I found your name in the telephone book,' Mrs Walsh said. 'I didn't know top police were listed. A matter of security.'

'I'm glad you did,' Harpur replied.

'These reporters have been getting at her, saying things,' Hazel told him.

'Mr Harpur, these are people who know a lot of the ins and outs. You know what I mean? They're a special kind.'

'Investigative,' Hazel said.

'We've had that sort here before,' Jill said. 'Dad sees them off. And Mr Iles, of course.'

'Mr Harpur, these people say that—'

'I think Mrs Walsh could speak more freely if you left us now, girls,' Harpur told his daughters.

'She's speaking freely, anyway,' Hazel said. 'She doesn't mind, do you, Mrs Walsh?'

'Go,' Harpur replied.

'Mr Harpur – please, could they stay?' She gazed around at the long sitting room and the shelves of books. 'I feel a bit nervous here and the girls . . . Well, I'd be happier if they stayed. Like friends?'

'If you're sure,' Harpur said.

'I don't suppose you think I'm much good, do you, Mr Harpur?' Rachel Walsh asked.

Harpur considered it. What did you make of a mother whose thirteen-year-old daughter was running drugs? What did someone trained up in police thinking make of it? And what did someone make of it whose own thirteen-year-old daughter still went regularly to school, as far as he knew, and had so far kept clear of much connection with drugs, as far as he knew. He was lucky, he was censorious. He was kindly and two-faced. He replied: 'Why do you say something like that, Mrs Walsh?'

'Of course Dad thinks you're fine,' Jill said.

Mrs Walsh looked around the room again. 'Oh, my daughter – into crime, yes, crime. No school. Me in the papers. Taking money for it.'

'Don't take any notice of the books,' Harpur replied. 'They were my wife's. They're going.'

'I loved Mandy,' Rachel Walsh said.

'Of course you did,' Hazel replied. 'Dad knows that. He said I don't know how many times what a terrible thing for you.'

'She goes and changes her name like she wants to be someone else, someone else's,' Mrs Walsh said.

'No, it's not like that,' Hazel replied.

Jill said: 'Kids at school do it. There's a kid called Esther and she hates it and we have to call her Blanche. Hazel hates Hazel. She'd rather be Anita.'

Harpur felt glad the children had stayed. When they wanted to they could produce a grand line in comforting.

'They go so deep,' Mrs Walsh said.

'Who?' Harpur asked.

'These Press.'

'I think they've scared her, Dad,' Hazel said. 'It's what's known as tabloid journalism.'

'I've heard of that,' Harpur replied.

'We do Press and Media in Civics at school,' Hazel said. 'The tabloid Press is often sensational, such as the *Sun*.'

Mrs Walsh said: 'They ask, have I thought it might not have been an accident – someone else in the street? Like there to get Mandy. I mean, *only* there to get Mandy.' She was in the dark blue dress she had worn to the funeral. Now, though, there was what might be a real diamond brooch on her left breast. He had not noticed that in the Gospel Hall.

Perhaps she had been spending some of the newspaper money. He hoped so. The brooch looked cruelly jaunty against her tired, desperate face. He had failed to look after this woman, as he had failed to look after her daughter.

'This is to do with new information,' Mrs Walsh said.

Harpur said: 'Around a case like this there will always be a lot of rumour, some of it disturbing.'

'What information, Dad?' Jill asked.

Mrs Walsh said: 'This information is to do . . . Oh, I can't stand talking about this . . .'

Jill crossed the room and put her hand on Rachel Walsh's shoulder and then pressed her cheek against hers. 'Don't say it if you don't want to. You don't have to, does she, Dad?'

'Of course not.'

After a while Mrs Walsh said: 'This is to do with bullets they found . . . and this is to do with the autopsy.' Harpur had thought she might weep, but bringing out this word appeared to daze her. Her face was white and rigid, her eyes dulled. Harpur longed to help her, but that word, that calculating procedure, the autopsy, stood in the way.

'How could the Press know about that?' Jill asked. 'This would be, well, private. Medical.'

'Grow up,' Hazel replied. 'Heard of leaks – reporters bribing and scheming? Journalists get two kinds of information. There's official information and there's leaks. What Mrs Walsh said – deep digging. We studied what's known as Watergate.'

**151**

'So horrible,' Jill said. 'Why don't they think they could be hurting people?'

'It's about truth,' Hazel replied. 'They have to try to find it.'

'Why?' Jill asked.

'Sometimes it's important,' Harpur said.

'Got rid of President Nixon who'd been swearing on White House tapes,' Hazel said.

Mrs Walsh said: 'Mr Harpur, they say this is kept secret, the bullets and autopsy. By the police, I mean.' She had turned away from him and was speaking towards the windows. Her voice was low and apologetic, but dogged. There was the tiredness in her, but something else as well. 'Why I had to come,' she said.

'Oh, is that true, Dad, about the secrecy?' Jill asked. 'Covering up? It's not true, is it?'

'Police have like an understanding with some of these people,' Mrs Walsh said. 'That's what they call it, the reporters – an understanding. They say it's happening all over. The police don't have a choice – Britain, France, maybe America.' Now she did turn and look at Harpur. 'Don't you want to catch who did it? Won't it ever be put right?'

'Oh, Dad,' Jill said.

'It's rubbish,' Harpur replied.

'I had to come and ask you,' Mrs Walsh said.

'Did they send you?' Harpur asked.

'The Press? They don't know I'm here.'

'I thought they stuck close.'

'I don't think they know I'm here.'

'It *is* rubbish, isn't it, Dad?' Jill asked.

'Of course.'

Hazel said: 'I've heard of this, called chaos theory. On TV and people talking in the youth club. Everything seeming to make things worse, even little, random things, so the police have to take allies – even crook allies.'

'Yes, Mandy was little,' Rachel Walsh said.

' "Chaos theory"? New to me,' Harpur replied.

'Oh, you'd lie, Dad,' Hazel said.

'The reporters have been asking for everything NOON might have told you, Mrs Walsh, have they?' Harpur asked. 'Names?'

'She didn't tell me anything.'

'I believe you.'

'Honestly she didn't,' Mrs Walsh said.

# 14

Mansel Shale kept in touch with the hospital about Jack Lamb's condition, and when Lamb came out of Intensive Shale told Ivis they should visit. Last year and the year before Shale had bought some art from Lamb and Shale considered a sort of friendship existed. A common love of art did bind people. There was a duty to drop in on someone local who had been so savagely knocked about. For more than a week it had looked like Jack would die.

Shale had bought an Arthur Hughes and two paintings by Edward Prentis from Lamb and they hung in the rectory now. Shale got a direct message from Pre-Raphaelites like these two. He loved the idea of a Brotherhood. This was the sort of relationship he wanted with the police. He paid a stack for all three works, so possibly they were genuine and possibly they had come to Lamb more or less honestly, or even absolutely honestly. Stolen stuff was always cheaper because people wanted to move it on fast. Shale had heard several folk say that Lamb did have this straight side to his business. As far as Shale knew, Lamb had never been successfully charged with anything, and Alfie had really looked into this through contacts. In fact, it looked like Lamb had never been charged with anything, successfully or not. Of course, Jack might have his own mutuality with police.

There were tales, though Shale had never managed full authentication. It was not clear whether Lamb gave a percentage on deals to someone useful, or whether he came up with decent information now and then. He had a manor house out of it all, and some young ex-punk girl cohabiting. Lamb was a real private fucker and slippery.

But Shale wanted to ask him now whether any of those three paintings, or even all, were stolen and on the Fine Art Squad's list. If Shale eventually got a wholesome law-and-order cooperative going with Mark Lane and other big police, it would probably mean they would visit his house on the quiet now and then for conversation. What he did not want was to upset them by pushing hot property in front of their fucking noses. You had to move gradually when things were so sensitive and think of others' prejudices. Lane, the Chief, was a man of real soul, admired by many. The Chief was a Catholic, and quite a few of these had a constructive outlook, apparently. It would be a big move for Chief Lane to accept a business arrangement, even for the sake of peace. A serious move for any Chief, but some of them had done it. Lane would have to be brought along with very nice care. If one day he agrees to talk at the rectory and the first things he sees are three framed bits of high price loot the arrangement might die.

Of course, Jack Lamb was not going to admit straight off and direct that he handled hunted goods. No bugger knew better than Jack Lamb how to brickwall and dodge. But the thing was Shale had told Alfie to do research on those three paintings and so far he had found nothing rough in their recent history. It could be they were all right. Shale reckoned he would be able to tell from the look of Lamb what the truth was, especially as he could not be at his strongest now after the thump. If Shale got the message that this art was dirty, he would bring the three of them down before any rectory conference with the Chief and his people. Obviously, he would have to get something else to cover up the patches. This would mean buying more works of about the same size, and they would have to be real works. He could not put up fucking posters or prints on ex-rectory walls because that would do him as much damage as hanging burgled paintings. Lane might have that proud sod Iles with him, and Iles would definitely not want an arrangement with someone who hung cheap rubbish in his drawing room. Shale would have to buy other paintings from a gallery that was definitely clean. Probably there were some.

'I'd really miss that Hughes if I had to sell or stick it in the cellar, Alfred. The girl's tresses. He's so bloody good on tresses. You'd never get tresses like that in art today, take my word.'

'With respect, not sell, Manse. If we were into delicate negotiations with Mr Mark Lane we would not want to be trading in tainted items. Should something go awry we'd have a worse situation than if you'd kept them on the walls. You could store them for a while. Then, once the arrangement was in place, there would be a different relationship between you and the police. One could reasonably look for give-and-take. You could bring the paintings back out for show then, with a reasonable expectation of no harsh repercussions. This, after all, is what an arrangement is about.'

'Good, Alf. Often you see so damn clear.'

They bought some flowers and Denzil drove them out to the hospital in the Jaguar. The flowers were a small bunch of lilies. Shale hated too many flowers together. They looked so bloody bland, like they bred so thick they were bound to be all right when Mankind was finished. Shale carried them himself in the car. The other thing about visiting Lamb was, if you played it right, Jack could be turned into a go-between. Because of the art and his house and the undoubted money, he knew all sorts, and he might know top police. Yes, it was likely. Maybe he did not know Lane himself, because the Chief kept pretty apart – this was the problem. But Lamb could have links with other main people, say that maniac, Iles, or, down a bit, Colin Harpur. One view was that Iles ran the outfit, not Lane. The Chief had soul, yes, but maybe too much soul for a police officer. The police wanted height, not soul. When Jack was better again, he might be able to give a suggestion to one of these police contacts about the advantage of an arrangement with Mansel Shale Inc. W. P. Jantice should be trying the same, but Jantice was low-level and would not have what was referred to as clout. There would be something in it for Lamb, naturally. Shale would get Alfie to think of a decent number and then double it. Lamb would probably be glad of an earning chance after being off work for so long.

Ivis said: 'It's a tonic to see you looking so well after reports of this monstrous incident, Jack.' Alf was always great and oily at this kind of thing.

Lamb said: 'If you want to know details – numbers and so on – at the Kimberley house, I can't help.'

'How did you get to be there, Jack?' Shale asked.

'I thought you might show here,' Lamb replied.

'Mr Shale said we must visit at the very earliest.'

Lamb was sitting by his bed in an easy chair, wearing a yellow dressing gown. Shale could not stand it in hospitals when people were like that. They looked crouched over and beaten and elderly, even someone as big and weighty as Jack. He would rather see them properly in bed. You knew where you were with an illness or an injury if the patient was in bed.

Shale closed the door. 'There's a good place for you, as things will develop, Jack,' he said. He arranged the lilies with care in a vase. Esteem was what he wanted to show. It was the ordinary National Health hospital. Probably Jack would of gone private for illness, but this was where emergencies came and with Jack's head pulped he was definitely an emergency. Shale preferred private hospitals. You got such a mix in the National Health, and some of the coughing by working-class patients was disgusting. But even in this place, Lamb had his own room. He must have been real bad. Ivis said: 'Mr Shale hopes soon to cement an arrangement with—'

'They won't look at you, Manse,' Lamb replied.

'Who, Jack?' Ivis asked.

'Mark Lane's never going to let you get close,' Lamb replied.

Shale went on with the lilies, still keen to suggest admiration of Lamb, but, Christ, this sod made him furious. The fucker sat there shattered, his head in a bandage, and that rancid dressing down around him, plus Rose's lemon barley water bottles on the cabinet, but he talked like a witch doctor who knew all prospects. Shale gave a friendly chuckle, stepped back to inspect the flower arranging, and then went to sit on the edge of Jack's bed. He could have leaned forward and ripped that bright bandage off him, so damn easy. 'I don't think you can have heard how I see things unfolding, Jack. There's bags of *quid pro quo*.'

'The tale was around before I came in here,' Lamb replied. ' "The arrangement".'

He put a sneering voice on so it sounded like shit.

Ivis said: 'Mr Lane had it in mind, Jack, that you'd—'

'I don't fucking go-between,' Lamb replied.

'Not what I'd heard,' Shale said.

'They won't look at you,' Lamb said again.

'You mean they won't do a peace deal at all?' Shale asked.

'They might. Not with you,' Lamb said. 'Mansel Shale? Jesus.'

'Why not with Mr Shale then, in your view?' Ivis asked.

'Because he's Mr Shale,' Lamb replied.

Shale began to yell: 'You mean because they think my people did that little girl?'

'No, they know that was someone else. The bullets. Your name was fucking dud long before Sphere Street.'

Shale, sitting stiff with rage, said: 'How the hell do you know about the bullets when you're in here?'

Lamb said: 'Heard of the phone? Mobile and otherwise. People are in touch. You should have asked Neville what went on in Sphere Street.'

Ivis said: 'With respect, Jack, Mr Shale might indeed if only—'

'I heard he was at your house with Mr Kalashnikov. Plus Nev's bird.' The sod looked at his watch, a huge, tired gesture. 'I've got my mother and girlfriend coming. You ought to be gone by then.'

Shale said: 'You talk in your big fucking way like you know Mark Lane personal.'

'I don't know him,' Lamb replied.

'So which of them *do* you know?' Shale said.

'I know *you*,' Lamb said. Again the way he said it said *shit*.

Shale reached out and grabbed the flowers from the vase. Gripping the stems, he hit Lamb with the top part across the face, water and bits everywhere, one really great stroke. 'Behold the lilies of the fucking field,' he yelled. There was a lump of leaf right in the middle of the head bandage. Shale felt sorry for him for a second then. It was bad to get plant life on medical material. Shale shouted again: 'You know me and I know you, you fucking crook. You sold me three mired paintings. This is criminal stuff on an ex-rectory wall. My God.'

'Oh, here's my mother and Helen now, as a matter of fact,' Lamb replied pleasantly. He wiped his face with the edge of a blanket. The door had opened. Shale saw an elderly woman in a terrible pink and silver print dress and a much younger one wearing tan lightweight slacks and a green waistcoat over a cream blouse. This was a true nimble beauty, as you'd expect with some scheming bastard like Lamb.

'Here are some fine business chums of mine – Mansel Shale and Alfred Ivis,' Lamb said. 'Mother flew over from the States where she lives, as soon as she heard of my little trouble. That's so like her, I'm proud to say, gents.'

'Business?' Mrs Lamb replied. 'Are you the ones who got him knocked about?'

She had some filthy, low, back-street American accent, like a TV heavy. Shale stood up and took care rearranging the lilies in the vase. Some of the flowers were still intact and he put those on the outside. Then he stretched across and removed the piece of leaf from Lamb's bandage. Lamb drew away. 'Good Lord, Manse,' he joked, 'for a moment I thought you were going to tear the dressing off.' Shale had a chuckle at this.

Ivis said: 'We were surprised to see how well he looks, Mrs Lamb, despite everything.'

'I told Jack ten years ago if he went with the people he goes with – people like you two, probably – I told him he'd finish with no head. Did you ever see a man of Jack's age look as old as this, Mr Shale, Mr Ivis?'

'How old *is* he?' Shale asked.

'This is my son. This is a man I gave life to and taught about life. This is the face of suffering. OK, you'll say he can still pull young broads like Helen here, but that's also to do with the money and property, isn't it, dear?' she asked Helen. 'You two here for some deal, yes? Did we interrupt? I hope so. To me you two look the kind who'd let Jack down even deeper into the cack. You wear that sort of clothes, both of you. And the hair styles. What you two do not look like is members of your Order of Merit, I believe it's called.'

'As a matter of fact Manse and Alf were just on their way,' Lamb said.

'Christ,' Shale said to Ivis in the car, 'she talks to us about *our* clothes.' He leaned forward from the back seat and spoke to Denzil as he drove. 'Have you been talking, you ponce?'

'What's your fucking trouble, then, Mr Shale?' Denzil replied.

'About Nev and the others.'

'Talk to who?'

'Did you talk?' Shale replied.

'I would not of thought so,' Denzil said after a while. 'This is the girl I brought down for Nev to bang on your bed linen, Mr Shale? It was a lovely gesture, but I doubt whether I would speak of it, so as to guard the girl's reputation.'

'What fucking reputation?' Shale replied.

They went to Ivis's lighthouse. Discussion was needed and Shale did not want to talk any more with Denzil listening. Shale had always drawn back from putting a partition window in the Jaguar: big-headed tycoonery, and he hated anything like that. Today he wished there was one, though. He really wanted to talk to Ivis while all the aspects of what Lamb said were sharp in his head – the feel of them, not just the words. It was grave. Shale said the lighthouse because Alfred was always more relaxed in his own place, and his mind sure of itself, what there was of it. This was natural. Shale's good furniture and the art could make Alfie realize he was socially nowhere. Often it was poor management to make people uneasy. Shale told Denzil to wait in the car or walk the cliffs and note various lichens.

'I despair, Alfred,' Shale said, as soon as they were inside the lighthouse.

'That's not a word I'd ever associate with Mansel Shale, Manse.'

'Before I even put our scheme to him I'm met with low abuse, Alf. We go there in friendly spirit, distressed by his injuries and carrying a decent offer of work – liaison work of the type Jack Lamb could so easily handle – and this offer is dismissed with contempt.'

'It was unpardonable, Manse.'

'This is some fucking skull-scrambled bastard in slippers who'd plastic-sack me for the rubbish truck.'

'Perhaps his injuries have unbalanced him.'

'As he spoke, Alfred, I saw the chance of a civilized deal between us and the police simply dying.' He felt like sobbing the word, but spoke it tersely, with control. 'This was a hospital, supposed to cure, but all I felt was destruction of a charming and positive scheme.'

Ivis said: 'But luckily we were not committed exclusively to Jack Lamb as intermediary. This is a vindication of your year-in-year-out policy, Manse: that policy which will not commit too much on one front.'

'W. P. Jantice?'

'I feel he will efficiently and subtly urge the case for a merger.'

This was the thing about Alfred – he could be so good at reading accounts or spotting a detail but he did not always pick up the flavour or the hidden bits of what was said. Intuition he was short of. If you put it all together – that was *all* of it – the rumour and what Nev Greenage said and what Earl said and what Lamb just said – if you held all that up to the light what it showed was the man who shot the child in Sphere Street was W. P. Jantice. Plus the bullet cluster: this was police-trained marksmanship that put two so close – lower neck, chest. This was a child who knew a lot through her little travels and such and probably somehow she had picked up too much about Jantice, with a danger she would talk about it somewhere. So, he arranges a scene where she ought to get killed and he's up there himself anyway to make sure. He most likely knew the times of all their movements – the Carlton, obviously, and the other two, obviously, because he had slid into God knew how many outfits. And he must have fixed the girl's programme, too, that day.

Ivis said: 'W. P. Jantice could not make the approaches in

the same one-to-one way Jack Lamb might have, but he can sow the idea, and that's often much more effective. This is a lad who's only a sergeant, yes, but he's also a lad with great street knowledge. His expertise would be appreciated by Lane and others.'

'We'll certainly need to talk to W. P. Jantice,' Shale replied.

It was wisest not to discuss with Alf at this point what Jantice had most likely done. Mind, perhaps Alfie and W. P. Jantice had some kind of quiet understanding, and Alfie knew already what Jantice had done. The gorgeous testimonial from Alf stank a bit. Shale did not want Jantice warned. 'It's the insulting nature of what Lamb said that leaves me desperate, baffled, Alf.'

'Don't dwell on it. These were the ravings of a sick man.'

'He spoke like Mr Mark Lane would regard me as something vile, someone impossible to accept as a colleague. And yet people like Panicking Ralph Ember or Vine or Stanfield, even fucking Misto, these were all right, that's what Lamb hinted.'

'According to Lamb they're all right. Only according to Lamb. He's playing his game. Jantice will tell us something quite different, I'm sure. And Jantice will further your bid so that all these others are left nowhere.'

Obviously, Shale could trust nothing to W. P. Jantice. If he was what all the signs said he was, the one who killed the kid, it made him someone who would act only for himself when things turned difficult, and fuck everybody else. It was how they could sink, these once fine lawmen. They went bad from despair, and then had to do whatever was needed to hide they had gone bad – because they remembered what it was like to be decent, and wanted to go on looking as if they still were. Wasn't it the same as Satan? He'd be able to recall when he was an angel, probably, and sometimes feel sorry he might look rotten. Jantice was someone supposed to organize an efficient and entirely justified counter-strike to take out intruders on Sphere Street and instead of that he uses it to make execution of an inconvenient little child, inconvenient to him. What happens then is the people who are supposed to be removed get nimbly away because Earl with the Kalashnikov won't put a little girl in danger. Shale did not hold that against him. There had to be boundaries. Only in very rare conditions could Shale approve of gunning a child.

If that was how W. P. Jantice had played it – but there was no fucking if, this was exactly how W. P. Jantice had played it . . . so, *because* this was how W. P. Jantice had played it, there were two people around now who could be perilous – Sailor Billy and the other one, flesh-pricked, nothing worse. And there was a kid dead, and the Press and the country and the police in a wild, unforgiving state and wanting to poke deep into the whole structure of the trade. It was so bad. Yes, there was some talking to W. P. Jantice to be done.

Ivis said: 'In many ways I see Jantice as better for our purposes than Jack Lamb, Manse. We know that the Chief favours him. This means direct access. Lamb has police contacts, or a police contact, yes, but we don't know at what level. What we do know, because he told us, is that it is not with Mark Lane. And on a supremely sensitive political matter, such as a treaty, only the Chief's word would matter. If Jantice is right and Lane wants to infiltrate him, it would be even better. Then, he could have picked up a buzz from inside the trade that Mansel Shale would be willing to consider an agreement. Jantice would be able to talk to the Chief about it straight out.'

The biggest trouble about being a leader of men was you could never have full faith in any fucker under you, not even the ones who seemed closest, like Alfie. Maybe Mark Lane had this kind of worry about people under him, too. Alf and Jantice probably had a scheme that would put something extra in Ivis's pocket. He looked like he needed it – the slimy, kicked-to-death carpets and the decor and slum furniture they were sitting on now. Even the Brer Rabbit mug Shale was drinking his gin and pep from had a big chip out of the rim. Maybe Alf and Jantice were taking from two, three, five outfits. That woman of Alfie's – she looked the sort who would be at him to get more. Plus the children would have to go to boarding school. Nobody could stand having kids like those around long. Shale was against boarding schools, but for some kids what else?

'Did you notice that fucker never told me if my pictures were honest?' Shale asked.

'This is another aspect where Jantice might be able to help, Manse. He could probably get an under-the-bedclothes look at the Fine Art Squad's list.'

Jantice, Jantice, Jantice. Oh, Christ, he was a holy wonder, especially when it came to shooting little girls. The other day Shale was reading the obituaries of that one-time prime minister, Harold Wilson. They said he was scared of conspiracies and betrayal from inside his own party. Of course, for fuck's sake. If you had it you could be sure everyone wanted to grab it, and especially your dearest friends, because they knew all about the power, through having been near it. Ivis handled one set of Shale's accounts. Naturally, these were not the main books, but they would tell Alf something about earnings. It was only to be expected if you lived in a fucking lighthouse full of junk that you would want to push your way to more funds. Alfie would hope to run this firm one day, and he and Jantice might have some scheme to make it possible. Poor old Alfie. Shale had had enough and went home soon after this. It was half term and the two children had gone away to their mother in Wales. He gave her plenty of access to Laurent and Matilda, although she did not want them full time with her and her new partner, whatever his name was. He missed the children and the house felt very empty but you had to let even a selfish cow like Sybil have some contact with them now and then. That was only decent. Of course, there was the abuse danger with some unknown man in the house, especially in an untidy place like Wales, but some risks you had to accept for the sake of humaneness. And he always asked the children when they came back whether there had been any particular fondnesses. But, Christ, wasn't life turning dark when you had to wonder about such things?

He spent quite a while now examining the Pre-Raphaelite paintings, standing in front of each for as much as ten minutes, looking at the way the paint was put on and thinking about the lay-out. When you discovered someone like Jack Lamb had a hate for you you had to wonder not just whether this art was on a most wanted list, but also if it was genuine. That could be the real reason Lamb had not wanted to talk about the paintings. Someone with a mother like that could be crooked in all sorts of directions at once. Shale went up very close to the works and spent time on the signatures. Eventually, he decided all three paintings looked right. To him they seemed exactly the kind of art that someone who wanted to be called pre-Raphaelite would make sure he turned out, the colours and dignity. They had that feel to them, the pre-Raphaelitish feel, and you had to trust your instincts. Of course, this was only half the problem, or even less. They could be more damaging hanging there if they were genuine than if forgeries, because it would be the genuines that would interest police.

In the evening he took a trip alone to see Stefan Bulmer. This was the street-level lad the kid NOON had done the running for, the one she dealt with direct. Shale cycled on his 1930s upright heavy Humber. He loved that bike for its three-speed hub and the case over the chain to keep the oil off his trousers. You could not wear cycle clips with a first-class suit, for God's sake, they would look quaint. He took a 9mm Beretta automatic in his waistband. A boy like Bulmer might be jumpy and impetuous at present and things could turn delicate. Bulmer was smalltime-to-middling and took his supplies from Shale. That is, not straight from Shale, obviously. Bulmer was too far down the league for that. As wholesaler Shale sold to a bulk buyer and he sold on to back-lane pushers like Bulmer. But Bulmer was part of the outfit, all the same. What he had was a district franchise and it was Shale who gave it. Stefan Bulmer had responsibilities. It might be an idea to ask him if the child ever said she had special fears of someone. It might be another idea to see who fixed the detail and the timing of that three-way meeting in Sphere Street. Shale felt the need of extensive background before he had words with W. P. Jantice. Jantice could be even more slippery than Lamb. He was police.

Obviously the name Stefan was annoying, but Shale definitely would not mock it today. He wanted a happy talkative mood at this meeting. He would not get at Bulmer for using children, either, though he had been told a million fucking times not to if he wanted to keep the dealership. The bastard had ignored that. This was why seeing Shale on his doorstep could make Bulmer edgy. He would think it was reprisals. He would see the lump of the Beretta under Shale's jacket and might get hasty. This was one reason Shale went on the Humber. An old-style bike took some of the menace from a situation.

Shale knew what the sod would say to defend himself for exploiting kids. It would be *special street conditions*, Manse, and *increased Drugs Squad activity,* Manse. Plus other ploys. They always came pouring out if things went wrong, and not just from Bulmer and not just about Sphere Street. What was under such words was the idea that these kerbside traders knew local conditions best and the biggie with his Jag and far-off ex-rectory and so on could go stuff himself. But, Christ, didn't Shale know the scene inside out and backwards? How did these people think he *got* the Jag and the rectory and so on? Through having an empty head? But generally he let them believe they were the jet-thrust of the firm. Best humour these valuable, seamy little folk – unless they went really unkempt, of course, when they had to be taken aside. He hated that kind of violence, but it could definitely be forced on you.

'Here's a bloke with a bike asking for Stefan.' This fat girl in a brown boiler suit yelled up the bare stairs without turn-ing her head. There were kitchen smells but nothing worse. She watched him all the time, hard, grey sentry eyes. Perhaps the people here had trouble with the owner's strongarm friends or bailiffs. 'I don't think I've seen him for a while,' she said. 'There's quite a few here, so you don't always notice who's about. You know what I mean?'

'Gone away,' a man shouted back. There was no furniture or carpet in the hall, no table for visiting cards.

'Are you sure he's not here?' Shale called up the stairs.

'What do you mean, is he sure?' the girl asked.

'I mean is he fucking sure, dear?' Shale replied.

This Bulmer was some sort of drop-out – from a university

or the army or men's wear in Next, something like that. He had a drop-out face – like aggression and bitchiness and blaming everyone for the trouble he's got. He was not much more than a kid himself, about twenty and lived in this squat up Logan Gardens way. This lad Bulmer had come on very fast in the trade. By now you might have thought he would have his own place, but some of them liked this sort of life, the company and endless swap-around fucks right on the premises.

The man came downstairs, young middle-aged, shaving soap on half his face and carrying a safety razor. The shaved side gleamed truly pink, a fine job. He had on a kimono-style thing over jodphurs and plimsolls. His grey hair had been brilliantly styled. Shale thought about asking him which barber, but probably they did each other's hair in here, a commune, exchanging skills and so on. Shale would not want to attend here for a haircut. 'Stefan left well over a week ago,' the man said.

Right after Sphere Street so it could be true. People did disappear then. 'Going where?' Shale said.

'He's very concerned about the environment,' the man said.

'The whales? Is he coming back?' Shale asked.

'You could definitely leave a message. We've got a cork board for notes et cetera in the kitchen.'

'This is the latest thing,' Shale said.

'Who should we say, if he does come back?' the girl asked.

'A bloke with a bike,' Shale replied.

# 15

When Shale went home he had the feeling as soon as he entered the house that someone else was in there. That was it, just a feeling. But one thing he always did was trust his intuitions. They were what made him. His mother used to say he had better intuition than even a woman, and his mother was sharp. He did not pull out the Beretta yet or anything like that. He hated panic. This might only be Alfie bringing one of his new urgent worried thoughts. Or maybe one of the more recent girls who had lived here for spells, Lowri or Patricia or Carmel. Alfie and all the women had keys and Shale never bothered to change locks after a girl left. It would seem so measly. If you had been sleeping chummily with a girl for weeks or even months it surely gave her an entitlement to look in on your property now and then, as long as she did not take anything much, and by and large these three were pretty good that way. As usual when he went out in the evening he had left lights on here and there, so the caller could be in one of three or four rooms, upstairs or down. If this was one of the girls in a bedroom it would probably have a meaning, and he did not know whether he wanted all that tonight after the stress. A girl had returned for a night not so long ago and that had been fine. Trying to recall it now, he thought it was probably

Patricia. Girls had their needs, for God's sake. He thought there might be a tiny trace of a familiar perfume somewhere in the air, so perhaps his reactions were not based entirely on intuition. It might be Red. Or possibly Brute. He was pretty sure one of the girls did Red. He had once given some as a present. Perhaps Alfie used Brute.

Shale had an Edwardian armchair upholstered blue and gold in the hall and he sat down there and listened. He did open his jacket for quicker access to the Beretta, but that was all. Although he waited for three or four minutes like that he heard nothing. This did not convince him he had been wrong, though. All it made him think was that whoever was in here wanted to stay secret and knew how to keep silent. The intruder would have heard him open the front door. All this changed the picture. It would not be Alfie, nor any of the women. They would have called a welcome. Now, he did bring the gun from his waistband. He felt glad the children were away. There were troublesome people about and all kinds of nasty currents flowing after Sphere Street. He was angry, not afraid. He did not like the idea of someone breaking into a former rectory. Shale was rarely afraid. He believed that if you had a brain you could think yourself around most hazards. No, he did not believe it, but he wanted to.

The stairs came down into the hall and were dark at the top. After another minute he suddenly sensed there was someone watching him from up there, but not a girl. Staring, he thought he could make out the outline of a man on the landing. The figure was in the deepest area of shadow, and Shale could not be certain. It was the wrong build for Alfie, and wrong for Neville Greenage or Earl, too – too slender. The light was on in the hall and Shale knew he was sitting there like a target, the pistol in full view. He pulled his eyes away and looked along the landing. There might be more than one. When he redirected his gaze towards the original shape, he saw it had moved and seemed about to come down the stairs. Definitely male, apparently unarmed. Shale stood and pointed the Beretta two-handed. 'Stay there a minute, old son,' he said. You had to sound relaxed.

'This is a business call, Manse.' Desmond Iles was illuminated gradually as he descended, starting with his shoes. 'You ought to get some more security, you know, post Sphere Street. Couldn't you be a target? Don't you ever pull the curtains across?'

Shale lowered the gun, then replaced it in his waistband. A great tingle of triumph went over him and he smiled. His anger disappeared. This was an Assistant Chief doing a pilgrimage to his property and breaking in for confidential talks, such as a treaty, what else? He wished that slandering sod Jack Lamb could see this. Iles would be here on behalf of the Chief, this was plain. Lane probably felt he must not make the first approach himself. Shale could understand that. It was a delicate process. Iles would be just the shag-around sort to bodywash himself in Brute.

'This ought to be a private matter,' Iles said. 'I thought I'd better check all the rooms with lights on. We don't want interruptions, Manse, sightseers. Who advised you on the fucking décor and furniture – Prince Albert?'

Iles would have to say something hurtful like that. This was how he worked. He had to down people, even people he entirely respected and needed. Remarks like that were part envy and part defence. 'Did Mr Mark Lane send you, Mr Iles?' Shale replied. 'Do you come as his sort of emissary?' The thing was, maintain complete civility, it would get to him, even to such a fucking famous savage.

'I'm talking to one or two people in entirely general terms at this stage,' the ACC said.

'I was expecting you,' Shane replied.

'Bollocks.'

'As a matter of fact, what's called intuition told me someone was in the house, Mr Iles.'

'Well, this *is* a coincidence,' Iles cried. 'I'm strong on intuition myself, Manse. Some call me "Intuitive Iles", or even just "Intuitive", for short.'

'When you say one or two people, which people?' Shale replied.

'But you headed my list, Manse.'

'You mean talking to Panicking Ralphy and Vine and Stanfield as well? Misto, even?' They went into the drawing room. 'You don't have to fret about curtains, Mr Iles. There are grounds outside.' He had read that the upper classes in big houses and with land around never pulled curtains over.

'Yet on the whole I like this old place, Manse,' Iles said. 'I've been through the desk and so on and came across no incriminating material or even indiscreet. You could be as clean as clean. I appreciate that care. The safe looks very sound.'

'Thank you, Mr Iles,' Shale replied. The thing about Iles was you had to watch for violence, and you could not trust anything he said. Obviously, you could not trust anything any officer said, and especially the higher ranks, but Iles you could trust ten times less. He had this thinnish, wonderfully gentle-looking face with very smooth skin, not like a policeman at all – more an amputating surgeon. 'Does Mr Lane say how he wants this treaty to operate?'

'I feel a considerable personal bond with you, Manse.'

'I'm glad, Mr Iles. A bond through intuition.'

'Your wife buggered off with somebody else. You could give me advice. The main reason I dropped by.'

This was more of it, the stuff to flatten someone before the fucker came up with his deal, to get advantage, his foot on your neck. 'Has yours gone then?' Shale replied.

'Not yet. But she looks around. You know the signs. I'd be finished if she went. Possibly I strike you as strong, Manse. But I'm nowhere without her. They develop this contempt for husbands. Did you notice? And yet I've seen much worse things than you able to hold on to their woman and stay apparently happy. Well, no, not *much* worse, but worse. Do you have any answer for it?'

Shale prepared some drinks. Iles wanted port and lemon. Shale mixed himself a gin and pep. He used the best glasses. Iles went and studied the Arthur Hughes. He stepped back for the long view, then suddenly moved forward again and bent quickly, as if to pick something up from the floor. Shale did not see what. Iles put whatever it was into his pocket. The smell of scent or toilet water seemed more obvious in here, so perhaps it did come from the ACC, wafting strongly as he moved about. Iles sat down on a sofa. He was wearing a grey, high-buttoned, lightweight double-breasted suit, which was supposed to Oyez, Oyez his slimness and did. He said: 'You get this Salem bookcase for her, Manse, and the art and yet she still goes. It's tragic. The art is shit, of course, but would she have the brain to know that? I doubt it. So she moves out to someone with a bigger dick. That what it amounts to, Manse? Your sensitivity treated any old how. Ingratitude and appetite. These are recurring themes with them. Men are such victims.'

'I heard quite a few lads in the Force put it to your wife, Mr Iles.' Shale said. 'Harpur, Chief Inspector Garland. These are the names that come up most often in soirées.' You had to give him a riposte now and then with a bit of international vocabulary, he respected you even more for it. Shale sat down opposite the ACC in a deep black leather armchair, like something from a first-class London club probably.

'I'd eliminated you altogether from among the possibles for alliance talks, Manse,' Iles said. 'Did I want intimate contact with someone whose people shoot down a child?'

'No, it's not true,' Shale yelled. 'Would I?' The slur could still pain him. 'Is that what you think of me, what Mr Lane thinks of me?' Suddenly, what Lamb had said looked right again. 'Never.'

Iles held up a delicate hand, like a blessing. 'I know it now. The autopsy and bullets say impossible.'

'Oh?'

'Well, clearly you've heard this.'

'What alliance?' Shale replied.

Iles spoke softly, in a voice that had loaded itself with consideration. 'I look at you, Manse, and I think here's someone who's had enough trouble from life. His wife's quit, gone looking for full satisfaction. I heard she was with someone in Wales. Well, my God, this is really desperate. And you're left here with children, plus these terrible daubs and the farcical furniture. You don't want any more suffering. You look for some peace now, and you deserve it. Especially, you want trade peace on the streets. One desires peace oneself, Manse. You crave relief from these various agonies. I feel we might be able to get an arrangement, if you're interested, that is.'

Shale sat forward in the chair, shortening the distance between him and Iles. 'I've been longing to hold out the hand of friendship, Mr Iles,' he replied. 'I can guarantee you and Mr Lane, of course, civilized conduct throughout the manor. This is so desirable. My lads and I will save you from this chaos I've heard you fear, and which is definitely a current factor. It's a role I would be proud of and, yes, might of been made for.'

Iles transferred his drink to his left hand and then also

leaned forward. He took Shale's right hand and shook it. 'As I said, Manse, a bond.'

'I think of it as comradeship in a fucking good cause,' Shale said.

'Exactly.' Iles released his hand then stood and prepared to leave.

Shale was startled. He also stood and offered to mix another drink for him. Iles said he had to go. 'Other aspects to be looked at, Manse.'

Shale said emotionally: 'But I need detail, Mr Iles. Full assurances. I mean, the various reciprocities. These must be itemized.'

'They will be.'

'And then – I must ask again, do you come plenary, with the authority of Mr Lane? I would need to know if you are official, Mr Iles, or mavericking, in your little way.'

'Myself, I think it would be better confidential at this stage.'

'But what stage is it, Mr Iles?' How they were, police. They gave it, they took it away. They were trained to it.

'When I've gone, see if you can find where I forced entry, Manse. I doubt it.'

'So is the fucking treaty in place as of tonight?' Shale replied. 'That's what I need to know. I'd have to give instructions. Will your people from now on do extensive blind-eyeing, as your contribution? Mr Lane agrees? Plus – I mean, you having to leave like this – are you going to talk to these other fuckers as well – Panicking and so on? Is this exclusive to us, Desmond? It must be, must be.'

'A bond, Manse. I feel honoured by it. I needn't tell you, I'm sure, this meeting never took place.'

# 16

The Chief called Harpur and Iles to a meeting in his suite. This was unusual for Lane. Normally, he liked to drift into someone else's room and let a discussion develop as though unplanned. The Chief despised formality. He dressed without care or much cost and often wandered about the building in his socks. The scruffiness was his answer to those who thought Chief Constables should be retired brigadiers. But Iles said it showed Lane's 'sad lust to seem ordinary and acceptable, the less-than-ordinary unacceptable jerk'.

Today the Chief looked pretty good. There was a jauntiness to his voice and stance, a throb of conviction. He seemed to have come through some period of self-doubt. You saw how he might have convinced a selection panel he could command. Harpur feared for him. Lane said: 'Desmond, Colin, I've decided to go ahead with my plan to put an undercover officer into one of the gangs.'

A change. Originally, the Chief had spoken as if Iles should not know about this operation. Lane said: 'I don't need to be told of the risks, believe me, and it is imperative things are handled strictly within the guidelines. Because of the perils, I want a very senior officer to act as our plant's Controller. This will be you, Colin. You will do it admirably. And then it is important to have another level of supervision.

You will handle this, please, Desmond. I'd like you to take the role of what would be Registrar, if we were dealing with an ordinary civilian informant. This whole thing must be immaculately conducted. I don't have to remind you that we once lost an undercover officer.'

'No, you don't,' Iles replied. They were seated at the long conference table in Lane's rooms and Iles stared down at it, perhaps for once defeated by the Chief. Lane had made him central to his project, probably to sink any rival schemes the ACC had. This might be the reason for the Chief's good spirits. Yes, Harpur feared for him.

'I've been in discussions with various chief officers from other Forces,' Lane said. 'The universal view was that infiltration of drug gangs is not only a practical policy, but possibly the only one, given the growing difficulties of producing effective anti-drugs-trade evidence by other means.'

Iles stirred. He raised his eyes and gazed over the top of Lane's head towards the window, his face blank. It was as though he wanted escape into a wider, more intelligent world, one which revelled in his merits.

The Chief said: 'I see no choice. We have recurrent grave incidents and no convictions. No arrests. Oh, I've heard the ACC's suggestion that we should establish some sort of unofficial, secret working arrangement with stable and powerful overlord villains. Desmond, you say that such pacts are already in existence – either acknowledged or *de facto* in some police areas here and abroad. I've found no confirmation of this among those chief officers I've spoken to.'

Iles said: 'They might have felt sensitive about admitting it to you, sir. These arrangements are simply unpublicized recognition of an existing state.'

The Chief nodded several times, but not in agreement. It was to relay a kind of wonderment at Iles's argument. To Harpur, Lane's assurance still seemed bonny. The Chief was in uniform today for some function later, and Harpur thought it did something for him. The blue of the fine material distracted from his pallor, and the silver-buttoned tunic seemed to bunch him up together, almost gave him presence. 'Shall I tell you what your proposal reminds me of, Desmond?' Lane asked gently, like someone speaking reproaches to a loved child. 'I don't know if you've ever seen a film called *Prizzi's Honor* which comes on the television now and then. It is a Mafia tale, comic in intent, and part of this comedy is that the mobsters and police cooperate – have an arrangement, as you would call it.' He bent forward and spoke in what was virtually a snarl towards Iles. 'Am I being asked seriously to contemplate such a stoop to gross and farcical contamination?'

'Ah, I like to think of you and Mrs Lane watching humorous late-night movies together, sir,' Iles replied. 'Shared laughter is a happy marital asset.'

'I don't want you to think I discuss any of these matters with my wife,' Lane said at once. 'A security matter.'

Iles raised one hand to show he nearly believed this. Then the ACC brought out a notebook and took a while writing down the name of the film, getting Harpur to spell Prizzi a couple of times.

'I think you know the officer who is my preferred candidate for this role,' Lane said. 'I would value advice, though. I decided on W.P. Jantice early, and I've stuck with him. You're familiar with his qualities, I'm sure, and above all his remarkable inside knowledge of the scene. But I am certainly open to other suggestions.'

Harpur said: 'There's a woman officer, sir, Naomi Anstruther who—'

'Look, none of this is on,' Iles said.

'Desmond?' Lane replied mildly.

'The risk is intolerable,' Iles said.

Lane nodded several times, as before, but, as before, not in agreement. Now, it was to indicate sympathy. His dark eyes warmed with understanding. 'I know you are thinking about the past,' Lane said. 'The loss of that officer has scarred you. It is understandable, commendable, Desmond. But this will be managed differently, believe me.'

'I was in Mansel Shale's place the other night,' Iles replied.

Lane was silenced. Harpur said: 'How do you mean, *in* there, sir? You called on him? Part of the inquiry?'

'Waiting for him. And I thought it wise to have a look around, in case we did decide on Plan B, Chief. If we were forced to it.'

Lane whispered: 'Do I understand this? You broke in?'

'He has a former rectory, like yourself, sir,' Iles replied.

'Overlaps are strange. I thought that if we did go for an alliance we ought to know more about these people.'

Still whispering from deep in the dark pit of his shock Lane said: 'But there was never any possibility that I would tolerate an alliance. You must have known that.' Two or three of those red lines that would appear in Lane's doughy face when he was angry or perplexed suddenly gleamed across his cheeks. His body seemed to have slackened behind the silver buttons. *Oh, God, sir, go to the Seychelles for a month.*

'People like Manse Shale have risen to a point where they no longer have to offend personally, sir,' Iles said, 'except, of course, on the largest scale, which we are unable to combat. As a result, our dossiers on him are pathetically out of date. It seemed to me absurd to walk into an arrangement with such an information handicap.'

Lane struck the table but still whispered. 'There is to be no arrangement and never was to be.'

Iles said: 'I found nothing detrimental. Manse seems to have established an admirably solid way of life. They gave him custody of the children, you know, sir. We could be fortunate to land him as ally.'

The Chief said wearily: 'He wholesales dope, for God's sake. He is somewhere in the murder of this little girl.'

'A woman came in while I was there,' Iles replied.

'You were found by the woman he lives with?' the Chief asked. Phlegm clogged his voice. 'His partner discovers an Assistant Chief burgling?'

'She's an ex,' Iles replied. 'Still good friends, and so on. I'm not sure whether you've run across her, sir. Patricia Devonald, a lovely kid, known around the city, and with a delightful way to her. Absolutely stuffed with amiability. Oh, yes.' Iles waited to see whether Lane would respond. In a while the ACC went on: 'She did something quite substantial for a while with Manse – I mean, full cohabitation and exclusiveness – and she looks in on him now and then, out of this amiability.'

'Dark haired, tall, about twenty-eight?' Harpur said.

'She's gone auburn and it really suits her,' Iles replied. 'Azure blouse, auburn hair, very striking. Amiable almost to a fault, in fact,' Iles replied. 'I can say this: she was not in the least non-plussed to discover me.' He had replaced the notebook in the jacket pocket of his grey double-breasted suit but now brought it out again. 'This is what she said, sir.' He read very slowly and in a girlish voice, though alto: ' "Why, Des, how nice! How many of you people has Manse got on his list now, then? Or are you replacement for the other one?" ' He repeated this. 'It wasn't written at the actual time of utterance, naturally. I didn't want to chill the moment. But as soon as she had gone I wrote it up.' He chuckled. 'Lord, sir, I feel as if I'm a constable again, justifying my notebook in the witness box!'

Harpur said: ' "The other one"?'

'Exactly, Col.'

'My God,' Lane said.

'Yes, sir. Shale has one of our people on his pay roll.'

'My God, my God,' Lane said. He raised an arm to his face and seemed to bite at his wrist in anguish. There had been the breakdown not long ago. Harpur wished the Chief would retire, or stop trying to fight Iles. It would amount to the same.

'Yes, it has implications,' the ACC replied. 'Clearly, sir, this is someone who might pick up a word around the building here that we're infiltrating an outfit. I imagine he's one of the Drugs Squad, or what use would he be to Mansel? So, the likelihood of his hearing something, noticing something, would be high. Oh, we'd try to ensure sealed secrecy, of course. But things leak, sir. Given time, everything leaks in this headquarters, and we'd need a lot of time to get things settled. And the hazard to our planted officer would be the same, whether our infiltrator went into Shale's outfit, or one of the others. Everyone hates a grass, even if he's in a competitor's team. Mansel wouldn't want someone undercover anywhere on the scene, picking up trade gossip, learning methods.'

'Did she know this officer who works for Shale?' Harpur asked.

'Male, that's all,' Iles replied. 'Mansel would never allow her to meet him. These girls come and go, sir. You know how it is, I'm sure. As I've said, Mansel is in most matters brilliantly careful and reliable. She'd heard our man spoken of, that was all.'

'A name?' Lane asked.

'Yes, a name,' Iles replied. 'Aladdin.'

The Chief sat back from Iles, gave himself distance, and said: 'Is this true, Desmond? Forgive me, but I have to ask that. Is it your attempt to destroy my proposal and further your own? I ask again, can it be true, the girl, the disclosure, Aladdin?'

'Aladdin would be a code name, sir, not "true" in that sense,' Iles said.

'But this woman,' Lane replied. 'It seems unbelievable that you should be illegally in someone else's house and meet a woman like this.'

'Those were her words, sir.'

Harpur said: 'Did Shale come home?'

'Oh, certainly,' Iles said. 'But quite a bit later.'

'What happened?' Harpur asked. 'Did she speak to him about any of this in your presence – about you and the other officer?' It sounded like an interrogation, but Iles seemed willing to put up with it.

'She had gone by then,' the ACC replied. 'I was having a browse upstairs. Nothing.'

Lane said: 'Gone? But she had come to visit Shale, hadn't she?'

'Well, I think she was embarrassed, sir,' Iles said. 'We'd talked and waited around. You probably know how it is, Chief.'

Lane said: "How it is"?'

'Waiting around, sir,' Iles replied.

Lane thought about this, then came near to a snarl: 'Are you telling us . . . when you say this woman is "amiable" . . .'

189

'This is a fine woman I'd already met elsewhere in quite friendly circumstances, sir. I'm not going to impose upon some total stranger, I hope.'

'You broke into the house and took an ex-woman of his to bed?' Lane muttered. He bit at his knuckles this time.

The ACC laughed. 'Oh, no, no, sir. That would be unforgivable. Not his bed.'

'Downstairs?' Harpur said.

'Shale would not even be aware she had called that evening, Chief,' Iles replied. 'This is what I meant about her embarrassment. I don't think she will speak about it. I cleared up the room thoroughly. A fine drawing room, with a decent carpet, some passable art of its sort – an Arthur Hughes and a couple of Edward Prentises, I think. She found all that exceptionally moving, I know – to be beneath these quite reputable works. But no trace of this little episode was left, believe me, sir. Absolutely no taint on the Force will ensue.' Iles smiled genially towards Lane. 'Who the fuck is Shale, anyway? Is shit like that going to call up the Police Complaints Board because some piece is floored by a senior officer in his trite fucking drawing room? I scarcely think so. I'm happy to say the subsequent interview with him was conducted on the very best of terms, but I certainly did not commit you in any way, Chief. That would be outside my remit.'

'Can I believe this, Harpur?' Lane mourned. 'Can I believe any of it, part of it, all of it?'

Iles had put the notebook back into his pocket again, and

once more drew it out now. 'There was time for quite a lot of conversation,' he said. 'As you can imagine, sir, I asked her repeatedly for more about the hired officer. But this I'm afraid is all I came away with.' He intoned girlishly once more the words on the page: ' "Why, Des, how nice! How many of you people has Manse got on his list now, then? Or are you replacement for the other one?" ' Now it was Lane who gazed down at the table, in distress. Iles appeared to have brought something else from his pocket with the notebook. While the Chief's eyes were still down, Iles suddenly flicked a small round object at Harpur, sitting opposite. It struck him in the chest and fell to the carpet. Harpur glanced under his chair and saw an azure fashion button.

When the meeting broke up, Iles went to Harpur's room with him and took a chair. 'She told you Aladdin was W. P. Jantice, did she, sir?' Harpur asked.

'Of course she fucking did,' Iles replied.

Harpur said: 'I—'

'Look, I've never wholly agreed with those who said you were short of insight, Harpur, despite their number.'

'Thanks, sir.'

'You sensed that because our Chief saw Jantice as the sun, moon and stars, he'd certainly turn out to be shit, did you?'

'I could feel you weren't telling the lot,' Harpur replied.

'Routine kindness to Lane,' Iles said.

'What I thought, sir, knowing you.'

'Would I further shatter a poor old uniformed wreck, Harpur, before a subordinate?' Iles asked.

Harpur said: 'I—'

'Yes, you think I would.' Iles considered it for a while. 'Oh, possibly. But I can stumble into humaneness now and then. This relic, the Chief, is ours, Harpur, and he has to be tended, deftly bandaged. That's how I see solidarity. When did you have a time with Patricia, then, Col?'

'Might Jantice be the lad with the 6.35mm SIG?' Harpur replied.

'Of course he fucking might,' Iles said.

# 17

Mansel Shale decided to have a trip up to Sphere Street. He would have liked to cycle, but people in that sort of area expected him to arrive in the Jaguar, and it was important to look after his image. They needed to see the big influential black car parked on main street double-yellow No-Waiting lines, with Denzil slouched behind the wheel, maybe wearing his cap, if the sod was in a decent mood. To these scuttling nobodies the luxury car in an illegal spot signalled Mansel Shale Inc.'s power. Humour them. Some of the drab pedestrians were sure to be customers, and their children would be customers after them, or were already. A Rolls would have been too much. It would have looked loud. The Jag had some edge to it.

He left Denzil and the car outside the Post Office and walked up Sphere Street towards where the child had been shot. It seemed that know-all sod Jack Lamb was right about the bullets and autopsy report. Well, of course he was right. When Lamb said something you'd better believe it. Obviously, Shale could not ask W.P. Jantice for confirmation from inside, but there was a general buzz about the report now, and even some hints in the Press. They said the girl was killed by two handgun bullets fired on an upward path and definitely not from a Kalashnikov. He wanted to see if there was a place near the fruit and vegetable shop where a marksman might have operated. The idea grieved and enraged him. This could be someone knocking down a kid to cover the filthy double deceit he was into. At least double. And this 'someone' Shale had an important connection with. He did not want that kind of association.

Many people spoke or nodded a greeting as Shale passed, some calling out his first name. He loved all that. Although he did not live on this estate – Christ, *live* here!, he would never live in an area like this and hated the ramshackle look of it and all-round decay – but he longed to feel he had a warm link with the community. He was in favour of communities, and before the incident as much as five or six per cent of the firm's profit came from the Ernest Bevin. Soon, things would be back to that. He thought he could read real affection in people's eyes, plus, naturally, respect. This respect might not have come so easily if he had been on the bicycle. People up here did not understand bicycles. They would not get the non-pollution aspect or the convenience. For them a bike meant poverty, especially a 1930s-style bike. He did a familiar little wave now and then to some on the other side of the street who recognized him. You could have status yet not be remote. Look at royal walkabouts.

Opposite the fruit and veg shop he saw a narrow service lane and crossed to look at it. He stood at its entrance on to Sphere Street and gazed back at the stretch of pavement where he knew from TV pictures the child had lain. Briefly, he went down into a sniper's crouch. At once he realized this position was perfect – a beautiful clear view if there was no traffic, and on the day there had not been. Someone had thrown up nearby and he wondered whether it was the gunman, understandably sickened by his foul role. Shale was still folded down like that when the man who ran the fruit and veg came out in his grey work coat and crossed the street to him.

'You're the third I've seen hanging about there, Mansel,' he said. 'I thought you'd care to know.'

Shale straightened up. 'One on the day of the shooting?'

'Well, of course.'

'Firing a handgun?'

'Correct.'

'Couple of shots?'

'Too much going on to count. But I should think so.'

Shale described Jantice: 'In his thirties, tall, very thin, a lot of fair hair?'

'That's it. Known around here. From another firm? Police? We got chaos like Bosnia on this estate.'

'So who was the second?'

'This would definitely be police. The big one. Also fair hair, cut with a hedge trimmer, and one of them dull suits.'

'Harpur?'

'That would be it.'

'Did he know anything?'

'Not from us, obviously. He vomited.'

'Yes, I heard he had a sensitive side.' Shale went back with him to the shop and ordered a lot of stuff, fresh and in cans. You had to. He said to deliver it to his place and Alfie Ivis's and paid by cheque. They liked that kind of gesture, people of this sort. It would have looked like a bribe or a tip if Shale had tried to give him straight cash for the information, and the shopkeeper might feel degraded. He wanted to think Mansel Shale was his friend and speak of him like that to neighbours and shoppers. Buying all this rubbishy stuff – that was different from slipping him a reward. This was the kind of act that would be talked about. It was the kind of act people would expect from Mansel Shale, sort of lavish, big, in line with the Jag. Probably he would have to throw away a lot of the fucking fresh, because there was only himself in the house at present and he could not cook. That was what lavishness meant, though, surely – buying more than you wanted because counting mushrooms or oranges was something someone like Mansel Shale would not be bothered with. He hated waste, but now and then it could be handy. It was important to keep your personality in front of this kind through the way they passed on good tales about your acts, and there was always plenty of conversation in shops, unless Harpur turned up.

In the evening, Patricia Devonald looked in at the rectory wearing amber mainly. She looked brilliant and smelled a treat. Her hair was auburn now, and this worked quite well. Shale felt delighted to see her. Of all the three girls who had lived here recently Patricia seemed to understand him best, especially his devotion to order and progress and the importance of will. Perhaps she even understood him better than

Sybil. Sybil had never tried much after the first year or two. The children had liked Patricia best, too. She was full of jokes and adventure. When she let herself in tonight, Shale was on the phone to Alfred informing him the fruit and veg would arrive. He said Alfie's kids could use the apples for William Telling in their archery. 'I did a little tour around Sphere Street and so on. Just to get seen and push their morale back into shape after the incident. To show I'm thinking of them. We got to stay a living factor, Alf.'

'Wise.'

'It's still a sadness to walk over that bit of pavement.'

'Well, I can imagine,' Ivis replied.

'Yes, I . . . Ah, I hear someone coming in at the front door.' At first he thought it might be Lowri, who had not visited for nearly a year. That would have been all right. Lowri had some fun to her, and she understood him pretty well, too. Then the drawing room door opened and he was thrilled to see he had been wrong. 'Here's Patricia,' Shale said.

'Oh?'

Alfie did not like these girls returning and having keys. In his narrow, accountant's way he thought they only came back when they needed help or a present. Alfie was useless on the emotional side, and sometimes Shale felt sorry for his poor scratchy wife, Zoë. If Shale had told him that Patricia could often reach his soul, Ivis would not have said anything rude or sharp, because he always stayed polite, it was his way. But by not saying anything he would have been showing what he thought. That was his way, too, fucking creep. Ivis did not go for souls. Shale rang off.

'Ah,' Patricia said, gazing around. 'How I love this room. The art and everything. No changes. Good.'

'It must be months since you were here,' Shale replied. Luckily, he had been feeling in one of his wine moods and had brought up a couple of good burgundies from the cellar. If she stayed tomorrow she could help him eat some of that fucking kiwi fruit.

'Will you make love to me under Arthur Hughes?' she asked.

'As ever,' he said. 'Eventually.'

'Here first. Then bed,' she said.

'As ever,' he replied.

He poured a couple of drinks and they danced for a while to a CD of Luther Vandross that she liked, carrying their glasses. When the music stopped he released her and was stepping across the room to put on another disc when he heard something outside in the grounds. 'Get down,' he yelled and threw himself at her legs, trying to bring her low in a rugby tackle.

'Not yet, Manse,' she giggled, 'I'll spill wine on the carpet,' and somehow kept herself and the glass upright for a few seconds.

# 18

Harpur heard about the rectory shooting from Iles's wife, Sarah. Now and then when the ACC was away Harpur would spend a night or part of a night with Sarah. They were flashback meetings, consolation meetings, that was all. The Control Room rang Iles to inform him of the gunfire and Sarah, swearing in that full-out way she had, climbed delicately off Harpur and picked up the bedside phone. Iles and the Chief expected to be informed at once of any incident involving a set list of notable figures, and Shale was high on it. Sarah lay very close to Harpur with the receiver, her free hand stroking his wrist under the bedclothes, and he could hear most of what the Control Room inspector said. The stroking became a gripping of his arm, as though she knew he would have to leave now and would like to hold him back.

'Mrs Iles? Sorry to wake you, but is the ACC there, please?'

She answered hesitantly, half grunt, half speech, as if just drifting up from honest sleep. 'He's not due back from Manchester until about 2 a.m. Someone's retirement party there.'

'We hoped he'd returned. We can't reach Mr Harpur, either. His daughter couldn't help. She said probably surveillance.'

'What is it?' Sarah asked.

The inspector hesitated about talking business to a wife. 'Well . . .'

'If Desmond rings me I could tell him.'

'If you'd ask him to get in touch with us.'

'Have you tried him on his mobile?'

'I will now,' the inspector said.

Sarah's voice grew more assertive: 'In case you don't reach him, just give me the basics, will you? He would expect me to ask that.'

There was another hesitation. 'Shots at or near St James's rectory.'

'St James?'

'What was. Mr Shale's place. We've got an ARV there. That's armed response vehicle.'

'Yes?' Sarah said.

Harpur eased her fingers from his arm and rolled out of bed. His clothes and phone were downstairs. The evening had begun there beneath a Victorian oil painting of some woman Iles once told Harpur was an ancestor, and who might be, given the happy malevolence of her face. They needed louder bells on those damn mobiles. He went down and dressed, and then returned quickly to the bedroom to say goodbye. It would probably be for a while again, by her choice, not his. This kind of evening was like reminiscing, really. There had been a lovely, difficult, long affair between him and Sarah once, when her marriage and Harpur's own were seeing trouble. The relationship could revive briefly in this way occasionally, very occasionally. Things between Sarah and Iles were a bit better now, she said, but only a bit. Off and on she would still want Harpur, and he would want her, too: perhaps more than off and on. At these moments it was as though they both craved a move back to their earlier times and thought it possible. It wasn't. They knew it. Large changes had come. Sarah and Iles were parents of a daughter now. Harpur's wife was dead, and he had a free-wheeling girlfriend: a student in the town, but away in France for part of her course at present.

Sarah said: 'It's always sweet to see you, Col. Well, it's like necessary to me.'

'Me, too.'

'Just intermittently. I even think Desmond might understand.'

'Possibly. Or then again, no,' Harpur replied.

'I have to make a go of things here for a while, clearly.'

'Clearly.'

'For a long while, I suppose.'

'True.'

'But I also have to know you're still about.'

'Of course I am.' He bent and kissed her, then made for the door.

'How are you supposed to have heard of the shooting?' Sarah asked. 'Via the Assistant Chief's bedside phone at midnight? Have you thought of that, fucking idiot?'

'I haven't heard of it yet. I've been on close surveillance, as one of my daughters said.'

'Yes it was close,' she said.

'I've had my phone switched off, in case an incoming call gave me away. Even a piffling bell like this one – because of the extreme closeness of the surveillance.'

'I see.'

'I'll do a check now with Control. It's standard after being out of touch. They'll tell me about Shale.'

'Who *is* Shale?'

'Your husband wants him as a pal.'

She was snuggling down in the bed. 'You're my husband's pal, too, aren't you, Col?'

'In a way. But you won't have to go to bed with Shale, alive or dead.'

'Why does he want him as a pal?'

'To help keep the peace in a chaotic world.'

'Keep the peace with gunfire?' she asked.

'That's what your husband means – chaos.'

She was almost asleep again. 'Sometimes I don't think it bothers you enough that I'll be tied up here for years.'

'It bothers me.'

'Enough?'

'More than,' he said.

Three police vehicles had taken positions near the rectory grounds by the time Harpur arrived and Mike Upton was getting the place surrounded before ordering a forward dash. Upton liked to go into danger areas mob-handed: some called him Montgomery, after the British Field Marshal who demanded big numerical superiority before he moved.

Lights burned upstairs in the house. Upton said: 'We think a burst of handgun firing, at least five rounds, about twenty minutes ago. It came from the grounds and was presumably aimed at the house. A neighbour heard glass breaking and a possible scream as well as the shooting. then two more shots about four minutes later. The first ARV was here by then and the crew thought this firing came from inside the house. We've tried to get Shale on the phone, but no answer.'

Upton went to check the spread of his people at the back of the rectory. He had on black overalls and a black combat jacket with his name and rank white-stitched on the right shoulder. He wore a baseball cap marked 'Police' in silver just over the peak. Probably it was all necessary. Costume made people brave. A stubby Heckler and Koch submachine-gun hung around Upton's neck. Harpur stayed watching the house for a couple of minutes and when Upton was out of sight walked quickly into the grounds and looked for some shadow from the trees. From there he took another long stare at the house, a gaunt but handsome greystone place. He went nearer, and thought now he could make out the shattered downstairs window Upton had mentioned, though the room was dark. A pity Iles was not here. He must know the layout inside. Fuck, no, it was not a pity. Iles would want to run things, and would have to lead in. Harpur ran crouched from one patch of shadow to another, progressing towards the house. He was not armed, of course. He could not request a gun for love meetings with Sarah Iles, and it never occurred to him to take Lamb's .32 from Megan's handbag: that was for a one-off.

Harpur stopped again. He got the trunk of a tree between himself and the house and called out fairly softly: 'Mansel. Mansel, it's Harpur. Are you all right in there?' For a few minutes there was no answer. Then Harpur thought he heard a voice come from the room with the broken window. He could not make out the words. He called again, a bit louder: 'It's Colin Harpur, Mansel. I'm coming in.'

'Harpur?' Shale said. Harpur could see nothing. The voice seemed to emerge from beneath the sill. It was clearer now, though. 'Are you with them, then, Harpur?'

'With them?'

'No, don't come closer.'

'Who else is there?' Harpur said. 'Someone screamed. Is it Patricia Devonald?'

There was a long pause. Then Harpur thought he saw a movement from inside the room, a head raised a little. 'How the fuck could you know that, Harpur?'

'Is she all right?' He came out from behind the tree and was about to run towards the window when he saw between two rhododendron bushes to his right an automatic pistol lying on the ground. Bent double, he moved across and picked it up. It was a 9mm Star. He checked the magazine. There were two rounds left: six gone.

Upton's voice howled from a loudspeaker. 'Hear this. In the grounds, in the house. You are surrounded. Armed police. I say again, you are surrounded by armed police. Put down your weapons and come towards the main gate of the grounds. Come in single file with your hands on your head. Do not attempt to leave by any other route. I say again, do not attempt to leave by any other route.' Spotlights from a couple of cars were played on to the gates and the drive beyond.

Harpur made his sprint. 'Hear this. I'm coming in, Mansel,' he called. 'I say again, I'm coming in.' He reached the window. As he did, Shale stood, that square-built short body and snub face under the heap of dark hair. He was pointing what looked like a Beretta two-handed at Harpur through the glassless frame. Harpur had the Star in his hand but did not raise it. 'You've done enough damage, Manse,' he said. Behind Shale Harpur saw the shape of a woman dressed in amber stretched out on the carpet under some paintings.

'Are you with them?' Shale asked.

'Yes, I'm with the armed police, who else?'

'No, with the others?'

Jesus. Harpur kicked out some bits of glass in the lower frame and climbed into the room. Shale stepped back, still aiming the Beretta. Then he lowered it, as if ashamed. He put the gun into his pocket and Harpur did the same with the Star. It would be best to wipe and replace this gun soon in the grounds. Some of those missing bullets might have done the damage here. Upton's call came again, much the same words but with an overlay of irritation at the delay in response to his first instruction. A telephone began ringing on a table across the room. Harpur stepped over the woman and went to it.

'I haven't had time to answer that,' Shale said. 'I had to keep watching.'

Harpur picked up the receiver.

'Mr Shale, this is Chief Inspector Francis Garland. We—'

'This is Harpur,' Harpur said.

'I told Upton you'd probably be in there,' Garland replied. 'This pathetic need to be first. The search for *Gloire.*'

'Fuck off, Francis. Tell the ambulance to come in. Someone's hurt. There might be armed people in the grounds.'

'Oh, really, sir?'

Harpur put the phone down and switched on the lights. Yes, Patricia Devonald. Harpur thought she had been struck by at least three rounds, one in the head, two in the back. She was lying on her side, her knees up like a demonstration pose for a mattress ad. A smashed wineglass was under her face and had cut her cheek. There was a wide wine stain on the carpet and two smaller circles of blood. Harpur had not seen her for a few years, but she looked as if she had kept her nice lean figure. And Iles was probably right about the hair, it must have suited her.

'We'd been dancing,' Shale said. 'She fell on top of me. So she's shot in the back. I pulled her down to save her, and she stops bullets meant for me. In the fucking back, Harpur.' He did not sob or weep. His voice was as dry as old books. Mourning filled his plump face. 'This was a worthwhile girl. This was a girl who could be meaningful.'

'How many out there?'

'Would I know?'

'Who are they?'

'Would I know? I thought you were with them.'

'I'm a police officer,' Harpur replied. 'Did you forget?'

'I thought you must be with them,' Shale said. 'Are you? There's all kind of connections these days.'

'Are there?'

'Chaotic.'

'Yes. You fired?' Harpur asked.

'I was afraid they'd come in and finish the job.'

Harpur heard vehicles and shouting outside. Upton believed in heavy noise as a frightener. His men and girls got bonus marks for yells. He appeared suddenly at the window and climbed in. Five of his people followed, all dressed in the gear. Three had Heckler and Kochs, one a Smith and Wesson revolver and one a gas grenade launcher. All the weapons were at the ready now.

'How many more in the house?' Upton said. He seemed hardly to notice the girl on the floor.

'None,' Shale said.

'We search,' Upton told his team.

'None,' Harpur said.

'We search,' Upton replied. Harpur heard them banging about from room to room downstairs then above.

'Once I got the light out I could take the bastards on,' Shale said. 'But too late.'

'They were here to settle with you for the ambush in Sphere Street?'

'Sphere Street? Was that the incident where the poor kiddy was killed?' Shale replied.

There was a hammering at the front door and Harpur went to open it. The Chief stood there with Garland. More armed men followed them in. Lane had on one of his tight tweed jackets and a brown roll-top sweater. He did not look too bad for this time of night – almost young and purposeful, like someone off on a badger dig. He went into the drawing room and stared at the girl and then at the genuine pictures hanging near her. Shale was on a sofa with a glass of wine in his hand. He had blood smeared across his forehead and a wine stain on the collar and front of his shirt.

'I don't understand,' Lane muttered to Harpur. 'This girl is the one that the ACC—?'

'She must have died instantly,' Harpur said.

'She was a fine woman in every respect,' Shale said. 'This is a terrible incident in every respect, obviously, Mr Lane, but I feel sure it will not . . . Well, what I mean, this incident surely illustrates the need for . . . It's terribly unfortunate that the first time you enter my property it's in such – it's for such a terrible incident.'

Harpur said: 'Well, here's the ACC now, sir.'

The front door had been left open. Iles came into the drawing room urgent and beaming. He had on his brown bomber jacket, narrow-cut grey flannels and a tasselled scarlet scarf. 'I came direct, Chief,' he said.

'I was mentioning to Mr Lane re the crying need for restoration of peace, Mr Iles,' Shale said. 'What I would hate to happen as a result of this incident is that a slur should fall upon this house and myself. Please accept that I—'

Iles squinting down said: 'I know this girl, I think. Oh, yes, she rings a bell, even now.' He went and bent over her, the scarf hanging low and almost touching her destroyed head and face. 'This poor lovely kid.' He flicked the scarf back and then went lower and kissed her forehead, as he had kissed the piece of pavement where NOON had lain. The ACC loved to simulate warmth and lack of arrogance. 'Yes, I've bumped into her here and there, Manse. My belief is that Mr Shale would have done all possible to stop this happening, Chief.'

Lane said: 'We have to ask why this shooting took place at all.'

Iles, still down by the girl, nodded several times and gazed up at the Chief. 'I'm glad you said that, sir.'

Lane said: 'What we are witnessing here is the—'

Iles stood and said: 'Oh, certainly I don't see that this can be held to taint Manse Shale, sir. Because a beautiful girl is shot down in one's drawing room one's own standing is not therefore damaged, surely. This was not some casual piece that Manse brought in for the night, sir. Correct me, please, if I misremember, Manse, but this fine woman was once part of your household, I believe, and during the time a grand acting stepmother to your children.'

'Did you know her well, then, Mr Iles?' Shale asked.

'As I say, bumped into her. And I know I've heard mention of her, in the best of terms,' Iles said. 'And I know the Chief has, too.'

Upton came in and said that nobody had been found in the house or grounds. Harpur went out with him as if to confirm his report and rubbed the Star thoroughly with his tie before pushing the gun under a rhododendron bush. He returned to the drawing room. Paramedics arrived and lifted Patricia Devonald without finesse on to a wheeled stretcher.

'My guess is that this evening was meant as a rather precious reunion for you two, Manse,' Iles said.

'It's months since she was in the house and then the very night she comes this foul, foul act,' Shale replied.

'As much as anything I've ever seen it symbolizes general accelerating breakdown, wouldn't you say so, Chief?' Iles said.

Lane did not like to hear the word breakdown and winced. Harpur saw Iles had noted this and felt the ACC would rephrase the thought. Iles said: 'Yes, general accelerating breakdown.'

# 19

Early next morning Shale went out to Alfie's place for a consultation about the media. The police kept the crowd of television people and reporters out of the rectory and grounds, but they lurked at the gates with their lenses and suede boots, and the phone went non-stop until he disconnected it – sharp voices, men and women, hunting private facts about the shooting and himself and so on. Shale wanted to get out of town now, just hide somewhere distant. Nearly everyone Shale ever worked with said keep the fucking media right outside everything, they were dirty and bought and only wanted to hurt. Shale thought Ivis could drive him to the airport. Get clear. But Alfie said: 'With respect, Mansel, if you run, the Press and broadcasters will draw all their information from the police.'

'Fuck the Press and broadcasters. What right they got to intrude on decent lives, Alfie?'

'We must think of a studio interview for television News, so you can present your points properly, Manse. Studio, not some bearpit scramble. The BBC will grab the chance.'

Shale had cycled to the lighthouse. The Press mob around the gates would have followed the car. With the bike, he could get out secretly on to a mud path at the other end of the grounds and from there reach the road. He had plenty of money and cards on him. If he had done a flit Alfie could have sent luggage on later. He had his key. Shale had told Denzil to get out on foot by the path, too, and then stay with his mother for a while or someone like that. Although Denzil was not in the house last night and knew nothing much about the incident, he did know enough about the business and it was better reporters did not speak to him, especially reporters flashing cash. Christ, Denzil should have been let go years ago. Tolerance could be such a mistake.

Alfie said: 'It's crucial your version – our version – of events is given. This cannot be if the police alone say what happened. You – we – are caught in a mighty political battle, Manse. Thank God, some within the police see the necessity to come to an intelligent agreement with Mansel Shale Inc. But other elements are opposed, thinking they can find a superior way out of chaos.'

'Idiots,' Shale replied.

'Quite. But the obvious danger, Manse, is that those against an understanding with us might use last night's unpleasantness to darken your character: taint it by association. They want to make an agreement look unthinkable.'

'Lamb said that.'

There was a bit of a paved terrace at Ivis's place and they sat out there this morning on cheap plastic chairs with gin and peps. Alfred said: 'The Chief himself might oppose an alliance. He'll instruct his people to feed the Press hints unhelpful to your business. You could be made to look almost dubious: gangsterdom around the property and a shot girl in your drawing room.'

'I had Lane in there, you know. Right in the house. I saw he might be into personal views.' Shale watched birds rush about around the terrace in that fucking showy way eating gnats. 'There's Patricia lying in front of him fusilladed and her amber garments ruined, so you'd think he'd feel some sympathy for one of her dearest friends, or loving partners as was. But I'm looking at him and I got to say your reactions could be right, Alfie, and his response might have been negative.'

'We must think in the widest terms,' Alfie replied. 'Television, the newspapers – these can be invaluable allies. The media reaches tens of millions in a flash, and it puts pressure where pressure can be of use. We have to fight a sophisticated battle here. Status. Then police will see you're worthy of partnership.'

Of course, you never knew what you were getting from Alfie, especially in his own place – truth or bullshit or something to help along a devious ploy of his own. Shale said: 'If you'd see Patricia with four-fifths of her fucking head blown away you would not say sophisticated.' It shocked him to find Alfie keen on media. Generally, Alf lived by caution, and then some more. But now, here he was telling Shale to take the risk.

It was getting cold on the terrace. Shale wanted a change and walked about a bit gazing at the sea with hate. 'The

Press are going to ask me what it's all about, Alf. Such as who was these people in the grounds? Why was I shot at?'

Ivis turned that slabby face up towards him then, the rough acres of it pink and joyous, his eyebrows full of victory. 'Right, Manse,' he said with quite a chortle. 'Our chance.'

'Yes?'

'It's as much a mystery to you as to them.'

'Is it?'

'I mean, that's what you'll say in the TV interview. Yes, as much a mystery to you as it is to the police. Stick to that.' Then Alfie spoke in a real tone – this was the real diamond. 'But you tell them that one thing you certainly do know – this kind of dastardly attack is typical of our time. How, you ask, can law and order be restored. How indeed can it survive? See the point, Manse? Well, sorry, of course you do.'

Shale nodded. Now and then Ivis did come up with a fair idea.

'Obviously, you would not say on TV that you expect an alliance with police as the only means of saving this manor,' Alf said. 'That would be spelling it out. But the police will certainly realize this is behind the words. What I intend, Manse. They'll feel pressured.' Ivis stood up too now and moved back towards the house. 'Yes, we'll do this in a selective, dignified way. I'll telephone the BBC and insist studio.'

Ivis drove him there. The interview would be filmed and

go out in the evening network News as part of a long item on the shooting. In the car Ivis said: 'Use the interviewer's first name. It makes them feel equal.'

Shale found he really loved that BBC building. The reception area was great – wide and light, because obviously visitors coming to broadcast deserved scale. Once you had passed Reception there was a grand busyness plus undoubted respect for him. These folk understood he signified or he would not be there. Everywhere he saw cables and shining equipment and people knowing what they had to do, mostly wearing jeans and trainers yet probably fucking gifted with wires and that sort of thing. The makeup girl appreciated his features. She said she did not need to do much to make him right for the screen. Probably she told every bugger that, even some drinker with mailvan skin, but she wanted to make folk feel good and unnervy. Well, it was like star treatment, so maybe Alf was wise. Alfie said going on TV could bring the required status for partnership. You had to think of Sir David Frost talking to Tony Blair – that kind of scale.

The woman who would interview Shale came into Makeup and introduced herself as Dawn Davies. She was round-faced and pretty in a schoolgirl way. About twenty-four, Shale thought. How could a shaggable innocent like this understand what was behind it all, the lack of simplicity? Never mind. These people thought it such a catch to get him, but really like Alfie said he was using them. He enjoyed this notion, though not crowing. How things operated at high level. You devised your opportunities. He felt wonderfully relaxed and sharp. It was time.

Dawn Davies spoke to the camera. Her voice now she was in the studio and working surprised Shale – so bloody strong, like a tom-tom.

*Last night the rectory home of prominent local businessman Mr Mansel Shale was attacked by one or more gunmen. A friend of Mr Shale, beautiful, 28-year-old Patricia Devonald, was struck by three bullets from a handgun and died instantly.*

Shale sitting opposite under the lights was watching her and listening, ready for when she turned to him and started the questions, but he glimpsed a flicker on a screen to his right and he glanced there and saw a monitor set. He was on it. He looked pretty good. This was just the right kind of dark suit and careful tie. He thought he looked sad yet fully reliable. This was a bad death they were talking about, and it was important to show grief. He thought if he was Mr Mark Lane he would trust a face like this, it had proper depth.

*Police have not so far identified the raiders, but it is thought that members of a gang from outside the city might be responsible. Police believe that this attack could be related to other recent local acts of violence.*

Film of the ambulance taking Patricia away last night came up abruptly on another monitor and then a still picture of her, a smiling picture taken what looked like a few years ago, full of hope and fun. It threw him for a moment. This was how Shale longed to remember her and any woman, but the way he did remember Patricia now was hunched and bleeding on the floor, that wineglass snapped off and its stem digging jagged into her neck. This was a fine person who had visited him out of respect for their past and he had failed to guard her. It would stand against him. Lowri and Carmel would not come to see him any longer probably through fear.

The clips of film ended and Dawn Davies started the interview: 'Mr Shale, have you been able to help the police to identify the attackers?'

'I'm afraid it's as much a mystery to me as it is to them, Dawn.'

'You mean completely unprovoked?'

This kid's voice could hit you like a fucking welterweight. It was calling him a liar. 'Absolutely. Like I said, a mystery,' Shale replied.

'It has been suggested that there might be a gang aspect to the shooting.'

'Gang? I heard you mention that earlier, Dawn. Well, it's a surprise to me. What would a gang want with a lovely girl like Patricia Devonald?'

'But might you, not her, have been the target?'

'Me? Personally? What would a gang want with me, either? This is an ordinary member of the public, spending an evening at home with a friend. But one thing I do know, Dawn – this kind of dastardly attack is typical of our time. How can law and order be restored? How indeed can it survive?'

'It's been suggested there might be a connection between this attack and another in Sphere Street recently when guns were also used and a child killed.'

'I heard of that dreadful incident,' Shale replied. 'Indeed, who in this city and, yes, nationwide has not heard of it? In fact, I was so moved I felt a duty – I mean just a duty as a fellow-citizen of that child – I felt this duty to attend her funeral. Do you understand, Dawn? But no, I don't see what you mean when you say that killing could be connected to violence at my home.'

'You went to the Timmy Montain funeral as well, didn't you, Mr Shale? The man who might have been involved in the Sphere Street shooting and later found blasted himself, a known criminal?'

The baby cow. This was the kind of thing Alfie would not have realized might come, long foresight was not his thing. 'As a matter of fact I did, Dawn,' Shale said. 'Timothy Astor Montain worked for me occasionally some time ago. I don't write people off, I hope, whatever way their lives might go subsequent.' He let his eyes move from her for a second as he spoke and on to his monitor. Shale considered he still looked solid, not pushed off his perch by the fucking cheek of this Dawn, digging out embarrassments.

When it was over they all went to what was called a hospitality room for some drinks. Wrong fucking name for it. They offered gin there but no pep only tonic so he said rum. Alfie came close and whispered: 'Brilliantly positive,

Manse. As I knew it would be. It has unquestionably taken your case forward.'

'Fucking Montain's funeral,' Shale replied.

'Ah, that can't be undone,' Alfie said. It meant, didn't he tell Shale not to go?

'Police fed them that shit.'

'Of course,' Alfie replied. 'What I meant.'

'They think I'm rubbish, like Lamb thinks I'm rubbish. Like Mark Lane thinks I'm rubbish.'

'Not at all, not at all, Manse.'

'I've got to do something,' Shale replied.

'What?'

'Got to do something.'

'Be careful, Manse.'

'Fuck be careful.'

The girl approached smiling like a gallows trap. 'Obviously I couldn't ask all the real questions, Mr Shale.' She had a tumbler half full of whisky and water. 'Libel dangers.'

'I enjoyed it, Dawn,' Shale replied. 'A useful chat.'

Dawn Davies said: 'You're in the middle of an unholy war, aren't you? These gunmen were the other side's soldiers settling up. Trying to.'

'War?' Alfie said, laughing for quite a time. 'You folk – always seeking the dramatic! Well, it's your profession I suppose.'

The producer was with them, another woman, tall, thin as an extension lead, her hair hacked down in tight little curls like a lavatory brush, maybe not to tangle cameras.

'What business are you actually in, Mr Shale?' she asked. It was some university talking, loud and matey, full of a briefing. 'You clearly live in style – Jaguar, chauffeur, pre-Raphaelites, rectory.'

'Are you an art buff?' Shale replied. Media did not give a fuck about privacy. This was their training in a basement in London or somewhere like that. They were taught just steam in and forget politeness.

Ivis said: 'Mr Shale has varied interests. They could be most conveniently summed up as "entrepreneurial".'

'Almost all the gun crime in this city is drug-related,' Dawn Davies said.

'You mean this is people made "high" as it's called so they just go mad with weapons?' Shale replied. 'That's a worrying idea.'

'No, I mean trade,' Davies said. 'People fighting for control, ready to blast any bugger opposing them because the money is so big. Thus, you get a corpse on your drawing room carpet, Mr Shale.'

'Perhaps we should be moving along now, Mansel,' Ivis replied. 'Mr Shale is understandably tired after what he has gone through lately.'

'And then again,' the producer said, 'one hears of a possible coalition between police and barons.' She had a glass of beer in her hand, trying to get some fat on.

'Coalition?' Shale replied.

'Barons, indeed!' Ivis said, with another good long laugh.

'We think this story will run and run,' Dawn Davies said.

'Story?' Shale replied. 'This is a woman's tragic death, you know.'

'Do come now, Mansel,' Alfie said. He turned to the two women. 'Mr Shale must not upset himself further.'

# 20

Harpur had an invitation to evening drinks at Mark Lane's house. It came in a brief office phone call on the secure line. The Chief muttered: 'I'd prefer this meeting were not known about, Colin.'

The call alarmed Harpur. He feared Lane was speeding towards breakdown again: a personal disintegration to match what Iles had termed the 'accelerating breakdown' of order, government, system. Perhaps Lane's worsening had been brought on by this other wider collapse, furthered, of course, by the ACC. For a while lately, the Chief had seemed to believe he could fight the all-round slide into anarchy: suddenly, he had become resolved, positive. There was a plan: infiltration. Although he had opposed that originally, he changed. It might or might not have worked. But at least he had shown he still knew he must act, and was still determined to fight. And then Iles had arrived with his disclosures of treachery. They might destroy everything. If he set his mind to it, Iles could always usher Lane swiftly into despair.

And so the Chief had withdrawn. He still came into head-quarters but was rarely seen. He stuck to his suite, rather than drifting amiably into other people's rooms for informal discussion. When Harpur did get glimpses of him, he thought Lane looked frighteningly haggard and dazed, like someone who had seen hell, and might still be seeing it and would see nothing else from now on. Or, meeting Harpur by accident in the lift, Lane would jack fierce optimism into his face for the moment. This was worse than the usual misery – a leadership tic. He had always shuffled about the corridors, frequently in his socks, but now, when he did leave his rooms, he shuffled with appalling slowness, as if near exhaustion. Did he sleep? Did he eat? These were the kind of symptoms Harpur remembered from last time the Chief went under. Iles had spotted the new decline, naturally. 'Tragic, Col. And, of course, classic: it's the archetypal good man whose very goodness misleads, obscures, and brings him promotion way above his artisan ability. Seeing Lane, I always think of St Peter.'

When Lane's call came Iles was in Harpur's room discussing the pair of beautifully slim black lace-ups he'd just had made, and then drifting on to suggest W.P. Jantice should be taken by Harpur and him somewhere that night or the one after and beaten pretty much to death until he talked the lot, and then beaten to death. 'I know a bank where the wild thyme grows, Col, and he could scream his fucking head off there and be heard by nobody but gypos.'

Harpur said: 'We have nothing certain against him, sir. I can't prove he's bought and I can't prove he was in the service lane.'

'His name came to me from a fine source.'

'You say.'

'Lane's got at you already?' Iles, wearing dress uniform for a function, was seated with his legs stretched in front of him so he and Harpur could relish the shoes from various angles. 'Imagine what it's like to make love to a quite young-ish girl of those qualities one night and then find her shot on the identical area of carpet the night after, Harpur.'

'I don't—'

'One is bound to feel very much at the core of things. Had you been close to her a while ago? I'm sorry. I wonder if you're seeing anyone special these days, Col.'

'They found the 9mm that did the damage.'

'Really?'

'Under a bush, I think.'

'You'll tell me that's why they didn't get it on the first sweep,' Iles replied.

'Must be.'

'Yes, must be.' The fine material in Iles's dark blue uni-form always seemed to bring out the wild beast ferocity of his face under the cropped grey hair, and its eternal loneli-ness. The outfit was an hilarious attempt to show him as civilized and social. Harpur's phone rang then and he took the call while Iles fiddled with his cuticles to prove indiffer-ence. When Harpur put the receiver down, the ACC said: 'Lane?'

'Garland. To say no prints on the pistol.'

'Lane,' Iles replied. 'Some addled plot.'

'We'll let Shale see the gun. He might be able to tie it to someone.'

'You and Lane and Mrs Lane forming a sweet little cabal, Harpur?' Iles had begun to yell. Harpur's door was part open and he crossed the room quickly and closed it. This drill was often necessary when Iles went into one of his spasms. 'Debased, Harpur. Empty. A betrayal. But you've done it before.'

'I don't think it's a weapon bought around here,' Harpur replied. 'Star automatic. Spanish. All the local dealers push stuff from East Europe these days.'

Iles's voice sank to near normal. He could be worse, more thoughtful, at this level. 'Lane's bound to stick with infiltration, isn't he, Col? His soul and brain are committed to it. Maybe his sanity. The brain's not much and the sanity's off-and-on, but his Catholic soul is at least standard issue and possibly valuable – to him, I mean. You've seen him lately. I feel for Lane, believe me, the shaking wreck. If he backs off his little project there's nothing of him left. Mrs Lane will want you to help save him. You have a handyman look, Harpur. She loves her husband, regardless. And why not, Col? Could that rowing-boat face and sideboard body get anyone else? This will be a little *causerie* – at his house, for confidentiality?'

'I might ask Francis Garland to lean on Leyton and Amy Harbinger at the Hobart, all the same. Perhaps ex-Iron Curtain supplies are drying up and they're selling Stars now.'

Iles brought out a slim, leather-covered notebook and gold pencil. He made a note or pretended to. 'I thought Shale had dignity the other night with the body and his pretty art.

And not pathetic on TV. To me he looks like the give-and-take future. Lane's decided to cut me out of it, after all, has he, Col? You're in the middle again, and I sympathize, you duplicitous fucking cur. Shale ought to have protection.'

'From us?'

'If we're investing in him.'

'But we're probably not.'

'These people are still out there. This will be the two pedestrians from Sphere Street. Or more than two, if they're part of an invasion team.'

'Yes.'

Iles said: 'Slack to leave a gun, even wiped.' He stood up and went to Harpur's desk. He glanced through papers in the in-tray. 'Of course, it might be an idea to let Marky go ahead and plant W. P. Jantice. Then we give the word to Shale he's double-agenting. Manse would get someone to see to him. It would remove W.P. But I'd miss the actual sensation of flesh on flesh, boot on temple, wouldn't you, Col? I'd need something chunkier than these.' He fondled one of the shoes.

'We must try to get—'

'It seems an age since I saw Hazel, you know. I'll pop in soon. And Jill, of course. I expect they miss me.'

'How's Sarah, sir, and the baby?'

'We are a lovely unit, Col, unbelievably preoccupied with one another.'

'I'd heard something along those lines.'

*

Like Shale, the Chief lived in a former rectory. Lane's place was almost a mansion and had a paddock and stables in the grounds, with a couple of horses for his children. As he drove to it tonight, Harpur realized suddenly that he expected to see W. P. Jantice there. This was a meeting to get Lane's project underway, and to hell with the dangers. That would explain the secrecy. Lane had decided to cut out the ACC after all. Iles's claimed link with the shot woman of a drugs wholesaler would nauseate the Chief: make Iles forever unacceptable. Perhaps Lane meant to act as Registrar of the operation himself. Iles was probably right and the Chief's whole being and role were now bound to the infiltration plan. He had to proceed or slip the other little distance into total defeat and irreversible collapse. There had been a terrible, quiet frenzy about the way Lane spoke the invitation. It was an order, and a call for loyalty and for friendship. Harpur would have liked to give both, but no longer felt sure Lane was fit to command. He had become weak and obsessive. Iles would have said *more* weak and *more* obsessive. It might be a painful night.

Mrs Lane came out into the drive to welcome him, large and anxious and intent, wearing a brown and gold cotton suit. She must have been watching for his car. Harpur felt surprised to see her. If this was meant to be a planning meeting, she should not be involved, or even close. He had thought she must be away. She spoke to him through the car window before he had switched off. 'He must resign, Colin. Now.'

'Is anyone else here?'

'Who?'

'Anyone else from headquarters?' He climbed out of the old Sierra.

'You're the only one we can consult. Chief insisted he would do nothing until he spoke to you. We thought it best done here.' Her face was long and handsome – a handsome rowing boat, Iles would have said. She was very agitated now, the eyes ferociously busy on Harpur's reactions. Power throbbed in her, probably too much for Lane. 'He trusts you, Colin,' she said. 'You've known each other a long time.'

Yes – those old days when Lane was a great detective: before the big job here reduced and filleted him. That plus Iles.

Sally Lane said: 'He'd be youngish to go, yes – children still at school. But there's his health. He could legitimately cite that. Many have quit earlier through stress. There are other jobs. We don't need a huge spread like this. Please, please, tell him he should quit, Colin. He cannot cope, knows he cannot, yet refuses to concede. A terrible impasse and the sure way to mental catastrophe. That's frighteningly clear, even without the previous sequence to instruct us. He will not give in to Iles.' She spoke these last words with a mixture of pride and anger. She did not want him to give in, and she did. She was talking quickly, perhaps expecting Lane to appear from the house. 'Persuade Chief this is a crazy simplification of matters. Tell him it is not just a supremacy fight between him and that brilliant lout.'

'It is.'

'Of course it is. Persuade him it isn't. That's why I agreed he should ask you out here, Colin. Convince him he can go with dignity. He can't, he's shambolic, shattered, but persuade him he can. He can't stay with dignity, either. He's lost, Colin. But I'd like him lost with some health and life left. He needs to be told what he must settle for – told by you. I've told him already, of course. That won't do.' She began crying, but it seemed to make no difference to her voice or determination. She let the tears roll, did nothing to conceal them and did not mop her face.

Harpur said: 'It's not for—'

Her tone became a plea. 'There's no need to fear you'd be under Iles. Not more than you are now. They don't appoint chiefs from assistants or deputies on the same patch, do they? But perhaps you are an Iles man. We've never been sure about you, Chief and I.'

Harpur was not sure himself. Lane appeared in the doorway and waved. He seemed no better: the wave was limp, heavy with exhaustion. He had on some terrible leisure clothes and looked like a mental-home patient only lately allowed into the gardens alone. Harpur waved back. He and Mrs Lane began walking towards him. 'Please,' she whispered.

'Has she been softening you up, Colin?' Lane said.

'I was admiring the beeches in your drive, sir.'

'Yes?'

They went into what Lane called the sitting room. He would find 'drawing room' pretentious. There were framed photographs of what Harpur took to be Lane relatives on one wall, most of them smiling easily, as if happiness was simple to get and keep as long as you acted decently. On the other walls were pale country-scene watercolours. 'Naff Gallery' Iles used to call the room. Lane said at once: 'Either way I'm being asked to surrender everything.' He had gone ahead of Harpur and Sally Lane and spoke now with his back towards them, standing at the other end of the big room and facing the wide fireplace.

'That's theatrical, Mark,' she replied.

Maybe it was. His voice was not theatrical. It would not have reached beyond the first few rows. Lane did not turn, as though not wanting to meet their eyes. 'If I go it's – well, it's literally a cop-out.' Christ, Harpur had hardly ever heard him make a joke before. It took tragedy. 'If I stay it will be to follow a policy I loathe and fear, in which my own powers and those of the people I lead will be whittled down and down until they are insignificant. We will be tokens. Oh, I know Iles would say our powers are hardly significant now – that people like Shale with their money and clout effectively run some areas, and that their rule will increase, as it does nationwide, worldwide. But to recognize that? Accept that? Give it tacit endorsement? Is that what he proposes? Can I? Is this not like signing a surrender document?'

He did turn now, his face with that foul slump to one side again, his skin patched with sweat. He gave another wave, this time pointing to chairs. When Mrs Lane and Harpur had sat down he took one himself.

'That second alternative is surely intolerable, Mark,' Mrs Lane said. She had stopped crying. 'It is not within your character to make treaties with evil. I'm glad. I know Colin will agree.'

Harpur was appalled. It unnerved him to see Lane even worse than he had expected. For a second then, he wished he had been right and this call-out was for a meeting to launch an infiltrator into one of the outfits: even W. P. Jantice with all the doubts and complications that would have brought. Harpur craved some sign of combativeness. Instead, Lane could speak only of different kinds of capitulation. Harpur felt appalled, too, by the extent of Sally Lane's knowledge. Although the talk had been general, it was clear Lane had discussed the alliance proposal with her. Perhaps he had even discussed infiltration. Harpur was out here for the sake of secrecy but found that Lane himself preserved no secrecy. Iles always said Mrs Lane knew everything and ran everything through the Chief.

She mixed Harpur his usual drink, gin and cider in a half-pint tankard. The Lanes drank white wine. There were vol-au-vents and cheese biscuits. Harpur would have preferred nothing. It seemed wrong to be acting the cocktail circuit while Lane decided which kind of collapse to pick. He was in a heavy plaid shirt and brown cord trousers. Yes, the outfit seemed wrong, too. It gave him that half-mad look, which Harpur had already noticed, but harmless mad, not wild.

'We watched Shale on television,' Sally Lane said. 'He made it sound as though the pact with him were already in place. The girl interviewer harried him. Yet he seemed to feel above it all, secure. Colin, I have to ask whether Chief has been outflanked. We have to ask whether resistance by him is too late – whether the only decent course is withdrawal. I believe so.'

Lane said: 'No, no, I cannot—'

'Let me put it clearly to you, Colin,' Sally Lane said. She faced him, her face still shining with tears, though she was not weeping now. 'Chief had his scheme. It was risky, but one which has been successful elsewhere. Infiltration. Virtually a routine these days, as you know. But the scheme was destroyed by Iles before it could even start. Destroyed by information he claims to have received from a woman friend of Mansel Shale whom he, Iles, charms and whatever else. The information says that there is a two-timing officer within Chief's force who would betray any detective infiltrated and bring about his death.' Mrs Lane did not seem to have drunk anything. She wanted her brain hard and quick and her voice imperturbable. 'And then, before this information can be confirmed in any way by someone other than Iles, the woman is shot dead, silenced. That is, silenced if she ever in fact said anything. Colin, do we honestly believe that Iles, having broken into someone's house, would then have the gall, the luck, the irresistibility instantly to win that woman's confidence, pluck her secrets and fuck her body, in her ex-partner's drawing room?'

Yes, Iles would have all that. The locale was irrelevant. The coarseness from Sally Lane hit Harpur almost harder than her argument. 'You mean that Iles and Shale simply agreed to fix the tale on to Patricia Devonald? That Iles and Shale are confederates?'

'Isn't that what he wants?' Sally Lane replied.

'Iles bought?' Harpur muttered. 'Iles or Shale himself killed Patricia Devonald?'

'Iles in the kind of partnership he advocates for the whole force. The so-called de facto argument: the barons have power, so acknowledge it and adapt to it.'

Lane, his body slack in an armchair, said: 'But would you have me walk away from such a situation, Sally, if it is as you think?'

'We *know* it is, don't we?' she replied. 'Don't we, Colin?'

Harpur said: 'You're moving fast and far.'

'I ask again, ask both of you, can I turn my back on such a situation, withdraw to cultivate my garden?' Lane said.

Mrs Lane stood and went to stand alongside his armchair. She put a hand on his shoulder. She was weeping again. The Chief covered her hand with his. She spoke gently down at him: 'Darling, you are sick, tired. You have fought and the fight has brought you down and then down again. You are no longer in a state to oppose these people. You are vilely undermined by at least one colleague. They all exploit your goodness and your fragile health. If you resign, it will not mean you are abandoning your beloved patch and folk to the barons. Someone else will come in, someone younger and fitter, who can find ways to smash Shale and Panicking Ralphy and Vine and Stanfield.'

Lane looked even sicker. 'I'm to hand over? Sally, would you want a man who white-flagged like that?' he asked.

She thought about it. When she spoke again it was even more gently: 'You would be less, it's true.'

'I would be nothing.'

Jesus, Harpur wanted to run from this house. A man was under dissection here, dissection by his wife and by himself. Spectators were not needed.

She said: 'Colin, you'll notice I often call him Chief. Not *the* Chief, even, but Chief. It's a habit, a tribute. I'm sure people find it quaint, funny.'

Harpur said: 'Not at all, Mrs Lane. I don't know that anyone has ever noticed it. It must come so naturally from you.' Iles now and then performed a Lane bedroom-scene at parties in which as a panting Sally Lane he gasped: 'Oh, Chief! Chief! Oh, oh, OK, Chief: all right to come now.'

She said: 'You would be less, Chief, it is true. We've always spoken straight to each other. You would not be the same. Although I might still call you Chief there would be tragic emptiness in the word then. But this is what we must accept, Mark. What I am prepared to accept to keep you alive and with me and the children.'

They became silent. It was like a pose for one of the

family pictures, though neither smiled. She stood as before close to his chair, and her hand remained on his shoulder covered by his.

Harpur said: 'No. Don't go, Chief. Please. We'll infiltrate.'

# 21

Mansel Shale had an invitation from the pair of wholesalers called Keith Vine and Stan Stanfield to an evening meeting at Panicking Ralph Ember's club, the Monty. Vine seemed to be really impressed with the TV broadcast. He said bring Alfie Ivis if Shale wanted to. Shale cycled up again to talk to Alf about it. Ivis said: 'We must certainly go, Manse. Frankly, this is just the kind of development I was aiming at in using the BBC.'

So smart. 'These are fucking nobodies,' Shale replied.

'With respect, Manse, they are not as minor as that. I did a little inquiry on them recently.' Alfie's children were back at school after half term and his wife out. Shale's own children would be home from Wales soon. 'And, in any case, Manse, the scale of these people is not quite the point. What we want is the appearance of unity among wholesalers, with yourself at the head. It will become even more impractical for the police to resist a pleasant working arrangement then. They will be powerless.'

'This Vine did say on the phone I'd be top banana,' Shale replied. 'How he talks, this kid, Alfie. I mean, do I want association with cunts who talk like that?'

'You've always been exceptionally sensitive to the way people express themselves, Manse. But perhaps we have to accept their crudenesses. Believe me, this would be a very useful advance. Did he say Stanfield agreed you'd be undisputed supremo?'

'Both of them. They had a discussion.'

'This is significant, Manse, Stanfield being so arrogant and weighty. He operated in France. All at once they see they need you.'

'Do *I* need *them*, Alf?'

'Certainly not, Manse. Not in the sense that they need you. You need them only to make it look like a happy confederation of suppliers.' Alfie was really cheerful, that slabby face on the move at all kinds of unusual spots. 'It's very useful to have this meeting in the Monty. Ralph Ember's another one trying to turn himself into a wholesaler, I hear. Perhaps he's already started. But, obviously, he'll have seen you so assured on TV. And he'll also see us conferring with Vine and Stanfield in his club. He'll deduce what's up and will want a closeness to you, too, Manse. These people cannot survive without it now. They're terrified of being outside our pact with the police.'

'There isn't no fucking pact yet.'

'They suspect there is. That's what counts, Manse. And this belief will itself help us get the alliance. Harpur and Iles have their little grasses inside that club, I've no doubt, so they'll hear about the meeting, too. We'll be irresistible.' Alfie smiled in that beigish, horse-tooth way he had and struck the arm of the filthy old leather chair where he sat. 'The appearance will create the reality.'

Shale hated shit phrases like that, but he thought he'd better float one back. 'It's dangerous, Alf. It's turning fucking moonshine into company policy.'

'There's a temporary risk, I admit. It will resolve itself. Mansel Shale is not one to baulk at risk, I believe, or where would we be?'

So Shale agreed to the meeting. He would cycle to Alfie's place again tonight and Alf could drive him to the club. Shale had come round again to thinking Ivis could manage real business flair now and then, and maybe it was best to let him shape the situation. It was a big switch from how Shale had thought right after the TV interview. Then the broadcast had looked like a foul mistake, undoing great years of low, low profile. It was Alfie's fault, no question, and Shale had begun to wonder even more about him once it was over and the rotten taste of it still in his mouth. Alfie got juicy money from the company, and why buy disasters? Plus Shale still wondered what kind of private link there was between Alfie and W. P. Jantice. That was a damn deep matter.

But then Shale had this eager fan call from the young loudster, Keith Vine, and he began to wonder. Maybe the TV was not so bad after all. Shale kept the phone unplugged most of the time, but he would reconnect now and then to make calls out. Vine had come through just as Shale was about to disconnect again.

'To offer congrats, Manse,' he said in that winner's voice, full of cosy blare.

'Yes?'

'I mean, surviving brutality at your place the other night. This is people afraid of you, Manse, afraid of what you've achieved already and what you might go on to. And then the broadcast. Masterly. Stan and I, we both said so. The brilliant concern for order.'

The thing about Vine and Stanfield was they would be hoping to make their outfit bigger, and suddenly Vine wanted friendliness. This broadcast had obviously hinted to him that Mansel Shale Inc had things all organized, one of those nice understandings with the police which were getting so fashionable. It was true what Alfie had said – Vine suddenly felt scared his outfit would be left outside, unprotected, just like any invading team from London or Manchester. Shale realized then that perhaps Ivis's TV gamble had not been so mad after all.

On the phone, Vine had said: 'We thought real weight in your performance, Manse. That child interviewer didn't know where she was. You've brought bonus dignity to the business world.'

'Thanks, Keith.'

'Look, Manse, Stan Stanfield and I both thought a meeting with your good self might be worthwhile.'

'What you got in mind, Keith?' Well, it was obvious what this one had in mind, but you had to show somebody like Keith Vine you did not just walk into the dark.

Then that good bit: 'Clearly you'd be top banana, Manse. You're the pacesetter, the pathfinder. Stan says so, I say so.'

Shale said: 'I'll get back to you.'

So now here they were in the Monty. Shale hated this club. In the old days it was a class spot, they said. Well, it slid, like everything else, and was sliding faster. Any time you did a count, twenty per cent of members would be fee-suspended because of jail and a few more were strapped to beds in secure hospitals. But this Ralph Ember who ran it acted as if it was still like one of those London spots such as Boodle's or White's, where there were power and distinction. You were supposed to feel wowed by the mahogany and brass fittings everywhere from those earlier times, plus Panicking Ralph Ember behind the bar, talking like Sandringham fucking Castle.

Vine said: 'Stan and I like to think we can see at least a little way into the business future.'

'I wish *I* could,' Shale replied.

'Manse, you *are* the future,' Stan Stanfield said. 'Hence the meeting. And thanks for turning out tonight, at a time of distress.'

The four of them had a table under an enlarged framed departure photograph of that famous Monty excursion to Paris when a tart was abducted for thirty-six hours and two pimps who came looking for her badly hurt.

'Ah, the twenty-first century,' Vine stated. 'I expect we all have loved ones, dependants, and we'll be thinking of how to make them secure in this coming era.'

'We have to be flexible,' Alfie Ivis replied. 'A time of rapid social and commercial change.'

Stanfield stood up and pulled the picture away from the wall, bug searching. He seemed satisfied and gave a friendly smile to Ember, who had pretended not to watch.

'As long as the police know they've got to be flexible too,' Vine said.

'That's the essence of things,' Alfie said.

Keith Vine said: 'We are definitely not going to ask for detail of how this arrangement you're brilliantly creating actually works, Mansel.'

'No, please don't ask, Keith,' Alfred said. 'Many confidences are involved.'

'Like at what rank, for instance – whether the very top itself or possibly a trifle lower,' Vine said. 'That would not matter very much, anyway. Everyone knows who really runs police here.'

This kid was asking questions by saying he was not going to ask them. He must think Shale was a fucking novice, like his fucking self. Vine was about twenty-five, burly, with cropped fair hair, like someone who tore rows of seats out for weaponry at soccer games. 'True power can sometimes be quiet and in the background, not showy,' Shale replied.

Stanfield said: 'We would certainly be prepared to consider putting our operation under your governorship, Manse.'

'What I meant about the future,' Vine said. 'Cooperation in a fine cause.'

'This is certainly a proposal we shall wish to look at very

positively,' Alfie replied, 'though obviously not something we can deal with off the top of our heads now here in the Monty.'

'Hardly,' Vine said, with a grand laugh. He and Stanfield were drinking Kressmann Armagnac, some smart bottle with a black label that was just the sort of item Panicking would tell customers was important. Shale and Alfie had gin and peps. That sod Ember had smirked when he mixed them. This was a lad who earned his name, Panicking, from so many jobs he fucked up, bank raids, building societies, security vans. But he always seemed to get away with it, and get away with a big lump of loot. There were people dead, or doing twenty years or in wheelchairs because of Panicking's panics. He stayed fine, though – he had the club, daughters in good schools, women.

Stanfield said: 'That was amazing, the way things soon went quiet after the kid was shot. This has to be genuine influence, Manse. Congratulations.'

'Mr Shale feels unceasing sadness over the death of the child,' Alfie Ivis replied.

Stanfield said: 'When Keith suggests we would not expect to be given the details of an admittedly very personal arrangement you might have created, Manse, we obviously know a bit about the basic nuts and bolts of it – say the go-betweening, for instance. We worry a bit about him. There's a certain wildness.'

'Extremism,' Vine said. 'We realize there has to be a link-man, but all the same we . . .'

Alfie said: 'I don't think Mr Shale and I understand what you are—'

'This is W. P. Jantice, clearly,' Vine replied.

'Who?' Ivis asked.

'Oh, come on, Alf,' Stanfield said. 'We don't say that what he did was unnecessary. Someone acting like Jantice gets a lot of stress.'

'A kid. Hellishly unfortunate,' Vine said.

'But we don't believe this would have been on orders from you, Mansel,' Stanfield said. 'This is not the way Mansel Shale would behave towards a child.' He was older than Vine, with a face nearly as big as Alfie's. Stanfield had a heavy fair moustache, straggly, more like armpit hair. Like Alf mentioned, he done some activity in France, that was the tale, and women went for him – some said even Jack Lamb's girl and Harpur's student.

Vine said: 'Jantice is a lad who might destroy patterns, whereas, as I understand it, what we all want to do is re-establish the predictable and ordered.'

Stanfield used to tell people he was descended from some famed painter last century called Clarkson Stanfield. Of course, women moistened up to an arty touch. 'We'd be better without W. P. Jantice,' he said.

Ember approached, carrying a tray on which were two more large gin and peps and the Kressmann bottle and three empty brandy glasses. He pulled a chair over and joined them. He put the new gin and peps in front of Shale and Ivis, then filled the three glasses with Armagnac, took one for himself and passed the others to Vine and Stanfield. 'Compliments de la maison, messieurs,' he said, giving a sort of little sitting bow to Stanfield because he had been abroad. 'This is the kind of tableau I love,' he said. 'It's a nice return to the old days of the club when a group of businessmen might sit here and discuss worthwhile deals, or perhaps just enjoy a civilized chat.'

'It's part business and part what you could call philosophy, I suppose, Ralph,' Ivis replied. 'We are seeking ways towards stability. We are searching for a hidden system in the seemingly chaotic happenings of our time. Then we must adapt ourselves and, at least as important, persuade others to adapt to this system.'

Ember nodded. A scar along his jaw shone under the lights like pork on a slab. Panicking never said where it came from but he let folk think it was some noble fight in his noble past. Some people said he got it falling over his feet when running from a girl bank clerk who turned rough in a raid.

'Stability,' Panicking said, 'that's some rare commodity these days.'

Ivis said: 'If we can unite and bring in other influential interests we—'

'Police?' Ember asked.

'United we will eliminate the random, the accidental, such as Sphere Street,' Ivis said.

'That was an accident?' Ember replied.

'Sense and justice cry out for this kind of coordination,' Ivis said.

'Well, it sounds really good to me,' Ember replied.

'But I'm top fucking banana,' Shale said.

It was late. Ivis drove Shale back to the lighthouse to pick up his bike for him to return by the path. Even at this time of night some of those media sods might be at the rectory gates. 'This Jantice is becoming a burden, Alf,' Shale said, but Alfie did not answer.

# 22

So Shale fixed a night meeting with W. P. Jantice. He put the Beretta automatic in his pocket. This could be a difficult little session one way or the other. First, would Jantice come? Christ, he must have a notion things were getting a bit dubious for him. There might be a word around on the street that Shale had been up in the service lane, and that Harpur had been up there before that. This boy Jantice was damn good at picking up the chatter. He ought to be – it was his job, one of his jobs. This boy Jantice was usually full of laughs and neck and slipperiness, but he must have an idea things might not be too good for him and could be getting worse.

Shale said a spot in trees and bushes near a stretch of foreshore known as Carnality Strand where lovers went. Two cars close together would not be noticeable. It could be husband and wife, but not each other's. People down there did not call the police about what they might see or hear because most of them should not be there, anyway, and they wanted no celebrity. It would be mad to let Jantice come to the rectory, especially with some media still adhesive, and Shale would not go to Jantice's own place even if Jantice had suggested it. You did not carry out a tense little encounter like this one on the other lad's home ground – he could have all sorts of tricky stuff hidden here and there, ready, and even mates waiting. Sometimes they would use Alfie Ivis's lighthouse for conferences, it being so remote. But Shale wanted this meeting to be just himself and Jantice. That was important. Of course, if Jantice and Alfie had something private going, Jantice would be on the phone to tell him about the meeting. That was bad, but not avoidable. Shale took five hundred in twenties.

Jantice did come. He was there before Shale. Shale knew his silver Belmont. Shale did not like him being there early. This could be to look around the ground and get the possibilities – quick ways out, hiding places for assistants, that sort of thing. He was the kind who might have a lot of rough friends, some bought for business purposes, some heartfelt. Shale was in the Escort. He parked close to the Belmont and joined Jantice in it. Shale would have thought it arrogant to sit there until Jantice came to his car, even though Jantice might have bits of trouble hidden about his vehicle, just like if it had been in his flat. Shale thought some risks had to be taken for the sake of decent politeness.

'I'm glad you called a get-together, Manse,' Jantice said. 'I'd have asked for one myself, otherwise. I heard of the Monty gathering. That was not too wise.'

'Social,' Shale replied.

Jantice leaned across from behind the steering wheel towards Shale in the passenger seat and spoke like a friend: 'I'll tell you how I read that gathering, shall I, Manse?'

This was the thing about this kind of sharp lad – they

turned things round so when you thought you'd take some-one to bits they took you to bits instead. Assertiveness was the name of it. 'I got a responsibility to think of things on a wide basis, W.P.,' Shale said. 'This business is more than just today and tomorrow and it's more than one or two deals, no matter how big.'

Jantice said: 'This Monty thing is teams coming together to convince Mark Lane you could deliver your side of a street agreement. And to convince him he can't do without you. You haven't got Misto's lot, but three is not bad. Or it *wouldn't* be bad – it wouldn't be bad if that's the way police thinking went. But it isn't, Manse.'

'We—'

'Just listen to me. This is the kind of thing you pay me for, so listen and get your money's worth, all right? It might be the way Iles's thinking goes, but he's isolated. Marky Lane's made a real recovery. Apparently, he thought of get-ting out, but he's come back, and he's come back with the same idea he always had: fight you, not join you. He doesn't believe he can't do without you. This is a spiritual thing with him, profound. He was taught young there's a difference between black and white, and it's stayed with him. Perhaps he's got Harpur on his side.'

This fucker was thinking of his situation and his money. If the firms and police got a good understanding going there would be no need for someone like Jantice to bring the inside police information because the inside police infor-mation would be outside on a plate as part of the agreement.

It was a bit sad and a bit quaint to see him struggling like this because the situation was going to disappear, anyway. It was going to disappear tonight, one way or the other. Shale had made the decision and he did not go back on something like that.

Jantice said: 'The Chief's still sure it has to be infiltration and he's still sure it has to be yours truly who infiltrates. This is going to be beautiful, Manse. But when I hear about this hobnobbing at the Monty, and the sniffing up Sphere Street, I'm bound to feel bloody angry and hurt. I'm bound to feel you'd like to drop me. So stupid, Manse. So disloyal. That's you personally, not Alfred. That's why you want this rendezvous.'

'Some kind of reciprocity between you and Alfie?' Shale asked.

'But, the point is, Manse, you need me, need me more than you realize, because you don't know how to read head-quarters. Iles is Iles, but only Iles.' He spoke quietly yet hammering it, all the same, like a teacher.

'You're a fucking liability, W.P.,' Shale replied.

'So you come here packing a pistol.' He nodded at the right pocket.

'Like you.'

'No.'

'I'm carrying something all the time these days.'

'No, you don't, Manse. You hate weaponry. This is special for me.'

This Jantice, he looked feeblish, the skinny body and the

blond locks, but he had some strength, too, and some bravery. He was a lurking, dangerous kind of sod, like so many
of them. Shale said: 'I've had people blasting off at me in
my own home and killing a dear friend, so naturally I'm
always tooled up now.'

'Let's walk a bit,' Jantice replied. 'It's muggy in
here.'

It wasn't. What Shale had to think was this lad could be
leading him to an ambush in the foliage. Jantice did not
need a gun himself because he had a little armed party
waiting. Christ, Alfie himself might be there. This could be
their move to take over. Jantice would have the flair and
slyness to plan something like that, he had police training.
But it would have seemed pathetic and rude to Shale to
refuse, so he climbed out of the car and they strolled through
the greenery and down towards the seawall. Shale did not
even put his hand on the Beretta. That would have been
such a slur. They climbed the grass slope of the wall and
stood on top looking out at the mud flats shining into the
distance under a huge moon. It was grubby as a view, but it
had scope. Tall, thin, perpendicular bits of frothy factory
effluent were picked up by the breeze now and then and
danced across the flats like escaped madmen. It was light
enough to see Jantice's warm brown eyes, shining with
cleverness and distrust.

'You got no fucking tact, W.P.,' Shale said. 'Gunning a
small kid in full view.'

'That was the most terrible thing I've ever had to do,'

Jantice said. He was whispering for a moment. The words came so slowly.

'Even for police I can believe that,' Shale replied. He meant it.

'This kid would have sunk me. Sunk you as well. I don't need to tell you. This kid knew a hell of a lot of people and a hell of a lot of dicey facts, Mansel.'

'There should of been another solution.'

'I didn't get offered one.'

'Did you ask? You should of consulted.'

Jantice was silent for a moment, seemed astonished. 'Well, I did, Manse.'

'Oh? So, who?'

'Of course I consulted.'

Shale thought about this. 'Alfie told you to do it like that?'

'I had to assume this advice was reaching me from you, Manse. Obviously, never to be spelled out by you or Alf or me, then or later, but, yes, from you.'

'You had to assume fucking what?' Shale replied in a groan that rolled out towards the far-off sea. 'To knock over a child? Did Alfie say it came from me?' Shale turned from looking at the mud and glanced back, in case Jantice had folk sneaking out from behind them. It was quiet, though.

'Oh, God. The last thing I want is to put any evil between you and Alfred, Manse. You've always been such a fine combo. That's the point. You think as one.'

'Alfie don't think. He leans.'

Jantice gripped Shale's arm for a second, maybe to stop

him getting at the Beretta. Shale did not break the grip. He hated inconsiderate movement. In the glare of white moonlight Jantice's long, dreamy face looked like a warning against too much tossing off. 'Manse, if I misinterpreted your wishes as to—'

'Misin-fucking-terpreted?' Shale replied. 'You thought I'm the sort who would . . .? Listen, W.P., I'm paying you off.'

'No, Manse.' Again he whispered, his voice gone weak.

'Paying you off fucking finally. After tonight, no contact, you understand? After tonight, you come anywhere near my operation and you're a spy, you're the enemy, just someone who snoops and kills kids. You'll finish out there, on the mud.' He produced the roll of twenties and counted off ten. He gave them to Jantice.

'I don't deserve this, Manse.'

'Take it.'

'I don't mean the money. I mean getting cut off.' Jantice fanned the twenties. 'This is a bit fucking low, isn't it, Manse? How long have I been feeding you? Two years?'

'Listen, I thought of killing you, W.P.'

'Well, I know. Obviously. I thought give you a chance. I don't know I'd care so very much. I look at myself now and then and puke. Do you believe it, Manse?'

'Maybe. You take one little step into your kind of life and suddenly you're lost. Yet all the time you can think back to how you used to be.'

'That's it.' Then he laughed. 'How I used to be was poor. And mind you, Manse, you'd have had difficulties: shoot someone in a car and the mess goes everywhere. Did you see *Pulp Fiction*?'

'I hate that sort of stuff.' Shale gave him the rest of the five hundred.

'Go easy with Alfie, Manse.'

They walked back towards the cars. Shale felt comfortable. This was something that had been settled in a decent style. It could be right Jantice deserved the five hundred. It could be right there had been a mistake in the communications, so Jantice thought the child should be shot. There were complications, errors, everywhere. He was glad Jantice had not fallen into fear or gibbering. Shale hated it when people screamed for mercy, it put you in an embarrassing position. Jantice was not too bad a lad. He still had a bit of conscience and some quite noble indifference. Jantice was the sort you had to get rid of, but not get rid of crudely. Shale knew that to be feeling good about him like this and all-round satisfied could be some mistake. This was the sort of lull time when people would hit you. He did put his hand on the Beretta now as they reached the trees. They went through them quickly and into their cars. Jantice drove away at once. There was no talk, like lovers who had had a quarrel.

# 23

Harpur decided it was time for a talk with Naomi Anstruther, the young Drugs Squad detective, to check if she was right for undercover work. And to check if she would do it. You did not order people into that degree of risk. He had looked through her papers, of course, and liked the profile. There were no children and she was unmarried. She had two official commendations for bravery, one for arresting an armed man when unarmed herself. Mark Lane would have met Anstruther personally to make these awards and might remember her. This could be a plus, might make it easier to move him away from the doomed fixation on W. P. Jantice.

Harpur still needed Lane to stay and to fight in the way he wanted. Any way was all right, as long as he fought. Lane had picked infiltration. That would do, then. It would have been unbearable to see the Chief finally crushed by Iles, or finally crushed by his wife and forced to retire. Lane was a good man and deserved more. But he had become weak, not always able to achieve what he deserved. He needed help and Harpur was willing to give it now and then. In any case, perhaps Lane really was right, and infiltration would eventually work – and only infiltration. Harpur could not allow this duty to go to Jantice, though. Harpur had nothing concrete or even half provable against him: nothing he could put before the Chief. If Harpur told what he thought, but could not stand up, Lane would decide it was simply part of Iles's plot to kill infiltration, and if possible destroy Lane himself. The Chief suspected alliances against him everywhere, and especially between Iles and Harpur. Sometimes those fears made sense. They crippled Lane's judgement. What Harpur needed to put before him instead of black rumour about Jantice was a different, irresistibly suitable candidate.

Harpur was shocked to find he now objected almost as much as Lane to Iles's wish for a working arrangement with the gangs. That would be massive capitulation. It would be regression towards chaos, not an escape from it. Iles and other high-rankers in this country and around the world argued that some such useful compromises already existed. Because the wholesalers had made themselves too powerful and rich, and too aloof from actual street business, they could rarely be touched. There was blind-eyeing, there was police toleration of large-scale, grossly illegal trade. You could hound their back-lane minions and give some inconvenience by locking them up, but that was all. For the sake of peace Iles wanted the next few steps towards an understanding formalized. It was a strong case, resting on that central unspoken gospel of desperate policing – that is, most policing – *quid pro quo*: something for something. When things were as they should be, the famous 'policing by consent' might work, because consent came from the general population, the people. When things were not as they should be it came from those strong enough to usurp that will of the people through terror. Iles believed the terror battle had been lost. Now and then Harpur believed it, too, but only now and then.

While he was still trying to work out where and how to set up a private meeting with Naomi Anstruther, he had a call from Jack Lamb, just out of hospital. On the phone, Jack sounded totally recovered, as full of self-belief and improper influence as ever.

'I couldn't risk visiting you,' Harpur said.

'Of course not. You'd have fingered me in bed, as it were. I had trouble without that. You've got trouble, too, Col.'

'Have I?'

'And more to come. Let's rendezvous. I was going to ask you up here to Darien for a chat, in view of my convalescent state. But my mother's a guest, tending me. She can be loudly contemptuous of police. With your sensitivity you can't take that.'

'Oh, I don't know. I get a lot at home.'

'Say somewhere else,' Lamb said. 'Not army.'

'Sainsbury's.' Harpur was glad to dodge a visit to Jack's manor house, and not just because of Mrs Lamb. He and Harpur occasionally used this supermarket car park. Half Harpur's career seemed to focus on finding safeish rendezvous spots. Lamb said he was off military settings for now. In any case, he had been unable to buy new army surplus garb while in hospital. He liked to glint freshly like the Sword of Honour cadet. They talked now in Jack's Land Rover. Every manor house should have one.

'You've still got a lot of people on the loose, Col,' Jack said.

'We're closing in.'

'Balls,' Lamb replied. 'When I say people on the loose, I mean the two pedestrians in Sphere Street, plus Neville Greenage and Kalashnikov man.'

'We'll get them all.'

'Balls. The lad called Sailor Billy,' Lamb said. 'William Charles Rich. I told you about him. My information says he's back, hunting.'

'Information from where, Jack?' A ritual. As a woebegone attempt to keep control of things, Harpur would occasionally ask Lamb questions about sources. They got no answer. They were impertinent.

Lamb said: 'Billy could be one of the folk who gave me my blows, Col. I owe him. Why I'm talking.'

And thank God he was. A meeting like this with Lamb forced Harpur to chuck many of his pieties. He was bound to see – see again – that much of his own detection depended on what Iles and others would call a working arrangement. Harpur had his pacts with informants, and above all with Lamb. They required Harpur skilfully to ignore some criminal behaviour in exchange for good pointers about other criminal behaviour. All successful detectives operated such neat balancing acts, probably even Lane before he soared high and grew virginal. Did these methods differ much from what the ACC proposed? Iles would say no, but Harpur thought yes. Christ, he had to. What Iles envisaged was bigger, more frighteningly fundamental, and probably irreversible. Once you handed people favoured status on that scale it was hard to cancel: see Hitler's Brownshirts. It was even hard to cancel on a lower scale: see Lamb. 'I checked with the Yard on Rich. All they told me was he had a lot of form and was out of jail for now.'

Jack said: 'Billy could also be one of the folk who went gunning for Mansel Shale and hit the girl in his house. He's got large grievances. It's worrying to be shot at by a Kalashnikov, even in dud hands.'

'I'm not so sure of that,' Harpur said.

'You think he was sparing the girl?' Lamb asked. 'Kalashnikov gent, then. But have you thought Sailor Billy – plus Quant, the other one, if he's still all right – plus the rest of the team who seemed to have been in Letchworth Avenue when I went calling – have you thought they'd be peeved above all with whoever crafted that three-sided Sphere Street scenario?'

'Manse?'

'Manse and his boys are only *one* side of it. There's also Sailor Boy and Quant, plus NOON.'

'NOON might have been accidental.'

Lamb sighed impatiently. He had lost weight in hospital and now sharpened his already sharpened features into a weary frown. 'I hear you've reasons to doubt that.'

'Hear from where?'

## Top Banana

People with loaded trolleys dawdled past the car, some staring in. Two men talking like this and not shopping might be noticeable. Harpur wanted to be away soon, and so should Jack want to be away soon. Supermarket car parks, hotel car parks, football-ground car parks – they had the advantage of busy crowds for cover, but they were also obvious. Jack's injuries had brought him Press fame. He might have a tail. And always Harpur might have a tail.

'Someone clever organized that noisy conjunction on Sphere Street, Col,' Lamb replied. Despite his run-down look, his voice was still thick and scorchingly positive. 'Do you know anybody clever?'

Harpur said: 'I—'

'Anybody clever who might have something to gain from a battle there. Impresario abilities.' Lamb must be down a couple of stone, bringing him to about sixteen and a half. For now he was not much bigger than Harpur. Jack's suit would billow a bit when he walked. Harpur saw why Lamb would require new army surplus. Ill-fitting civilian clothes might be tolerable, but slack military gear would offend him. His features were mildly shrunken, like a heavyweight boxer trying to get to light-heavy too fast. 'Is he around? Or they?' Harpur replied.

'Sailor Billy and the rest? They come and go before you and your boys are awake. Ask Mansel Shale. Ask the late Patricia Devonald. Ask me.'

'Who the hell's been keeping you so well up to date while you were sick, Jack?'

'I'd say whoever set up that incident is in real peril, wouldn't you, Col?'

'Peril's general.'

Lamb said: 'But the next question is, so what? Do you care? Why protect someone capable of that?'

'We're a police force, Jack. We have a duty to all.'

'I've heard about it,' Lamb replied. 'One tale says this clever lad might even be a cop – someone juggling his loyalties and afraid everything might fall to the ground if the girl spoke. Probably not you, though, Col.'

Harpur said: 'So, is Sailor Billy around, or they?'

'Why else did I bring you out here?' Lamb replied. He squinted hard through the windscreen. 'I feel exposed. Sailor could be under sliced bread in that trolley, a Sainsbury gunship. Cheers, Col.' He boomed: 'Yes, I'm feeling more myself now. Thanks for asking.'

Dismissal. The tip had been given. Harpur climbed out of the Land Rover and went back to his old Lada from the police pool. It was a worry to think W. P. Jantice might be targeted, but not much of a worry, as Lamb guessed. Jantice was owed no protection. The supermarket had closed and its car park was swiftly turning into a wasteland. All the same, Harpur would still prefer this spot to Darien. At Jack's house Harpur knew he would have been confronted again by some of the brilliant, worrying items Lamb dealt in professionally. Very expensive art hung on Darien's walls. Harpur knew nothing about paintings except what Jack told him, but if Jack said this was a Hockney and this a Jackson

Pollock and this a Tissot, you'd better believe it. You could also believe him when he told you the price he would sell them on for. What you could *not* have believed was his account of how they reached him, if he had ever given one. He did not. The pictures came and went at Darien and were replaced by others, but the general aura of distinguished costliness remained. Harpur's embarrassment at looking at them would also have remained, if he had been forced to visit Darien very often. He managed to blank them out of his mind otherwise. This was another necessary and routine piece of detective flair.

*

'Well, if we go into any it's got to be Manse Shale's,' Naomi Anstruther said. 'His operation's the biggest. Should they ever get a merger going, he'd be top banana. Get into his and you're into the lot. Keith Vine and Stanfield are on the way up, but nowhere near Manse yet. Panicking? He's really only just starting, looking for a steady gold mine to invest his loot. Misto *was* pretty big, but he's come off damaged in a couple of tussles lately. He's thin at the moment. They haven't even invited him into their confederation.'

'Our object is to stop any confederation.'

'I do understand that, Mr Harpur.'

'They'll only want a united grouping if they think they could do a deal with us.'

'I do understand that, Mr Harpur.'

'You're the alternative.'

'Yes.'

'Or you will be, if we proceed.'

'Yes.'

They were in a launderette. Harpur had brought a bag of washing. His visit was natural enough for a one-parent family and would go on being natural enough, if Anstruther took the job and needed to meet her Controller now and then. Headquarters would have been useless for meetings. Leaks squirted all ways there. No leaks but steam leaks in a launderette, with any luck. She said: 'Can you guarantee that if—'

'I can't guarantee much at all. Don't press for guarantees or I can't use you.'

But she persisted, talking very precisely to get to him above the chunter of the machines. 'Mr Harpur, can you guarantee that all our confidential meetings will be in public places like this?' she asked.

'Oh, yes, something like that I can guarantee, if you want. I thought you were talking about panic button response.' He looked at her for an explanation of what she had meant, and thought he knew.

'You're regarded as a bit of a shagger-around, Mr Harpur.'

'Thanks.'

'I could name names, of course. I'd be a poor detective otherwise. All right if I make my statement?'

'Certainly.'

'I don't fancy you.' A woman filling one of the machines glanced around at Anstruther, then at Harpur, as if considering an Anstruther reject.

'Good,' he said. 'It won't get in the way of work.'

'I wanted you to understand that from the beginning. My man could get fed up if he found out I was in secluded meetings with you.'

'Fuck your man.'

'I do.'

'Listen,' he snarled at her, 'we're talking about your life, not your fucking sex life. Your life's my responsibility. We might need a secret spot – a "secluded" spot – at some stage. More than once. If that puts you off, you'd better say now. And your man is not to find out anything at any stage. Not about where we meet, not that you're doing this work at all. He might get awkward about you being close to Manse, as well. Perhaps he's heard Manse is a shagger-around, too.'

'My man doesn't get told anything, I realize that, but he might find out.'

'He doesn't find out. If he does, your part in the operation is closed.'

'He wouldn't talk.'

'If he finds out, your part in the operation is closed. Do I know him? He's not in your papers.'

'How *would* you know him?'

'You made it sound as if I might.'

'You mean I made it sound as if he knew you were a shagger-around?'

'Is that what I mean? Yes, that he thought I was because you'd fed him gossip. Is he a police officer?'

'No. I'm not obliged to pick a cop to live with.'

'Many do and regret it. I knew one woman well who made the mistake. Have you ever had a habit?'

'No. I look as if I did, don't I? Sort of unfocused face. I have trouble with it in mirrors, wonder if I'm who I was when I began the day. Of course, if you've got a habit you're *not* who you were when you began the day. That's the attraction – you can become someone else. Is my druggy face what got me on your shortlist?'

'No.' Or yes: there was the seeming dreaminess in her eyes which would at times turn to horrifying emptiness, and the impression that her features were aslant – her nose, cheekbones, chin and jawline, as if some muscles had decayed under a dope onslaught into permanent relaxation. It seemed especially noticeable in here among all the shining hard box edges of the washing machines. None of it stopped her being attractive, though. It stopped her being beautiful. Did Manse go for beauty? Patricia Devonald was beautiful. Harpur said: 'It's not at all necessary for you to have been a user. Maybe better not. A lot of dealers don't use. Your basic background is so right and I get nothing but fulsomeness on you from the Drugs Squad.' He did not pause then and spoke the next words like an official caution. 'I've got to remind you about Raymond Street while there's time for you to back out.'

'Killed undercover,' she said. 'You don't need to remind me.'

'I need to remind myself.'

'Don't,' she said. 'It's sentimental. It will get in the way, like sex might have. Tell me how I infiltrate. Or shouldn't I ask? Should I be able to see for myself how it's done?'

Through the front panel Harpur watched his shirts and pants and the children's bits and pieces going around in the washing machine. It seemed such a simple, ordered procedure. Even the bubbles looked systematic. Was it Newton who said life was like that, or Sam Goldwyn? 'Yes, I suppose you should be able to see for yourself, really.'

'This is a point against me?'

'There are bigger points,' Harpur replied. 'If you agree to do it you're a possible, that's all. The Chief wants someone else. And the Chief is likely to name himself Registrar. He's important.'

'Lane? I'm an Iles person in that divide. I thought you were.'

'Sometimes. When he's right.'

'Lane's the past, if that.'

'We can't be Iles groupies on this.'

'On this?' she said. 'It's pretty basic, isn't it?'

'Yes.'

'So, is preferring Iles a point against me, too?' She was concentrating. Her face seemed to become even more bizarrely askew, and even more winning. 'I think you'd have to tell me about a small-scale drugs bust we had planned, and I would warn Shale and they could make sure nothing was found. That would get his trust.'

'Not *too* small scale,' Harpur said. 'Manse reads us pretty well.'

'Oh, he's bloody bright.'

'We'd have to arrange two or three major fiascos before he'd start believing in you, paying you. He might not believe it even then, because he'd expect us to plant something if we didn't find any. Why have we suddenly turned scrupulous?'

'Yes,' she said. 'Naturally, I've done that when I knew for a fact people were dealers but seemed clean in a raid.'

'Policing is only part a science. There's the creative side.' They moved up on the row of light blue seats among the light blue décor to make room for a heavily built woman with what seemed a bag of hotel table napkins that began to tumble and rise in the machine like a rain of plates or a launch of frisbies. Harpur lost sight of his clothes in the far washer, but knew they would still be moving around on their consoling predestined route. 'We'd get bad press for these muck-up raids and maybe Manse's lawyers after us. So, in the long run, we've got to bring it off to justify the knocks.'

'Keynes said that in the long run we're all dead.'

'Does he write mottoes for Christmas crackers? Anyway, Naomi, don't be dead, long run or short run. Street was brave but foolish for a moment or two.'

'I don't mind you calling me by my first name. But I'll call you Control. It's what you're supposed to lack, isn't it?'

'Iles thinks it's all I've got. Says it keeps me down among the dull. We'll use code names for phone or radio. I got them from one of my children's homework books. You'll be Mole.'

'Le Carré got there before you.'

'Who? I'll be Rat.'

'Who's Mansel?'

'I'll have to take another look at Jill's book.'

'There's a character called Toad,' she said.

'You know this tale then? Education's damn widespread. Yes, Toad will do.'

'Toad's the only one we're interested in, yes?'

'Nobody lower. It's not worth—' He had been about to say, 'It's not worth risking you for small fry' but changed it to, 'It's not worth setting up an elaborate thing like this for small fry. We let minor people get away with it. That's what happens in the failed raids you warn him of. It's the reverse of what we usually did . . . do – nab the nobodies while top banana stays safe and still top. After Manse we move on to Vine, Stanfield, Panicking.'

He opened the machine and pulled his stuff out into a plastic sack.

'Who does your ironing, Colin?' she said.

'Not you, Mole. Your man wouldn't like it.'

'He wouldn't know.'

'It was Toad not Mole who dressed up as a washerwoman. Look, just concentrate on the secrecies that matter, will you?' Harpur said. 'If you get the job.'

'You rat, Rat. You knew about Toad all the time.'

# 24

Harpur went home with his washing. As often as possible, he liked to be there when the children came in from school. That usually turned out to be two or three times a month. He was not sure whether it mattered much to Hazel and Jill, but it made him feel worthy. He would go out to the front gate when they were due, so the neighbours could see the girls were not neglected after their mother's death. Harpur had been brought up to to take account of what neighbours thought, and some traces of that had stuck. His daughters considered it pathetic. Although he was now a widower, he still worried about the nextdoors when he brought his student girlfriend Denise home for the night. But it did not worry him enough not to do it.

The children were late this evening and he went out to the gate three times before they appeared. Then he walked down Arthur Street to meet them, an affectionate, slow, paternal kind of walk, so they would not think he had been anxious, though he had, and so that the neighbours had plenty of time to enjoy the sight of a happy family.

'We went to see how Mandy's mother was getting on,' Hazel said.

'Mandy?' He thought of the dead child only as NOON these days her own choice for her later years.

'Mrs Walsh,' Hazel said.

'I told you she doesn't like people to call Mandy NOON,' Jill said. 'It takes her away from her.'

Something else had taken her away from her, but Harpur said: 'Understandable.'

They went into the house. He had their tea ready. They did not switch on the television, so he knew they must have something to tell him or ask him or both. He wondered whether it had been a good idea to come home.

'Dad, Mandy's father has been back,' Jill said. 'He read about her in the Press.'

'This is her true father, not . . . This is her *true* father,' Hazel said. She was eating cereals in cold milk, one of Iles's favourite dishes – might have picked up the taste from him.

'I didn't know her dad had shown. We wanted to talk to him,' Harpur replied.

'Mrs Walsh said he didn't stay long,' Jill said.

'Where is he now?' Harpur asked.

'She didn't know. She said he was angry,' Jill replied.

'I expect so,' Harpur said.

'Very angry,' Jill said.

'I think she's afraid, Dad,' Hazel said.

'Of what?' Harpur asked.

'What he might do,' Jill replied.

'She said he was a bit tasty, knew people who were very tasty,' Hazel said. 'That means violent.'

'Oh?' Harpur replied.

'Don't pretend you knew,' Hazel said.

Jill said: 'She talked about him like he was . . . well . . .'

'A heavy,' Hazel said.

'Not *like. As if,*' Harpur said.

'As if he were a crook,' Hazel replied. 'She said he knew guns.'

'Did she want you to tell me this?' Harpur asked.

'I don't know. Maybe,' Jill said.

'Why?' Harpur asked.

'So you could give some protection, maybe,' Hazel said.

'Who to?' Harpur replied.

'Yes, so you could give some protection,' Hazel said.

Jill and Harpur were eating tinned mackerel in mustard sauce with canned spicy vegetables. He liked to spread himself a bit on teas when he was home in time. He wanted these meals to stay in their minds when they were older so they could think back to the mackerel and know he did his best for them: thought of treats, paid out. Hazel was sniffy about the fancy quality of such food and would never eat it. She put down her spoon and took a long drink of tea. Harpur had an idea something important was on the way. 'Dad,' she said, 'a reporter was there with Mrs Walsh when we arrived.'

'She's still a star because of Mandy,' Harpur replied.

'That terrible place,' Jill said. 'So tiny. He didn't stay all the time, but he's asking us things. Rotten things. It was sly the way he asked them – yes, rotten things.' Her voice trembled, as it had when comparing her age with Mandy's, but again she recovered.

'That's the sort of job they're in,' Harpur replied. 'Take no notice.'

'Like did we know if you thought Mandy might of been killed by a police officer,' Jill said.

'Might *have* been killed,' Harpur said. 'You sound like some town rough.'

'Oh, might she have, then?' Jill asked. She crouched lower over the yellowed bits of mackerel, and Harpur saw she was cranking herself up for the next question. 'One of your lot shoot a child?'

'Of course not,' Harpur said. 'It's rubbish.'

Hazel said: 'He was saying but not saying – you know how they do it, Dad – he was saying but not saying that the police did not want to catch anyone for her death because it would mean getting one of their own officers.'

'It's rubbish,' Harpur replied.

'Is it, honestly, Dad?' Hazel asked.

'Of course it is, of course it is,' Jill cried, as if ashamed of what she had started. She stood up and went and stared from the window, head up now, full of gravity. 'Dad would want to get someone who did anything like that, wouldn't you, Dad?'

'Certainly.'

'This reporter said the killing was to silence her,' Hazel said.

'Rubbish,' Harpur replied.

'Oh, don't keep saying rubbish, Dad,' Jill screamed. 'It

makes it sound like it's true. *As if* it's true.' She had not turned, was yelling at the window.

Harpur said: 'Do you know if the reporter told her dad this rub— this nonsense?'

'No, we don't,' Hazel said.

'Did the reporter meet him?' Harpur asked.

'He didn't tell us,' Jill said. 'He went off.' She frowned, came back to the table and began to finish her meal.

'Did Mrs Walsh say?' Harpur asked.

'What?' Jill asked through the food.

'If the reporter met Mandy's father.'

Jill looked at Hazel. 'Did she, Haze?'

'I don't think so,' Hazel said. 'Why, Dad?'

'Well, spreading an evil rumour.'

'Are you scared he might go looking for this cop?' Hazel asked.

'There isn't any such cop,' Harpur replied. 'If there was, don't you think this reporter would have published it?'

'He said they were trying to stand it up, trying to prove it,' Hazel said.

'That means he wants to turn rumour into fact,' Harpur replied.

'Is there a rumour about this officer?' Hazel asked.

'And he thought I knew about it and might have told you?' Harpur said. 'They're mad. That way he imagined you could turn it all into fact for him.'

'You haven't told us about it, but do you know about it, Dad?' Hazel asked.

'Of course he doesn't know about it because this officer does not exist,' Jill shouted.

'Exactly,' Harpur replied.

'This reporter said they even had a name,' Hazel said.

'What name?' Harpur had to ask.

'He wouldn't tell us,' Jill said.

'He said he couldn't tell us because it might leak to some other reporter,' Hazel said. 'He wants a scoop.'

Jill gazed at him, grease gleaming on her upper lip and chin. 'You're worried he told her father this name, aren't you, Dad?'

'If there's a rumour, maybe you know this name, anyway,' Hazel said.

'I don't deal in rumour,' Harpur replied.

'Why not, Dad?' Jill asked. 'Some rumours turn out true. There was a rumour the deputy head was pregnant. Suddenly she's big.'

Hazel stood. Harpur said: 'No, I'll wash up.'

'You're always like trying to make up for something, Dad,' Jill said.

'Not always,' Hazel replied. 'He's hardly ever here.'

# 25

The media pack had dispersed from around Mansel Shale's gates so it was all right for Laurent and Matilda to come home from their mother. He had let them stay a few extra days after half term, but now was worried about their schooling. He also recalled Denzil and asked him to drive him in the Jaguar up to Alfie Ivis's place. Shale took the fully loaded Beretta. He wanted to arrive in the Jaguar today and not on his bike because there was a certain lasting significance in this visit that required style. He liked the important sound of the Jaguar on Alfie's gravel. It was a Saturday and Alf's family were around the lighthouse, those fucking foul kids Alfie had brought on himself, yet which he did not seem ashamed of enough.

Shale and Ivis walked the cliff again. Shale loathed it, yes, but he loathed any contact with Alfred's family more. There was a bit of wind and the sea came in in big waves. He hated that, the way they were so plump and pushy, and the regularity. If you took away these cliffs that fucking sea would be all over the landscape and civilization shattered. He handed the Beretta to Ivis. 'It's time to kill W. P. Jantice, Alfred,' he remarked. 'When you do, he might have something left from five hundred quid he took from me. I'll have it back.'

Alfred did not accept the gun, not at first. He had been smiling at some cormorant or parakeet or something like that that was flying fast just above the water looking for a pilchard probably. 'Jantice?' Alfred said. 'There are problems attaching to him, I'd concede that willingly, Manse, but on balance I would say he's still an asset.'

'I sacked him, but it's not enough. I hear the papers are going to splash W. P. any day now for Sphere Street and the child. If we're still associated we're finished. Panicking and Vine won't look at us. I wouldn't blame them – the inhumanity, the stupidity. All right, Jantice had his reasons – *his* sort of reasons. No good now. Do him, Alfred. The police will see we can deliver.'

'With respect, Manse, what we'll be delivering is one of their own people, dead.'

'He's an embarrassment to them. They can't do it themselves, but they won't protect him. They'll be so pleased to know he's been taken out they're not going to hunt you too much. We'll be very in.'

'This is a tricky one, Manse,' Alfred replied. 'Jantice is alert to perils these days. Naturally.'

'Have you got some special deal going with him, Alfred?' Shale asked.

'Deal?'

'Do him and I'll believe you haven't,' Shale replied.

'Manse, with respect, that's preposterous.'

'I sack him, but he could still have a link to you, Alfred. I don't want that. Do Jantice and I'll believe there's no private connection. Well, there fucking won't be, will there, because he's dead?'

They went on together in silence for fifty yards. Then Ivis said: 'Well, now, as you'll appreciate, Mansel, it's a long time since I did any shooting.' He stared out to sea for a while, getting reminiscent about the more struggling days. 'Nineteen eighty-three? Even eighty-two. I mean shooting a man.' He waved towards a string of most likely ducks in the air to show he still did those of course. 'The last would be Big Paul Legge.'

'But when you *were* knocking over men and so on you were top quality, Alfred.'

'You're very kind, as ever, Manse,' he said, taking the Beretta and weighing it fondly in his palm.

# 26

MURDERED POLICE OFFICER WAS CHILD KILLER
*by Malcolm Pitts*

*A police detective found shot dead in bed yesterday was himself the killer of a child drugs runner, gunned down in the street two weeks ago.*

*On the surface, Detective Sergeant Wayne Patterson Jantice was an experienced and devoted Drugs Squad officer. But he had another hidden life in which he systematically betrayed his position and his colleagues for high rewards.*

*The tall, slim officer was on the pay roll of at least one major drugs trader. He provided highly sensitive police infor-mation to the dealers, for example about planned raids and general police anti-drugs strategy. He killed 13-year-old Mandy Walsh, known as NOON, because she had stumbled on his secret and he feared she might reveal it.*

*Jantice, aged 32, always known as W.P., was found by his landlady shot twice through the head in the flat where he lived alone since his divorce three years ago. It is believed that Jantice had organized the street battle between two gangs as cover for his execution of Mandy Walsh. She also was shot twice and it is likely there is a connection between that Sphere Street shooting and the murder of Jantice.*

*A police spokesman said yesterday: 'We are keeping an open mind on motives for the killing.' There is no official police admission that Jantice was suspected of the Mandy Walsh murder, but the local community and particularly the local criminal community are sure that a police officer was the killer and that it was Jantice.*

*Mandy's mother, blonde, 34-year-old Rachel Walsh, said yesterday: 'It is terrible to think my little girl might have been killed by a police officer – one of those who should be guarding children from harm.'*

*Forensic experts are seeking to identify the weapon that killed Jantice. Mandy Walsh was killed by two 6.35mm bullets believed to come from a SIG-Sauer pistol. No gun was found in Jantice's flat, but an experienced police officer would know that the first precaution for a murderer to take is to dispose of the weapon.*

# 27

Iles said: 'This is the sort of mistake I could have made myself, sir. And so could Harpur, couldn't you, Harpur?'

'In a way it's odd,' Harpur replied. 'Witness silence, which is normally used against the police, in this case protected a police officer. There must have been people who saw him in the service lane. He's distinctive. Yet nobody says anything – anything to us.'

'This was an officer, Chief, who was so far into duplicity because of the nature of his proper work that he had lost all sense of what loyalty amounted to. This is what I meant when I said I might have been deceived just the same as you, sir. Jantice did look a natural infiltrator to you, because you instinctively recognized that he no longer had any central, constant identity. He could become anything for a while. He adapted to where he was. A chameleon. It does happen to detectives. Did you ever see that Woody Allen film, *Zelig*, the man who became obese when he talked to the obese and Greek when he met Greeks?'

They were in Iles's room, Lane folded deep and destroyed in an armchair. His face was the colour of elm veneer but without the shine. He was in uniform and today that made his aura of absolute defeat worse, like a PoW. 'I am not fit to lead,' he whispered. 'I know only the route to error.'

Iles was in front of his long mirror, placed for the checking of his uniform on ceremonial days. He had found some hefty blemish in the skin of his right cheek and leant forward to examine it properly. Then he ran his thumb over the glass, obviously thinking any fault had to be in the mirror. He had gone as far as he meant to go in consoling Lane and ignored him now.

'We should abandon infiltration and do things your way, Desmond,' the Chief said. 'Some sensible arrangement. Why didn't I see it before? We cannot go on countenancing these appalling deaths. Isn't this your view now, too, Colin?'

Harpur said: 'I've got a first-class girl who would infiltrate.'

Iles spoke to him via the mirror. 'You fucking what, Harpur?'

'I think it would work,' Harpur said.

'Do you? Do you?' the Chief whispered. He sat up a little, his face grown almost unsluggish.

'It never works. This is some piece you want to get it away with, yes, Harpur?' Iles asked, still concentrating on the looking-glass. 'Ideal intimacies via this sort of operation. My Christ, why didn't I realize you'd see a chance and pick a woman?'

'Oh, Desmond, please.' Lane stood up, as though eager to leave the discussion while there was still hope and before the full acrinomy from Iles erupted. 'Good, Colin,' he said. 'If you approve of her, I know I will. And tell me, would you allow me to act as Registrar in this, as I'd envisaged for Jantice?'

'She makes it an absolute condition of accepting, sir,' Harpur said.

'Does she, does she?' Lane cooed.

When he had shuffled from the room on his thermal socks, Iles said: 'I'm glad, Harpur.'

'I knew you would be, sir.'

'You've behaved with charity here, Col, you scheming shit, Harpur.'

'Thanks, sir.'

'How long have you been bringing this girl along on the quiet? You'd risk her in work like this because of your dirty urges?'

'The Jantice killing was exceptionally skilled,' Harpur replied. 'Well, as you know, sir. I mean from the reports.'

Iles said: 'There's a point beyond which destruction of another human being, even one like Lane, should not go. We are there. Infiltration will fail, of course. But it will take time to fail and by then Lane might have gone and be spared the knowledge and suffering. We'll slip even faster into collapse and reversion to the Middle Ages then. This, in fact, is the essence of chaos theory, Harpur. You have contributed to it in your pigmy style. The small, slimy, generous gesture you've made in recruiting this girl, so that our Chief is not devastated, will eventually lead to appalling, uncontrollable consequences. It's like the leaf falling in a rainforest.'

'Is that right, sir?'

'The leaf that starts a chain of results which finally wipes millions off Wall Street or starts a revolution in Latvia.'

Harpur said: 'We might be able to—'

'I've got this damn streak of gallantry in me, Col.' Iles spoke disgustedly of it, as if it were like the growth he had found in his face. 'Lane will drag us all down and yet I cannot enjoy the thought of him finally broken.'

'It must be a pain, sir.'

'You're noble, Col. Dim and endlessly two-timing but with these fragments of nobility also.'

'Thank you, sir.'

'Yes, I was relieved when you threw the jumped-up jerk a lifebelt.'

'It will work.'

'Plus if you can get this girl emotionally and all other ways dependent on you you might leave my fucking wife alone for a while. I can tell her you're nicely preoccupied.' Iles began to yell, as he did sometimes when he spoke of his wife. Harpur glanced around to check that the ACC's door was closed. 'She cannot understand how she ever came to see anything in you, Harpur. Or Garland. Absolutely fails to understand it.'

'There have been one or two women like that in my case, sir. I don't begrudge them their second thoughts.'

Suddenly Iles yanked something from his face and examined whatever it was on the ball of his thumb. Then he opened the window and flicked it into the street and fondly watched its descent. 'Jantice. Who did him?'

'Well, sir—'

'I'd say it could be Manse or one of his people, possibly Alf. Or one of those walkers on the day of the incident. The beret or the long overcoat. Or the child's mother or father, of course, if the father ever showed up. Did he, Col?'

'Nobody was seen near the flat.'

'As ever, no witnesses, I suppose,' Iles said. 'An expert job.'

'For a time I wondered whether you might have killed him, sir. He was in the way of the pact and he was an evil disgrace to policing and to humankind.'

'Yes, he was that all right,' Iles remarked. Blood oozed from a wide hole in his cheek but he seemed satisfied.

# 28

Shale cycled up to the lighthouse again. There was no need to travel big-time today. Just social. Although he could have asked Alfie down to the rectory, that might have seemed bossy. You had to be considerate. Alfie's family were around somewhere, but stayed clear, thank God. Shale and he drank gin and peps on the terrace again. The sea was still out there, grousing away, wanting to be the centre of everything. 'These various developments should of been a real help getting credibility with our possible colleagues and the police,' Shale remarked. 'Yet I don't see us getting an agreement. Not at once.'

Alfie handed back the Beretta.

Shale examined it. 'This hasn't been fired.'

'He was dead when I got there, Manse. With respect, I asked myself whether you'd decided you couldn't trust me in view of everything and did it yourself. I wonder if you came across any of your five hundred pounds. There was nothing on him when I searched.'

The thing about Alfie, with all his terrible fucking furniture to replace, he might have taken that money, whatever was left, for himself. Shale could never even think about going through a dead man's garments personally. It would be so disrespectful. He would hate it.